"I intend to seek a bride from among the merchant class."

She was quick-witted, her reaction more curiosity than confusion. "Whatever for? Despite the current state of your finances, you would still be accounted eligible."

Could she not simply say, "Indeed, my lord" and leave it at that? Annoyance sharpening, Sinjin said through clenched teeth, "I do not think a lady of my—your—class would meet my requirements."

"And what might those requirements be?"

Uncertain even a sharp set-down would curb Miss Beaumont's unladylike persistence, he grudgingly took the more polite path of answering. However, not having yet progressed in his own mind from what he *didn't* want to what he *did,* he had to grope for a reply.

"Modesty. Simplicity. Temperance in all things."

"And ladies of breeding are not modest, simple, or temperate?" she asked in a silky voice.

"In my observation…generally not!"

Acclaim for Julia Justiss's bestselling book
THE WEDDING GAMBLE

"A scintillating, thoroughly engaging love story!"
—*Romantic Times Magazine*

"Ms. Justiss's first novel is excellent.
The characters leap from the page and take up permanent residence in your heart…this is a story to savor."
—*Rendezvous*

"Julia Justiss proves to be top-notch in this exciting Regency adventure. You will find a new writer to put on your shelf. Splendid!"
—*Bell, Book & Candle*

"This is a fast-paced story that will leave you wanting more…you won't want to put it down!"
—Newandusedbooks.com

The Proper Wife
Harlequin Historical #567—July 2001

JULIA JUSTISS

THE PROPER WIFE

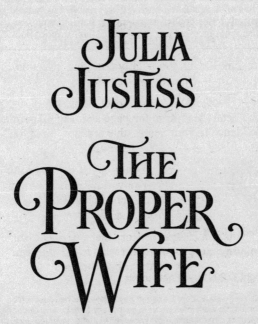

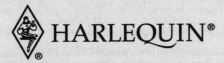

HARLEQUIN®

TORONTO • NEW YORK • LONDON
AMSTERDAM • PARIS • SYDNEY • HAMBURG
STOCKHOLM • ATHENS • TOKYO • MILAN • MADRID
PRAGUE • WARSAW • BUDAPEST • AUCKLAND

ISBN 0-373-29167-1

THE PROPER WIFE

Please address questions and book requests to:
Harlequin Reader Service
U.S.: 3010 Walden Ave., P.O. Box 1325, Buffalo, NY 14269
Canadian: P.O. Box 609, Fort Erie, Ont. L2A 5X3

For my children, Mark, Catherine and Matthew,
truly life's most precious gifts.

Chapter One

Gloved hands gripping the windward rail, Colonel Lord St. John Sandiford braced himself against a gust that threatened to rip the shako from his head, and gazed into the gray curtain of wind-whipped fog. Through a momentary cleft in the drizzle, he spotted the faint outline of the approaching shore. England. *The conquering hero, home from the wars at last.*

As his lips twisted at the bitter irony, a loud "halloo" redirected his attention. He turned to see Lieutenant Alexander Standish approaching, his awkward limp worsened by the rise and fall of the pitching deck. When their ship slammed into a cresting breaker with a hull-shuddering crash that seemed to threaten the soldier's precarious balance, Sinjin leapt toward him, hand extended.

"Grab on, Alex," he shouted against the wind. To his relief, the lieutenant didn't hesitate, but took the help offered. Together they stumbled back to the firmer support of the rail.

"Thank you, Colonel," the young man gasped, still panting from his exertions. Sinjin inspected him closely, relieved to see the glow in the lieutenant's eyes apparently derived this time from excitement rather than fever. "Guess I'm still none too steady on my pins."

"Shouldn't have ventured on deck in this blow." Sinjin delivered the mild reproof with a smile. "Fine thing for me to nursemaid you through a battlefield and months of hospital, only to have you wash overboard within a mile of landfall."

The lieutenant smiled back. "I expect it wasn't prudent, but...but I couldn't wait any longer for a glimpse of home! I admit I was surprised to see you up here. Should have thought you'd had experience enough on the Peninsula being soaked through and frozen. You must be as anxious as I."

Reticence honed in the months spent with the Duke of Wellington's diplomatic train curbed his replying it was precisely to *escape* the eager talk below decks that he'd ventured topside. Turning the question, he said, "If *you're* anxious enough to risk becoming fish-bait, Lady Barbara herself must be awaiting you on the pier."

A blush stained the soldier's thin cheeks. "Certainly not, though that would be the most gloriously welcoming sight I could imagine. I...I can only hope she's still waiting in London. Nothing formal was announced before I joined the Regiment, you know, and now..." He took a deep breath and swallowed hard. "Her parents may want someone better for her, someone who's still—whole."

How often things change whilst soldiers are off fighting and dying. That thought stirred the embers of a rage three years hadn't managed to extinguish, and once again Sinjin had to bite back his first reply. "Nonsense," he said instead, giving the lieutenant's shoulder a bracing slap. "What better man could her family wish for her than one of the peerless heroes who vanquished the tyrant Napoleon for good and all? A rich hero at that, if the gossip of your father's wealth is accurate. Besides, you can always tell them how much worse off it was with the horse. Him, we had to shoot."

As he had hoped, the young man laughed. "Despite the leg, holding rein with my good hand, I can still ride, thank God. Regardless of what Lady Barbara's father decides, I'm much more fortunate than many."

For a moment both were silent, thinking of how few, how precious few of their comrades had ridden away from the killing ground of Waterloo.

"What of you, Colonel? After a long year abroad, surely some lady impatiently awaits your return?"

A visage flashed into mind before, with a grimace, he could banish it. "I've been gone a deal longer than that," he evaded once more.

"You came to Brussels before the rest of the Army, then?"

"Actually, I never left the Continent. After Toulouse, the Duke was posted as Ambassador to the Bourbon Court and needed a retinue. I volunteered, and then remained in Paris with the Duchess and the Embassy staff when Old Hookey went on to the Congress of Vienna."

The young man whistled. "Must have been unpleasant duty. I hear the Frogs grew rather nasty toward Bourbon supporters in general and the English in particular while Boney was drumming up support for his return."

"Madame de Stael and other returned exiles kept us entertained well enough." Some of the lovely ladies in her train had even seduced him into a temporary forgetfulness.

Raising an eyebrow, the lieutenant grinned. "Ah, that's why you lingered. The delights of French damsels notwithstanding, you're still an Englishman, and must be yearning for your land."

"Every mortgaged acre of it," he responded wryly. Indeed, letters from Jeffers, his batman whom he'd sent on ahead after Waterloo, had become increasingly insistent that he must return to begin setting the shambles to order. Now with the peace secured and the regiment ordered home, he could avoid that onerous duty no longer. A duty that might have been a joy, were he able to have the woman he loved beside him. *Sarah,* the name whispered in his ears like a sigh.

"Is that how things stand? A pity." The lieutenant shook his head. "Still, if you've no sweetheart waiting, you are free to find yourself a wealthy bride. I daresay," the lieutenant made a show of looking him up and down, "any lady's papa should be happy to snare you for his daughter, an officer of handsome mien, distinguished title, and service gallantly rendered in that most accomplished of all Hussars regiments, the glorious Tenth."

So sour was the idea of marrying for money, he had to grit his teeth. "I doubt a scarred and pockets-to-let old soldier like myself shall be accounted quite the catch you claim, but I shall do my possible."

"Then I shall see you in town for the Season. I should like that. And if you encounter a spot of bother before you find your heiress..." the lieutenant shifted uncomfortably at something he must have seen sparking in Sinjin's eyes, "don't hesitate to approach my father. Gossip didn't overestimate the Earldom's wealth, and I owe you more than I could ever—"

"Balderdash, 'twas nothing, though I do appreciate the offer. I daresay it won't come to that."

"Doubtless not. But I say, do you see it? Over there, through that break in the fog?"

Turning his chin in the direction of the lieutenant's pointing finger, Sinjin suddenly perceived, looming close ahead, high white cliffs ghostly in the shifting mist. The Dover bluffs.

In spite of himself, the vista held him mesmerized. From within the frozen, stoic lump in his chest that had once been his heart, a frisson of excitement sizzled up.

He was returning to a bankrupt estate and a spendthrift mother, inescapable realities that would likely force him to barter his body and breeding for the gold of a bride he did not want. Yet at this moment he still felt a sense of…limitless possibilities. He must, he concluded acidly, be more the ''mad Englishman'' than he thought.

In the early morning chill a week later, Sinjin rode his last remaining horse from the offices of his solicitor in the City back to Westminster. As if compelled, he drew rein for a moment on the street before Horse Guards, as unobtrusive now in his nondescript brown jacket and worn riding breeches as the uniformed guards outside Army headquarters were resplendent in scarlet coats and gold lace. None of the pickets glancing casually toward him would suspect his shabby apparel—faded garments he'd worn while riding as an intelligence gatherer—concealed an officer of the Tenth Hussars.

Former officer, he amended. A poignant regret stabbed him, as it had yesterday when, after resigning his commission, for the last time he removed the blue tunic and furred pelisse and packed them away. An outsider now, no longer part of the Army that had been his life this last six years.

Not that he'd miss the war, he thought as he nudged his horse to a trot. Any notions of glamour died long ago with the first man he'd seen killed in battle, and a bloody, brutal business it had been for the five years since. But the camaraderie, the bond forged between men facing privation and danger to struggle in a common cause, and his sense of accomplishment at doing a difficult job well...yes, he would miss those.

Bloody sentimental fool, he thought with a flash of irritation. After the unpalatable news delivered by his solicitor an hour ago, 'twas a good thing he had determined to sell out—even that relatively small bit of cash would be welcome. Jeffers' laconic letters had not overstated his dire financial condition; if anything, matters were worse than his batman imagined.

He'd already, with a sense of grief nearly akin to the losing of a friend, turned his other horses over to the staff at Tattersall's for the next sale, keeping only Valiant, the surefooted companion of many a hard march. Unless he took the exceedingly stringent measures outlined in prosaic detail by his man of business, he'd very soon not be able to afford him.

The last of his solicitor's recommendations was hardly unexpected: find a rich bride. Mr. Walters had even added, with a small smile, the same compliment offered by Alex on the ship last week—that for a man of his birth and address, the procuring of a suitable heiress should prove no very difficult task.

To that end, his man concluded, running a pained eye over Sinjin's shabby coat and breeches, he believed the beleaguered estate could stand a small advance of funds to allow his Lordship to procure suitable garments for the upcoming Season.

Trussed up like a prize trout, he thought grimly, and realized that despite all his ruminations on the subject, not until this morning had the stark reality struck home. He must marry an heiress, and soon.

True, at odd intervals in the six years since his father's death revealed the catastrophic total of the late Lord Sandiford's debts, he'd considered the notion. But each time he'd advanced on the idea only to retreat in distaste, vaguely trusting at some future date he would discover an alternate attack on his pecuniary difficulties that might allow him to outflank the prospect.

Time for such an alternative had run out, Mr. Walters had just demonstrated with chilling clarity. Unless he wished to see the remaining lands and possessions of his ancestors put on the block, Viscount St. John Michael Peter Sandiford must now rig himself out to enter that unholy assemblage of social events known as the Marriage Mart, there to hawk his looks and lineage as shamelessly as a harlot strutting her wares outside a Haymarket theatre.

He took a deep breath and swallowed, the bitter taste of bile in his mouth. No wonder he'd been so reluctant to return to England.

Enough, he told himself. Time to stop bleating like a raw recruit at the first cannonade and get on with the sorry business.

He could drop by the establishments in St. James on his way back to his modest rented rooms at North Audley Street, or perhaps pop in to the Albany and visit Alex. His young lieutenant, plump in the pocket and eager for the beginning of the Season, could doubtless advise him which of the gentlemen's shops he should patronize to bring his wardrobe up to snuff. Even to his own admittedly non-discriminating eye, in his current attire, the only civilian clothes he possessed, he looked like a groom.

Not exactly husband material for one of the over-dressed, overcoiffed and overbejewelled damsels over whose perfumed hands he would soon be bowing. He allowed himself a sardonic smile at the thought of the probable expression on one of those hothouse flowers were he to present himself at her feet in his current garb.

By now he'd reached Piccadilly, but his mood was still too uncertain for company. Perhaps a hard gallop would settle him. At least the air and the bridle path of Hyde Park were still free. Turning his mount, he headed west.

Instead of continuing along Piccadilly, however, he entered the hubbub of traders going to Shepherd's Market, picking his path north until he reached the relative calm of Curzon Street. As he neared the handsome Georgian house set back from the roadway, he pulled the horse to a halt, his heartbeat accelerating.

'Twas the disorienting changes of the last few days— his life once again turned upside down—that had brought on this fit of black melancholy, he told himself. He'd indulge it but a moment longer and then ride on.

As if in a dream he dismounted, looped Valiant's reins around a post, and silently approached the quiet dwelling.

Though it was early enough for most of the aristocracy to be still abed, somewhere within those stately walls he knew Sarah would be working. Not his Sarah anymore, the girl who'd grown up his neighbor, friend, and confidante, companion or instigator of dozens of childhood adventures. The girl who'd metamorphosed from boyish hoyden to young lady and taken his heart with her. The lady who for the last three years and three months had been wife to the Marquess of Englemere.

What little was left of that organ he believed long since shattered seemed to convulse, sending a shudder marrow-deep. *Ah, sweet Sarah, my one and only love.*

She was well, he knew. Though after he rejoined his Regiment three years ago he'd resisted opening her first two letters, intending to destroy them unread, in the end he'd succumbed to the need to preserve at least the feeble link of friendship. Reception of a new letter, full of the most interesting of the events taking place back in London, had rapidly become a high point in the mostly dull routine of his days. He'd kept them all, including the latest received just three weeks ago, tied in a neat package that now resided on the bedside table in his North Audley Street rooms. All but one.

A slight noise at the front door riveted his attention. He'd best be moving along, before someone came out and discovered him standing like a beggar at her gate.

Before he could retrieve his grazing mount, a horse rounded the corner and galloped toward him at a reckless pace. A peddler scurried out of range, his display of pans clanging to the pavement, several housemaids squealed and abandoned their feather dusters on the roadway, and he himself had to step back as the rider pulled the huge black brute of a stallion to a clattering halt.

A rider on a sidesaddle. He looked up at a feminine profile whose classic perfection of shape and smoothness of skin doubtless inspired slavish adoration in men and envy in less-favored damsels. Long curling lashes shielded the Beauty's eyes, which were turned toward the horse whose neck she patted with one expensively gloved hand.

His lip curling with distaste, Sinjin noted other accoutrements which, given his experience in discharging the bills incurred for his mama's finery, he knew represented equally lavish expenditures. The wool superfine of her habit, Italian by the look of it, and a sovereign an ell at the least; the dashing bonnet of velvet and Ostrich plumes, the finely-tooled leather of the riding boot in the chased silver stirrup. The price of the gold lace lavishly embellishing the bodice in, he realized, pale imitation of a Hussar's uniform coat could have fed his unit of skirmishers for a year.

And the stallion—having just undergone the painful business of having his own horses evaluated for auction, he judged that prime bit of blood pawing an impatient hoof before him would fetch upward of five hundred pounds. In addition to being totally unsuitable for a lady's mount, a fact that precipitous bolt through the London streets had just demonstrated.

Behind the rider, the peddler stoically regathered his pans. Sinjin felt irrational anger flare. What could her lackwit of a papa have been thinking, to purchase such a horse for his daughter? And the chit herself—how dare that pampered, protected, frivolous creature usurp a uniform he had just put away with such pride and regret, a uniform worn by so many in valiant struggle through the sweat and blood and filth of countless battles? He thought of Uxbridge losing a leg and Alastair his arm, of the decimated ranks of the charging Seventh, of the Twenty-seventh Foot who had stood, and died, to a man in their square atop the bluff at St. Jean's wood.

While she, no doubt, had spent her mornings asleep in her boudoir, her afternoons primping at her mirror, and her evenings dancing until dawn.

Had his brain not been fogged with fury, even one as scornful of beauty as he might have been impressed with the brilliance of the emerald eyes now turning in his direction, or the perfection of the full soft lips opening to speak.

"You, sirrah! Hand me down, if you please, and take my horse to the mews."

His attention distracted to the butler now opening the door of Sarah's townhouse, a long, incredulous moment passed before he realized the Beauty was addressing *him*.

"Take him yourself, Miss," he spat back.

Still too angry to think, he turned on the heel of his worn boot and strode away. With one motion he snatched up Valiant's reins and flung himself in the saddle, then spurred his mount toward the park.

Her lips parted in an *O* of surprise, Clarissa Beaumont watched the tall blond man ride off without a backward glance. Clerk or farmer or—gentleman? At any rate, *not* the servant she'd taken him to be. Though in that garb, and in front of Sarah's house where a groom usually awaited her after her morning ride, she could hardly be faulted for the mistake.

With an experienced horsewoman's eye, she noted the quality of his mount and the effortless grace with which he controlled it. Quite possibly a gentleman, she concluded. Though if he were, he was the rudest and most deplorably dressed she'd ever encountered.

And, she concluded with a wry grin, the most unimpressionable. Her oft-praised beauty had elicited from him none of the awe, astonishment or reverence she'd come to expect after four Seasons as the ton's reigning Belle.

A flicker of feminine interest stirred. If he *were* a gentleman, and she *were* to meet him again, it might be quite interesting.

She saw Glendenning waiting by the open front door and waved as a groom arrived to take Diablo's reins and hand her down. Before turning to the house, she gave the stallion's velvet nose one last pat. "Allow my prince an extra ration of mash, Stebbins, if you please. We've had a marvelous gallop. And to think, I nearly turned him over to a stranger."

A stern mouth and a flash of blue eyes was all she'd

glimpsed of the man's face, she mused as she mounted the steps. And a scar—she was quite certain he'd borne a scar above his right eye. A handsome scarred man of mystery, a desperate character right out of the pages of one of Mrs. Edgeworth's novels.

Her chuckle turned to a groan. Lud, her life had indeed grown dull if she must be weaving gothic fictions about a chance-met stranger. Who was, no doubt, some penniless clerk with a wife and a hopeful family whom she'd never encounter again. With a pang of regret that surprised her, Clarissa dismissed him.

Chapter Two

Her ladyship Sarah Stanhope, Marchioness of Englemere, awaited her in the morning room, Glendenning informed her. He bowed her in, but before Clarissa could
greet her dearest friend, a projectile hurtled against her.

"Clare! Clare! Play soldier!"

"Heavens, Aubrey, you'll knock her over!" his mama
protested. "Young gentlemen who cannot greet a lady
properly will be banished to the schoolroom to improve
their manners."

"Stuff, I'm not so easily overset." Affection swelling
for the most precious being in the very small circle of
persons dear to her, Clarissa knelt to hug her godson.
"I'm delighted to see you, too, poppet," she said,
smoothing back the curly black hair and smiling into earnest green eyes nearly as brilliant as her own. "We shall
play soldiers as soon as I've had my tea."

Lady Englemere shook her head. "Really, Clare, how
can I train him to behave when you encourage him
shamelessly?"

"Fiddle, Sarah. He's time and more to learn all the
tiresome rituals that hem in the rest of us. Let him be
free while he may."

"You're as unrepentant as he is."

"Of course. Have I not always been so?" Heedless of her new habit, she sank to the floor and lifted her godson into her lap. "Now, general, where is my tea?"

"Careful of your gown," his mama warned. "Aubrey's already finished, and in the inevitably sticky-handed way of boys, is sure to be all-over crumbs."

"Piffle, what's a few stains among campaigners, eh, my general?"

Lady Englemere shook her head at Clarissa. "Yes, cleaning spots off that habit will be your *maid's* problem."

"Which is why one employs a batman," Clarissa said with a laugh.

The little boy on her lap was tracing the elaborate frogging of her bodice with one admittedly grubby finger. His face lighting in a smile, he turned to Sarah. "Clare soldier! See, Mama. Clare soldier too."

"Clever boy. I had this habit made just for you, and fine it is indeed, do you not think? Now, what unit?"

"'Zar!"

"Yes, Hussar. Excellent! Would he not make a brilliant campaigner, Sarah? Too bad Wellington was deprived of his services."

His mother shuddered. "I, for one, am quite happy he was too young to serve."

"I almost forgot." Clarissa lifted the child off her lap. "Look in my reticule and see what I've brought you."

"Soldiers!" the child said gleefully, swiftly untying the strings of the bag to pull out the uniformed figures one by one.

"Oh, Clare, not *more,*" his mama groaned. "You've bought him half a battlefield's worth already."

"Then we require only the other half."

"You are as fascinated with soldiers as Aubrey!"

"And why not? At least soldiers have been somewhere, done something grand and useful." She held out two of the lead figures. "See, Aubrey, these are Prussians. This old fellow is General Blucher himself."

"Aubrey, take them to the nursery and set them up with the others. Then you'll be ready to play when Aunt Clare finishes her tea."

"Yes, Mama." The lad climbed to his feet. "Thank you, An' Clare." He made her a solemn bow, then dispelled that image of propriety by scampering to the door, soldiers clutched to his chest. "Come fast," he commanded as he skipped out.

"What an excellent son you have," Clarissa said, her eyes following the child fondly.

"The fact that he's nearly as great a scamp as his godmother doubtless enhances his charm."

"Stuff." Clarissa rose and brushed off her gown, then came to sit beside Sarah on the sofa. "I've grown entirely dull and respectable."

Lady Englemere made a rude noise. "Indeed. Do you intend to finally stop letting Mountclare dangle and accept his offer, then? It's been fair on three months, and you've done nothing to discourage his devotion. Englemere tells me the odds at the clubs favor him."

In the midst of stirring sugar into her tea, Clarissa made a face. "Do they indeed? As I always prefer the long shot, it appears I must refuse him." Irritation, and a long-familiar blend of restive dissatisfaction welled up in her. "Oh, I don't know! He's amusing, certainly, and altogether too devoted. But how could I marry a man who fancies yellow waistcoats?"

"Was that not your objection to Wexley's suit?"

"Wexley? His were puce, and besides, unlike Mountclare, whose conversation sometimes contains a modicum of sense, Wexley never has a thought in his head more profound than the cut of his coat.''

"But eventually you must marry someone. You've already refused most of the eligible men in London. Viscount Albright and Lord Manton this Season alone, and—"

"Please." Clarissa waved a hand to forestall her friend. "Must we discuss such a dismal business as marriage?" She gave her friend a mischievous grin. "Only conceive of becoming riveted to such dull propriety as Englemere. Are you *sure* you've never regretted it?"

Ignoring the bait, Sarah replied calmly, "My husband being the most excellent and intelligent of men, that's a subject on which we shall never agree. Are you sure *you've* never regretted jilting him?"

"Not for an instant. And that is one subject on which we *can* agree."

"Still, there are other inducements to marriage. Such as those related to a warm bed on a cold night." Sarah looked on her with a fond but worried eye. "With all your passion, I should hate to see you deny yourself that."

Unfulfilled desire was certainly part of the restless yearning that pulled at her, Clarissa acknowledged. "One need not endure the bondage of marriage to experience that," she offered, only half-jesting. "Gentlemen surely do not."

Somewhat to her disappointment, Sarah seemed not at all shocked. "True. But never forget, my dear rash darling, ladies, unlike gentlemen, bear passion's consequence. A consequence, however, I believe you would much enjoy. Your mind being so little removed from a child's, you should make a wonderful mama."

"I think I've just been insulted."

Sarah grinned. "A compliment, I assure you."

"Children are an inducement, I admit. But unless one wishes to create a scandal, they come with a bitter price attached—that unavoidable husband."

Sarah inclined her head, surveying her friend. "So we come full circle. Granted, you are rich enough to do without the husband, but if you persist in this disinclination to marry, what shall you do with yourself? You've already taken over the reins of the household for your mama, and handle them quite skillfully, yet despite the extra duties I sense you are still dissatisfied."

"Mama is a ninny, albeit a sweet one. Mastering the tasks you've performed since girlhood held a certain challenge, but 'tis accomplished now. Were marriage not such a permanent estate, I might be more tempted. As it is, I've yet to encounter a gentleman who didn't become a dead bore within a fortnight. If I'm presented one more poorly-rhymed paean to my eyes or lips or Titian hair I vow I shall jam the missive down the author's throat and exit the room screaming."

The ever-present compulsion to *do* something brought Clarissa to her feet. "My opinion of gentlemen sinks lower the more I know of them," she said as she paced to the window. "When I restrain myself to be polite and ladylike, I might understand why, given this *beauteous* frame," she indicated her body with a scornful gesture, "they flock to me. Yet even when their attention vexes me and I lose my temper, the more quixotic or preemptory I become, the more they seem to fall over themselves to fulfill my every supposed desire."

When Sarah merely raised an eyebrow, Clarissa had to laugh. "Ungracious you think me, and you're right. Oh, I grant 'twas flattering, even exciting at first, but I've long begun to suspect the lot of them are as bacon-brained as dear Mama. To set such store by eyes and lips or a full figure! I daresay not one has any idea of the character of the woman behind the ivory skin and emerald eyes. Even more daunting, I believe none really cares.''

The tone of despair behind that statement must have revealed more than she intended, for Sarah came over to envelop her in a hug. "*I* happen to think the woman behind the mask has a purity and strength of character even more beautiful than her face.''

Unaccustomed tears pricked Clarissa's eyes as she hugged her friend back. "Considering how often you scold, I shall treasure that rare compliment. Indeed, you are the only person I know—save one,'' she added, rolling her eyes toward the portrait of Lord Englemere which hung over the mantel, "who has ever attempted the daunting task of trying to restrain me. I allow I'm the better for it, though at those moments I scarcely relished your opposition.''

"Yet I lived to tell the tale.''

"Only because my aim is sometimes off." Memories of vases and various other projectiles which had at times served to express her dissatisfaction made them both laugh.

Releasing her friend, Clarissa walked to the door. "Still, I'm so damnably *bored.* Surely life holds more for me than this endless round of silly parties and sillier people. Despite all my good intentions, if nothing more exciting happens soon, I swear I shall be compelled to do something quite outrageous.''

The sudden vision of unsmiling blue eyes and thin lips pressed in a disapproving line came to mind. "Like running off with a penniless married clerk.''

Sarah laughed out loud. "You'd drive him to distraction in a week."

"Probably," she acknowledged with a smile. "But now, I must run off to play soldiers."

Sarah's face sobered. "You are so good with Aubrey. For a son like that, do you not think marriage might be worth the price after all?"

A bittersweet longing filled her. Ah, to have a child of her own, to play with and cosset and cherish, to love with all the chaotic passion churning within her for which she couldn't seem to find direction.

From the doorway she gave Sarah one last smile. "Until I discover a man even half the equal of your son, I shall be content to borrow Aubrey."

Early that evening, Sinjin stood sipping a glass of wine while his batman, Jeffers, newly returned from his country estate Sandiford Court, unpacked the boxes just delivered from his afternoon shopping expedition. Apparently the merchants had not yet gotten wind of the precarious state of the Viscount's finances, since he escaped their premises having ordered far fewer garments than the smiling owners had tried to press on him.

More likely it had been Alex's cheerful presence beside him that inspired them to such courtesy, he concluded. The proprietors of the establishments at which Alex introduced him must have concluded any friend of the wealthy Lord Standish would have no trouble settling his accounts. Remembering the total of the bills now reposing in his desk drawer, he gave a scornful laugh. If only they knew how dubious an investment his custom was.

Jeffers, hands full of the white brocaded waistcoat he

was folding, looked over. "Aye, Colonel, sorry threads these be, compared to the tunic of the Tenth."

"Colonel no longer, Jeffers. And I suppose we'll both have to get used to black, buff and green."

"I expect I can learn to 'milord' ye, sir, but to me ye'll always be the Colonel. It's a soldier through and through ye are. Waistcoats may change the look of ye, but 'twill never turn ye into one a' them idle dandies, thank the Lord."

Recalling some of the strolling exquisites he'd seen on his excursion to Bond Street, Sinjin shuddered. "I sincerely hope not. But now we fight a battle of quite another sort. Walters gives me two months, maybe three, to gain an heiress's gold to reinforce us, else I'll be selling much more than my commission."

Placing the folded garment in the wardrobe, Jeffers sighed and turned to his master. "'Tis a distasteful stratagem, I ken, this relying on the reserves of a woman, but ye're the best officer I've ever served under. If any man can find among all the fluff and feathers of the nobs a woman worth having, 'tis ye."

Sinjin gave a deprecating laugh. "The boot is rather on the other leg, Jeffers. I must find one who'll have me. This titled hand, you recall, bears a very empty purse."

His batman sniffed. "Not that I know the workings of a woman's mind, gentry-mort in particular, but if a female can't tell ye're worth a battalion of those jackanapes strutting the Lunnon streets, she's daft."

"Indeed, she should deem my offering for her a signal honor," he jested with bitter sarcasm.

Jeffers straightened as if on parade and stared straight at Sinjin, seeming affronted. "A Colonel of the Tenth Hussars, veteran of Vimeiro and Sahugun, Corunna and

Vittoria and—'' He stopped at Sinjin's impatient wave. ''I should bloody well think so.''

''We shall see. If you've finished with the boxes, Mrs. Webster's holding dinner for you in the kitchens. We've both eaten enough cold mutton to enjoy a meal hot.''

''Aye, Colonel.'' Before Sinjin could remonstrate, with a half smile Jeffers saluted and walked out.

Shaking his head, Sinjin took his wineglass and eased into a wing chair in the small sitting room. ''Fluff and feathers,'' Jeffers had described the ladies from among whose ranks he must secure a bride. An old soldier like himself, who'd slept in the rain on freezing ground, counted himself lucky to dine on stale bread and half-cooked fowl, and watched comrades of a dozen campaigns blown to bits beside him, was hardly likely to find anything in common with a lady like that. Nor was it likely that such a lady, inhabitant of a society that prized looks over substance, wealth over character, and appearances over all would find much to appeal in a man who cordially despised her world.

A world whose preoccupation with gambling had lured his father to ruin, beggared his estate and left him in the despicable situation he now faced.

His mind replayed the image of that expensive daughter of aristocracy he'd encountered this morning before Sarah's house, and once again his lip curled.

An accredited Beauty, just like his mother who had always deemed Sarah too plain for her only son. A girl, haughty head held high, used to commanding a squadron of grooms, butlers, footmen, maids to her bidding. When she married, she would trade that porcelain of cheek and perfection of body for an endless run on her hapless husband's purse, her sole other function to breed his children and perhaps manage his household. Companionship would be limited to escorting her to a ceaseless succession of social events, conversation to gossip or details of her latest shopping foray. And she'd look down her well-bred, well-connected nose at those of lesser wealth or birth, like Jeffers, whom after half-a-dozen years of campaigning Sinjin accounted more friend than servant.

Was the price of salvaging his estate to be a life of misery, wedded to such a one?

No, he decided, rising to refill his glass. He could endure marrying a woman he did not love, but he must marry one he could respect. If, as Jeffers commented, such a woman was likely to be as scarce among the aristocracy as accurate cannon shots in battle, he must look elsewhere.

Perhaps among the middle class? A faint interest stirred. Two of his men, Master Sergeant Trapper and Lieutenant Fitzwilliams, both of yeoman stock, had brought their wives to the Peninsula, and finer, more competent, courageous women of character he'd never meet. Why not choose such a woman for his wife?

Of course, a simple solicitor's daughter wouldn't do, but perhaps among the merchant class there might be some captain of industry wishful of securing the social advancement of his daughter through marriage into the gentry. A man who had spent years, as he had, in hard and bitter enterprise and emerged by his own exertions with wealth and power, as a soldier skilled in battle rises through the ranks. Such a man's daughter surely would prize her husband's character higher than his bank balance, lack the self-centered haughtiness of an aristocratic beauty, and possess an ingrained distaste for idleness, profligacy and waste. She might not be too proud or vain to set her own hand to mending and cleaning as she worked beside her husband to restore a grand and ancient estate.

By Heaven, he decided, he would look for just such a bride, and no other.

The solution settled in his mind with a solid, convincing ring, like the sense of rightness he'd always felt after the best order of battle had been determined. His spirits rising for the first time since he'd made port at Dover, he held his glass high. "To a sensible middle-class bride," he saluted and downed the rest of the wine.

A light rapping sounded and he turned toward the door. Probably Alex, come by to introduce him at his Club, as Sinjin had never stayed in London long enough to join one. He'd not have the blunt for it now, certainly. Still, Ponsonby, Wetherford and some of his other fellow-officers had already returned from Paris. It would be good to see old comrades again.

"Come in, Alex," he called. "I'll pour you a round."

Hands busy with decanter and glass, he glanced up to greet his guest. Surprise jolted the smile from his lips, carried away his words of welcome on an exhale of breath.

Poised on the threshold, smiling faintly, stood Nicholas Stanhope, Marquess of Englemere. Sarah's husband.

After a few startled seconds, Sinjin pulled his wits together. "Englemere, this is an unexpected—" he couldn't get his lips to form the word "pleasure" and opted for "visit" instead. "Please, come in. I'm not settled yet, but I can offer wine." He motioned the marquess to a chair.

"Thank you." Englemere sat and took the proffered glass. "I learned through my contacts at Horse Guards that the Tenth was due back. Then Glendenning spotted you on the street this morning, so I knew you'd arrived."

"He must have a sharp eye. And with the help of those same contacts, you ascertained my address?" Sinjin asked, taken aback at the swiftness of Englemere's action—and the accuracy of his sources. "Rather good intelligence-gathering on your part."

"As you once told me, 'tis a useful skill. I see you've sold out. Are congratulations in order?"

Sinjin smiled wryly. "I'm not sure yet. The change is still too new."

The Marquess paused to take a sip, and Sinjin knew they were both remembering another call in another room over three years ago. "Kind of you to welcome me home so speedily, but I assume you had some other purpose in mind?"

His guest smiled back. "Ever one to proceed directly to the point. You may recall, when last we had private chat, you indicated the business we discussed would, in your estimation, remain 'pending' until after Bonaparte was vanquished."

Since the "business" they'd discussed was Sinjin running off with Englemere's wife, he knew exactly what the marquess wanted to settle.

When she'd written to him of her predicament, Sinjin had bent every effort to obtain leave to return from the Peninsula and rescue Sarah from the loveless marriage her family's desperate financial condition was forcing upon her. Only to find he'd arrived too late. The anguish of that discovery had never left him.

Nonetheless, the matter was well past mending now. He should inform Englemere of his tentative plans to wed an heiress, to get on with the duty of recovering his estate. But though he had previously determined, with a wrenching pain his heart would carry forever, that Sarah had come to love the man circumstance compelled her to marry, for some perverse reason he couldn't seem to make himself assure Englemere he no longer had any designs on her. And sever the last tenuous link to the days when her affection had been his alone.

Instead, he took a long, slow sip of wine before replying, "Your recollections are quite good."

"I assure you," Englemere said, the smile fading from his lips and his eyes like flint, "every word was indelibly burned into my brain."

"And mine."

"So you will understand that I ask once again what your intentions are concerning my wife. She is well, by the way, though I'm sure you know that."

"Yes. I received her last letter just a few weeks ago," Sinjin couldn't help adding that baiting comment.

"I thought it best to allow the correspondence. You are, after all, her oldest *friend.*" Englemere added subtle emphasis to the word.

"You think she'd not have written had you not 'permitted' it?"

"Certainly not. Her strong sense of *duty,* you know. But it would have…saddened her to break off all contact, and I didn't wish that. I assure you, I place my wife's well-being above all things."

"Indeed."

"And so I felt it might be wise for me to see you before Sarah knows you've returned. And to ascertain your…plans."

Once again, Englemere gave him an opening, and once again, he couldn't take it. "That depends on Sarah."

The marquess raised frosty green eyes to stare straight into his. "Once you claimed to love her, to want to make her happy."

"I've always loved her."

Englemere's expression softened. "She is a matchless treasure. I admit, I understand your feelings better now than I did three years ago. To have won Sarah's love, and then been forced to give her up, would be a nearly impossible task. But circumstances did require it, and we must all move beyond that. She *is* happy, Sandiford. I intend to see she stays that way, with no...disturbances to distress her. She's...in a delicate condition again."

The long-simmering rage he'd never quite mastered boiled up, choking off reply, even had there been one he could give. Rage at two rakehell fathers and a beautiful, selfish mother whose carping at him to do his duty and wed an heiress had driven him into the Army, taken him so far away he'd not managed to return in time to prevent Sarah marrying another man. Rage at Englemere's half-pitying look that said she now loved *him,* and finally, rage at the unspeakable image of another man, this man, holding her, touching her, making love to her.

Englemere, who with Sarah and her children now had everything he'd ever wanted. He clenched his fists at his sides and took a deep breath, trying to stifle the furious desire to pummel that handsome face.

The marquess's voice, when he spoke, held sympathy rather than triumph. "You're welcome to try and plant me a facer, though you wouldn't succeed. No doubt I'd feel the same, did I stand in your boots."

Another echo from the past—a deliberate one, he felt sure. And their positions were reversed. Englemere now had law, family—and Sarah's love on his side.

"You do love her?" was all he could think to ask.

"Absolutely. And since, by your reaction, I judge you still care, I invite you to call. See for yourself that she is content and cherished. If you truly desire only her happiness, it will set any concerns on that score to rest. And it would please her if we could be on friendly terms.''

Sinjin made a choking sound, and Englemere nodded. ''Perhaps too much to ask. Still, all I've heard of you from Sarah and from others tells me you are a gentleman of honor. I made this call, and issue my invitation, with that understanding.'' Once again his face sobered and he looked Sinjin in the eye with deadly intent. ''I promise you this, however. Regardless of your conclusions on the matter, I will protect what is mine.''

As a man of honor, he ought to now give Englemere the assurance he was looking for—that Sinjin accepted their marriage and relinquished his claim to Sarah. But between the tightness in his chest and the constriction in his throat, he couldn't get the words out.

Englemere drained his glass and put it on the side table. ''Thank you for the wine. Sarah usually receives in the afternoon. She'll soon learn from the on-dits that the Tenth has returned, so I'll expect to see you.''

Sinjin stood as his visitor rose, then walked him to the door. ''Englemere.''

The marquess extended a hand and, reluctantly, Sinjin shook it. ''Welcome back to England, Colonel.''

Much as he thought he'd steeled himself to it, as he stood long moments by his door after Englemere departed, trying to still the trembling in his hands and subdue the fury churning in his gut, Sinjin finally had to admit that though he'd swallowed the concept of Sarah married, he'd not been able to countenance the idea of her possessed by another man, carrying his child. Not been able to accept that the girl who threw herself in his arms and covered his face with kisses in a barn at midnight before his departure for the Army all those years ago, vowing to love him forever and never marry another, had eventually turned to Englemere.

As she'd been compelled to. As she should have. He should thank Heaven the man who'd been near enough to rescue her was as fine as the marquess.

He went to the sideboard and poured himself another glass with unsteady hands, then wandered to the window to look out over the gray London sky.

Six years. Since then he'd endured hunger and thirst, the burning heat of a Peninsular summer and the frigid winds of a Pyranees winter. He'd suffered the thrill and terror of battle, the agony of being wounded and the anguish of friends dying beside him. It was time, past time, to put an end to a dream born in the lazy days of an English summer long since past.

But first, he would see her again.

Chapter Three

The next morning Sinjin dressed with care in a new jacket of deep azure over a cream figured waistcoat and buff breeches. Despite the blue of the coat, the figure reflected in the glass as his fingers worked the unfamiliar stiffness of the starched cravat still seemed a stranger. He felt another sting of longing for his old dolman with its panels of braid.

He'd never paid much heed to his looks, but now he paused to inspect the face staring back at him. Skin still bronzed a shade darker than his English counterparts, though not so tanned as it had been after months under the strong Peninsular sun. The scar over his right eye, remnant of a saber slash at Corunna, was fainter now, matching the fine web of lines at the corners, the lips thinner and more compressed under a sharper nose. Altogether a harsher face than three years ago.

Would Sarah find in it any echo of the boy she'd once loved?

He was about to find out. Though Englemere had told him she received in the afternoons, he did not intend to risk meeting her again after three long years in a drawing room full of visitors. He would go this morning, early and unannounced if he could prevail upon Glendenning to permit it. Hopefully before she learned of his return to England, before she could prepare her response. He wanted to see the unrehearsed reaction on her face and judge for himself if she was, as Englemere claimed, content. And though it was probably selfishly unfair to test her thus, he craved to know whether the aching burden of love he bore her was now entirely unrequited.

As it happened, his call being so unfashionably early he was lucky enough to catch Glendenning gone from his post. The young footman who admitted him was much easier to manage, and with his Colonel's commanding manner he swiftly overrode any protest.

Lady Englemere was working in the back parlor, the footman reluctantly revealed. As the servant ushered him down the hallway, memories rushed back of the last time he'd been in this house.

She'd been abed, recovering from injuries suffered at the hands of that now deceased blackguard Findlay. Her gray eyes shadowed, her pale blond hair a mass of braid-bent ripples about her shoulders, she'd taken his hand and kissed it, thanking him for coming to her rescue. He'd clutched her slender fingers, his eyes recording every feature of her face, knowing with the vicissitudes of battles to come it might be the last time he ever saw her.

Close his eyes and he could see her visage still, as he had on countless nights lying in a cot in his tent, bedded down around a campfire, or shivering under sodden blankets on the soaking ground. In that twilight time between waking and sleep, when years and distance and the harsh realities of her marriage and his poverty dissolved, for a few magic moments she was again his own true love.

A beautiful dream that had sustained him through

lonely, dangerous years. A dream he had come today to confront, most probably to bury forever.

The footman halted before a paneled door. "Are you sure, my lord—"

"Yes. That will be all, thank you." At his gesture of dismissal, the boy slowly retreated down the hallway. Sinjin's lip quirked as he heard the footsteps stop. The lad would probably creep back to listen outside the door and send the first passing housemaid to fetch Glendenning. The staff seemed properly protective of their mistress.

Despite his firm intent, his footstep faltered on the threshold. Taking a deep breath, he unlatched the door.

As he would expect in Sarah's well-run household, it opened soundlessly on oiled hinges. Behind a desk across the room, framed by windows overlooking a garden beyond, Sarah sat, pen in hand, head bent over an account book.

For a timeless moment he stood spellbound. Hair pinned up in her usual coronet of braids under a small lace cap, skin pale but glowing with health, in her sea-green morning gown she looked beautifully serene as she marked an entry in a firm hand. And then glanced up.

Her glorious gold-flecked silver eyes widened, the quill dropped from her fingers and her lips opened in a gasp of surprise. "Sinjin?"

"Hullo, Sarah."

Then he saw it, a flash of gladness that lit up those starry eyes, and his splintered heart exulted. "Sinjin, how wonderful to see you!"

Her face brightening in a luminescent smile, she jumped up and came toward him, arms extended. Halfway across the room, she remembered herself and halted, a delicate blush creeping to her cheeks as she lowered her arms and clasped them behind her.

"You rogue, sneaking up on me like that! I shall have to read Glendenning a royal scold!"

So poignantly strong was the desire to take her in his arms, he stumbled over his reply. "D-don't blame him. I more or less crept in. I wanted to catch a glimpse of you unawares. And how lovely it was."

"You're looking fine as fivepence yourself, despite half-scaring me to death! And out of the Army at last. How good it is to have you back."

Smiling still, she held out both hands. He caught them, brought them to his lips, closing his eyes to savor her nearness. Ah, the satin touch of her, that sweet lingering scent of lavender.

The piping sound of a young voice shocked his eyes open. "Mama! Aubrey soldier gone. Mama have?"

Sarah pulled away to intercept the running figure of a small boy. Facing him toward Sinjin, she said, "Aubrey, make your bow to Mama and Papa's dear friend, Lord Sandiford. He's just back from being a soldier."

The child bobbed a bow, then inspected him up and down with curious green eyes. Englemere's eyes. "Soldier?" the child said doubtfully.

Though he knew she'd borne a child, still he scarcely heard Sarah's soft explanation to the boy whose cheek she stroked. A wave of emotion engulfed him as he stared at Sarah's son, the child that might have been, should have been his. *Their son.*

He must have looked as stricken as he felt, for after a glance at his face, Sarah instructed the child to search under the desk for the missing soldier, then turned to him.

"I wrote you of Aubrey's birth. You did get the letter?" she asked as she motioned him to a chair.

"Y-yes. Yes, I knew. Somehow, seeing him…is different." He swallowed. "Harder." Beyond all expectation harder, he was finding, to witness the demise of a dream than to merely contemplate its ending.

Her gentle voice mirrored a sympathetic sadness. "Sinjin, everything is different now."

"I know that too," he replied, unable to keep the bitterness from his voice.

"But an end is also a beginning. When life changes, it can bring undreamed-of blessings. Like children. Until you experience it yourself, you cannot fully imagine the joys of a family."

The bitterness cut deeper, striking the flint of anger. "No, doubtless I cannot. Nor do *I* ever expect to."

Her eyes flashed with an answering ire. "Do you think yourself the only one ever to have lost his heart's desire? Recall, sir, that you were the one to ride away! Whilst those you left behind had to deal as best they could with the circumstances life dealt them. I make you no apologies for that! Indeed, I thought we'd settled this long since."

Paradoxically, her anger snuffed out his. "So we did. Still, understanding the reasons for it makes seeing you—him—now no less…difficult."

"Which is why it serves no purpose to linger in the past. No matter how splendid it may have been."

"Move on briskly?" he asked, perilously close to a jeer.

She shook her head a little, wincing. "Never briskly. By slow and halting degree. But forward nonetheless. Toward something as fine, or better."

"I move, Madam—what other choice is there?" He grimaced, thinking of what he, at least, would move to. "Though I don't expect to find much joy in it."

"Then search harder." She leaned toward him, her face intent. "Oh, Sinjin, if misery taught me anything, it was never to abandon hope! Only recall, when Wellington found the fortress of Burgos invincible that first winter, he did not give up, but retreated to regroup his forces."

"Assault once more the fortress of love?" He laughed shortly. "Madam, I've scarce any heart left, far too little for the attempt, I assure you."

"Shall I believe so valiant a soldier's turned coward? Ah, Sinjin, pain is inescapable in life, do what we may. Only know, and I think I speak from experience wretched enough to judge, that regardless of the cost, loving never diminishes us. It only enriches."

He could read deep affection in her silver eyes, vibrating in the timbre of her voice, but the rejected lover in him still craved to hear her say it plainly.

"You...still care for me?"

"Care for you?" She shook her head in bewilderment, as if the words made no sense. "Of course I care for you. I grew up loving you—it's part, blood and bone, of what I am. But so do I love Aubrey and Mama and Nicholas. Our hearts are not a single room, but a vessel with chambers for many. New love need not supplant the old."

"But it must, if the love is the special kind between a man and a woman. The heart can contain but one emotion like that."

"Perhaps. But if one values it enough, even that love can be refashioned to a form honor permits."

"Ah, but the 'refashioning'—'tis a dreadful business."

"A trial by torment," she agreed, a fleeting shadow crossing her face. "As well I know. But," she focused her gaze back on him, "unless I'm much mistaken, a trial you too have passed through."

Her son came over, soldier in hand. "Found, Mama!"

"Very good, Aubrey." She lifted the boy into her lap.

Something in his chest twisted again and he shook his head. "I'm not so sure. Having once survived, I doubt I would choose to risk such vulnerability again."

She smoothed her son's curls and looked over his head at Sinjin. "Did you love me so little?"

"You know how much!"

"If you truly loved me, then, and in tribute to the affection I still bear, I ask this pledge. Do not harden your heart. Oh, Sinjin, the boy I loved, the man I knew, was altogether too warm, generous and fine to shut himself off in bitter isolation. Nor would I have you hide behind a pedestal of my supposed perfection, judging no other woman my equal. Promise me you will not deny the possibility of love. If you will not seek it out, at least be open should it find you. After all, my dearest friend," she added, her voice unsteady, "how can my happiness ever be complete, until I know you too are happy?"

"Guilty, my lady Englemere?"

"Certainly not." Her silver eyes flashed in a gesture of annoyance so familiar, he had to smile. "Just wishful that you act sensibly in your own best interest rather than in the pigheaded fashion of a man, scorning what is precious merely because it does not assume the precise form you had envisioned." Her tart tone softened. "You will promise me?" She held out her hand.

"Could I ever deny you?" With a wry smile, he took her slender fingers. "Very well, Madam, I promise. Should we seal the pact in blood, as we did when we were children?"

Obviously bored with adult talk, Aubrey squirmed, and his mama set him down. Stepping toward Sinjin, he once again surveyed him from boots to cravat, the man's height such that the action nearly overtoppled the boy. "Not soldier," he pronounced. "Play soldier?"

Eyes so like Englemere's beseeched him. Sinjin inhaled sharply, regret still too trenchant for proximity. "Not now, my good man. Perhaps another day."

The child's face dimmed in disappointment, then brightened again. "Papa!" he cried, and ran to the door.

But Sinjin had not needed the boy's shout to warn him who entered. The joy that illumined Sarah's face when she caught sight of her husband announced Englemere's presence only too eloquently. And like the morning mist on the hillsides overtaken by sunrise, the last shreds of Sinjin's dream evaporated in the brilliance of her smile.

The marquess caught his son and tossed him in the air, to the child's delighted squeals. Lifting Aubrey to his shoulder, he walked to Sinjin and offered a hand.

"Sandiford," he said, as Sinjin grasped and shook it. "I'm pleased you've come to visit us so speedily. I trust you've found my family well?"

Despite his casual stance, Englemere's body was stiffly alert, his eyes assessing Sinjin's face. For a moment the two men's glances held, both knowing the question transcended those simple words.

Though still aching, this time Sinjin pulled out the necessary reply. "Indeed, I find them perfect, my lord."

Englemere exhaled, some of the tension seeming to leave his body. "I am glad of it."

Still carrying his son, he walked over to kiss Sarah's cheek. "You look lovely this morning, sweeting. Sandiford, you will take tea with us?"

Such a picture they made, Sarah smiling down at the son who'd climbed back into her lap, Englemere standing behind them, his hand on her shoulder. A perfect family.

And he forever an outsider. Bleakness filled him and for a moment, he couldn't summon words.

"N-no, I must be going. I interrupted Sarah at her work, and I've errands of my own. Master Aubrey, a pleasure to have met you. Sarah, Englemere, a good day."

"I'll see you out," Englemere said. "Order us some tea, won't you, my dear?"

"You are sure you can't stay?" Sarah asked. "Then you must visit us again. Often," she added, and gave him that sweet Sarah smile he'd so often longed for and dreamed of. Then squeezed the hand her husband rested on her shoulder.

"I shall see you, of course," he replied, feeling hollow inside at the sight. *But not often.*

"Play soldier now, Mama?" he heard Aubrey coax.

Englemere escorted him out in silence. After the frowning butler handed him his coat and retreated, no doubt in disapproval of his unorthodox arrival, Sinjin spoke.

"I give you my word as a man of honor, you have nothing to fear from me. My congratulations. You have a fine s-son." His voice broke over the word, and he had to take a breath. "Lord willing, may you have many more."

Once again, Englemere's eyes held his for a long moment. Then, swallowing hard, the marquess nodded.

Sinjin turned to go, but Englemere stayed him with a hand. "I am fully cognizant of the…cost of that pledge," he said gruffly. "I cannot offer in return anything nearly so valuable, but rest assured, I shall be delighted to assist you in any way. You must restructure your estates to pay off some debts, I understand. Land and crop values are down, but I know a banker who is quite clever. I'd be happy to introduce you.''

Taken aback by the unexpected offer, Sinjin hardly knew how to reply. The truth would serve best, he decided. ''You're very generous, but I'm afraid matters have gone beyond that. If I'm not to lose the whole, I shall require a massive infusion of capital in the very near future.''

''Ah. You must look for an heiress, then.''

Sinjin couldn't stop the grimace. ''I'm afraid so.''

To his further surprise, Englemere grinned and clapped him on the shoulder. ''I'm here to testify speedy matches are not always a bad thing. But if your affairs must be resolved quickly, there's no time to lose. Having just arrived, I daresay you've not yet been introduced about. You must accompany us to Lady Devonshire's ball tomorrow.''

''I shouldn't put you to so much bother, and I—''

''Nonsense. Besides, when crucial decisions need to be made, 'tis best to reconnoiter the ground and gather as much intelligence as possible, yes? Sarah's friend Clarissa will be joining us. She's quite the belle, and can present you to the loveliest of the ladies present.''

A vision of a younger version of his mama rose up, to be dismissed with loathing. ''Perhaps, but I've already determined to seek a bride among the merchant classes.''

Englemere raised an eyebrow. ''Indeed? 'Tis your own affair, to be sure. As for me, I'd not make any firm decision without reviewing all the possibilities. Besides, several regiments have recently returned from Paris. I daresay you will find many friends. Pray do join us.''

It would be churlish to continue spurning an offer so kindly extended. Reluctantly Sinjin nodded. ''Very well. I should be delighted.''

''Excellent. I'll have a card sent round.'' The marquess extended his hand.

Sinjin shook it this time less unwillingly than on any previous occasion. Glancing up from that firm grip, the expression he read on Englemere's face underscored the marquess's words. He'd won the gratitude and support of this wealthy and influential man. Perhaps even his friendship, should Sinjin be able to accept it.

'Twas too soon for that leap, he thought as he nodded a goodbye and exited down the marble steps.

He'd taken a hackney to Sarah's house this morning, dismissing the driver a street away to attract as little notice as possible. But with his mind still churning, he waved away the footman's offer to summon another jarvey, choosing to walk the few blocks to his lodging.

He was finally facing the reality he'd been skirting ever since he saw Sarah after her wedding and realized she'd come to care for her chance-given husband. The page of time *had* turned, and there'd be no going back. Sarah was where she now belonged, with the husband she loved and their son.

Despite the wrenching ache of acknowledging her lost to him forever, he felt the rightness of that conclusion bone-deep. It was time to stop railing at fate, his papa, Sarah—even at his mama for the various parts each had played in the death of his dream. Time to extinguish the final embers of his anger and move on.

With a sigh, he vowed to banish for good both the rage and the restless yearning that had driven him these last three years. And felt some semblance of peace descend, a balm of ointment soothed over the abrasion of grief.

Damn, but Englemere was a clever rogue. He'd doubtless intended all along for Sinjin to call immediately, unannounced, catching Sarah at her work and with her son. So he might see for himself the depth of her content.

Still, he'd obtained one reassurance his lonely soul craved. He could face whatever he must, knowing that though muted, the affection Sarah felt for him endured and always would.

He recalled her challenge—not to let the hopeless passion they once shared wither into something bitter and harsh, a wall to close off emotion. To leave himself open to the chance that love might come again.

To complete her happiness by building a home and family of his own.

He made a wry grimace. Despite his promise freely given, he'd had a surfeit of love and its effects. Indeed, given the speed with which he needed to contract a marriage, an honorable bond based on mutual respect and perhaps a bit of fondness was the best he could hope for.

He reached his lodgings and mounted the stairs. After pausing in the sitting room, he proceeded on to the bedchamber. To the bedside table on which rested a neatly bound bundle of letters.

He would pack them away and save them for Sarah's son. If the boy persisted in his fascination with the military, perhaps one day he would enjoy reading the letters his mama had written to a soldier abroad fighting Napoleon.

As for the other…he fingered the inside pocket of his jacket, feeling the wisp-thin, aged piece of vellum he'd kept beside his heart from the moment he'd received it. Sarah's last letter before she left for London to make that unavoidable marriage of convenience.

Carefully he withdrew the paper. Were he to lift it to his nose, despite the sweat, rain, and several bloodstains on its fragile surface, he could swear the missive still bore the faint fragrance of lavender.

She'd explained her dire circumstances, apologized for having to break her vow. And concluded with words he read one more time, even though he'd long had them by heart.

"So tomorrow I depart, my dearest love, leaving behind the dream that has been to me more precious than life. Though I shall never again call you my own, as long as this wretched heart beats, you will be at the center of it. Always, your Sarah."

He walked to the sitting room, poured the last glass of wine from the decanter and carried it to the wing chair before the hearth. Pulling the chair close, he held the letter to the banked coals in the grate. Dust-dry with age, it caught immediately.

He held it to the last moment, while orange flame licked up the ragged surface and turned it rapidly from blackened edge to cinder. *Ashes to ashes, dust to dust.*

When it was no more than a smoldering fragment, he sat back and downed the wine.

The dregs at the bottom of the glass were acrid, and he grimaced. The grimace deepened when he recalled he'd acceded to Englemere's insistence that he attend the ball with them tomorrow night.

By force of will, he damped down the bleakness. Alex would likely be present, and others of the returned officer corps. He would have someone with whom to converse, could perhaps renew some contacts that might prove helpful.

As for the other—he recalled again that expensively-turned-out chit on horseback. Despite the marquess's recommendation that he not dismiss any prospects without examination, he was absolutely sure among the females attending what would doubtless be a glittering assembly tomorrow night, he would find not a single one he would consider for wife.

Chapter Four

Having successfully repinned an errant curl, Clarissa turned from the mirror in Sarah's bedchamber to glance at her friend. "You're sure you feel well enough to attend the ball tonight?" She inspected Sarah with some concern. "You ate almost nothing at dinner, and you seem very pale."

"I'm a bit tired, but nothing to signify, and entirely normal," Sarah said as her maid draped the heavy evening cloak around her shoulders. "I'm increasing again."

Clarissa dropped her pins and jumped up to hug her friend. "What wonderful news! Oh, make it a daughter this time, a lovely, curly-haired darling I can dress up, take to Gunter's for ices, and giggle with over confidences."

"Your preferences are duly noted. Though I shouldn't mind another son first, to insure the succession."

Clarissa made a face. "That sounds like Englemere's preference."

Sarah gave Clarissa a reproving look. "Actually, Englemere has no preference at all, other than for a healthy child and a speedy delivery. I believe Aubrey's leisurely meander into the world taxed him nearly as much as it did me. He's already trying to wrap me in cotton wool, and nearly forbade my going out this evening."

Clarissa regarded her friend with some anxiety. "Are you sure he isn't right? Granted, the Devonshire ball shall be the most opulent of the Season, but you care little enough for that. Perhaps you should remain home."

"As it happens, I especially wanted to attend tonight." With a wave, she dismissed the maid, then waited for the woman to exit before continuing. "A dear friend, my neighbor from Wellingford, Colonel Lord St. John Sandiford, has just returned from Paris with his regiment. Englemere invited him to join us at the ball tonight."

"A soldier—excellent."

"He's sold out, actually. I'm afraid Sinjin stands in much the same position I once did. With his estate dangerously encumbered, he must marry an heiress as soon as possible."

Clarissa frowned, a vague memory stirring. "Sinjin...was he not your childhood sweetheart? The soldier you continued to write even after your marriage?"

"Y-yes." Sarah made a study of her toe. "You will remember him, I think. He returned to England briefly just after Englemere and I were wed. I was hoping you might introduce him to the nicest of the eligible ladies."

A sharper vision focused: the glittering sconces of a ballroom...Sarah flinging herself at a broad-shouldered, blue-coated figure...the soldier's disbelieving face. "He was shocked to find you married, yes? And none too pleased, I recall. You'd been engaged, had you not?"

"Never officially. As neither of us had any fortune, no prudent parent would have permitted us to marry."

Clarissa inspected her friend's downturned face. "But you would have wed him, had it been your choice alone?"

"Most assuredly. I was devastated at the time, but you know I haven't remained so." She looked up, smiling. "Nicholas is a treasure for whom I thank heaven daily."

Clarissa chuckled. "We're unlikely to agree on that score. Still," her eyes assessed Sarah's face, "will it pain you to see him court and marry another?"

"Not at all. He's a fine man, Clare, possessed of many admirable qualities—even without the attraction of a Hussar's furred coat. Though he seems harder now, harsher than I remember." She shook her head, her face pensive. "Having so little control over our lives, I believe women adapt more easily to the necessities forced upon us. Gentlemen are used to shaping events to their satisfaction. After all Sinjin suffered in the war, returning to find himself compelled to marry must be distasteful indeed."

Clarissa shuddered. "Thank Heaven I need never submit to that. I doubt I could."

"Were it truly necessary, my dear, you would do as you must. And have the courage to make the best of it."

As you did, Clarissa thought, not voicing a truth that would surely induce Sarah once again to defend the husband fate had thrust upon her.

"I should like," Sarah was continuing, "to see Sinjin marry a gentle, accomplished, virtuous woman who can dismantle the walls of reserve he's thrown up and dissolve the bitterness that makes him seem so unlike the warm, generous man I know him to be. Someone who will help him restore the home he loves and make him happy." She smiled at Clarissa. "I'm counting on *you* to find just the right candidates to present to him." A touch of sadness tinged her face. "'Tis all I can do for him now."

Clarissa felt a flare of sympathy for them both. "I shall

mount a campaign with anticipation. It will be amusing to see just which paragon your paragon chooses.''

"Paragon, stuff.'' Sarah wrinkled her nose at Clarissa. "Let us go down. The gentlemen should have finished their port, and I don't wish to give Englemere time to conjure up more reasons for me to stay home.''

Clarissa gathered up cloak and reticule. "You know I'm seldom late now.''

"Yes, you've much improved. If you are tardy, 'tis only because you wish to make a grand entrance.''

Clarissa grinned. "Good timing is essential.''

"Indeed.'' Sarah raised an eyebrow. "Such as at Lord Alastair's costume ball, after Miss Glover had whispered to ten or twenty of her most intimate friends that she would appear in a gown so remarkable as to cast 'that conceited Miss Beaumont' in the shade?''

Clarissa shrugged. "I would not have troubled to show her up, but when she issued a clear challenge—''

"You could not help but respond,'' Sarah finished dryly. "So you let the ton speculate, then made a very *late* entrance in a simple white Grecian gown that so accentuated the excellence of your physical charms, poor overdressed Miss Glover was entirely routed.''

"She should have known better than to make me the target of her pique. I'd hardly exchanged a word with that precious Lord Mansfield she was so mad about.''

"Not before the incident. But afterwards—you must admit you deliberately set out to enslave the poor fellow.''

"Merely to complete Miss Glover's lesson.''

"Perhaps. But the innocent suffered along with the guilty. You did lead Mansfield on, though you had not the slightest intention of accepting the offer your encouragement prompted him to make. I saw him shortly afterwards and he was devastated, Clare. You simply cannot play with a gentleman's sentiments like that.''

"There now, we are back to scolding. Really, Sarah, I didn't *make* the poor fool lose his heart, if such he did. For the most part, 'twas all posturing and vanity. Indeed, I'm not at all sure gentlemen have hearts to lose."

Sarah stopped short, her gray eyes impaling Clarissa. "Sometimes, my dear friend, I wonder if *you* have one."

Clarissa felt something like shame heat her cheeks. "Come, Sarah," she coaxed, urgent need filling her to remove the disapproval from the face of the one true friend she possessed. "If I promise not to tamper with the heart of your friend Sinjin, will you cease chastising?"

A long, unsettling moment passed before Sarah replied. "Sometimes I think the best thing that could befall you would be for someone to tamper with yours. But," she allowed, her face finally breaking into a smile, "enough scolding. My fondest wish is that someone or something may touch your fierce soul and direct that energy and courage into some productive channel."

Clarissa released the breath she'd been holding in a chuckle. "You fancy turning me into a 'gentle, accomplished, virtuous woman?'" She shook her head. "A hopeless wish, I'm afraid. But if doing so will return me to your good graces, I shall do my best to find just such a lady for your friend Colonel Sandiford."

Vexation at being late and worry overlaying his original disinclination to attend the ball, several hours later Sinjin ran up the stairs of Lady Devonshire's mansion. As he suspected, the receiving line had already broken up and he would be forced to wander through the overcrowded rooms searching for his hostess before he could join Englemere's party.

"Damn and blast," he muttered as he entered the airless ballroom. His mood inauspicious to making himself agreeable either to his hostess or the friends who awaited him, doing the pretty to the passel of society chits Englemere wished him to meet was, he decided on the spot, completely beyond him this evening. He would escape at the earliest possible moment.

Pausing at the edge of the teeming mass of dancing, strolling, and conversing guests, he scanned the crowd for a lady fitting the description of his hostess. The sharp edges of his high starched collar scratched at his freshly shaved chin as he turned his head. Fashion be damned, he thought irritably, running a chamois-clad finger under his ear and recalling with longing the moderate height of his braided uniform collar. After tonight he would throw these blasted neck cloths out and purchase something sensible.

Mercifully after a few moments he located the Duchess and was able to pay his addresses. Proceeding to his next mission, he surveyed the guests until he found a cluster of uniformed men among whom, he was relieved to discover as he edged closer, were two familiar Grenedier Guards.

"Milhouse, Allensby," he called out.

"Colonel Lord Sandiford!" Captain Milhouse exclaimed. "Good evening to you, sir. But how plain you look!"

"We heard you were to sell out," Lieutenant Allensby said. "With Boney holed up for good, 'tis just as well. There'll be no decent fight now short of the Americas— and who wishes to venture to that godforsaken land? All red Indians and upstart Colonials."

"Former colonials, I believe," Sinjin corrected with a smile. "Could either of you present me to Lady Barbara Childress? I have a message to deliver."

"From Alex Standish, I'll wager," Allensby said. "I thought sure he'd be here to toss his cap back in the ring with the contenders for the hand of the fair Lady Barbara."

"Fair and *wealthy*," Milhouse added. "An irresistible combination."

His worry reviving, a frown creased Sinjin's brow. "An unavoidable matter precluded his attending tonight. I promised to convey his regrets. If one of you gentlemen would be so good as to point out Lady Barbara?"

"Brave man, to confront her dragon of a mother," Milhouse replied. "Countess subjects any buck venturing near her darling to a general's inspection. Nothing but perfection will do for Lady Barbara, her mama told mine."

"I hear she dismissed Upton on account of his squint, Norfolk wasn't tall enough, and she thought Westminster's countenance too red of hue," Allensby said.

"Aye, so adept is she at finding defects in every suitor the girl may never marry," Milhouse agreed. "But come along, Colonel, if you're determined."

As they inched their way across the room, a dusting of anger settled over Sinjin's worry. Unless Lady Barbara's papa were less bacon-brained than his wife, given what he'd just heard of the mother it appeared his war-injured lieutenant's chances of obtaining the girl's hand were slim. No wonder Alex was so uneasy.

His ready contempt for the ton in general resurfaced. Horse droppings, to judge a man by his height or the coloring of his complexion—or his wealth or birth, for that matter. Lud, he realized with a grin that lightened his irritation, he was turning into a flaming republican.

He sobered as he mulled how best to express Alex's regrets. How did he make excuses that showed sufficient cause for his lieutenant's absence without drawing attention to the physical limitations Alex hated to admit?

His face turned grimmer as he remembered their ill-fated ride this evening. Having dined at Alex's club, they were headed down Piccadilly toward the Albany in a hubbub of pedestrians, carts, and carriages when Alex's horse had suddenly shied violently to the right. With the muscles of his left knee still weak and his left hand useless, the lieutenant lost his balance and tumbled into the roadway, striking his head on a passing cart as he fell.

Summoning a physician over Alex's protests, Sinjin hustled him back to his rooms. Fortunately the man ascertained that, though bloody and painful, the lieutenant's injuries were not serious. Only by obtaining Alex's grudging admittance that he would attract far too much unwelcome attention by attending the ball with his head swathed in bandages had Sinjin convinced him to remain resting in his rooms. And by swearing to personally convey Alex's regrets to Lady Barbara.

"Over there," Milhouse's voice in his ear recalled him, "that pretty chit in green. Which reminds me, a party of us are leaving soon for the green room at Covent Garden. Allensby's negotiating for the company of a delectable little actress. Be happy to have you join us."

An actress from the green room—now there was a thought. A woman whose artifice was honest. A pity actresses did not amass fortunes, else he might seriously consider wedding one.

He had no blunt for enticing a mistress, but anything

was better than remaining at this curst ball. "I should
like that," he replied. "Shall I meet you there?"

"Capital. Must warn you, old man, once I make the
introductions I'm going to bolt. Not in the petticoat line
myself, and I've no wish to be snubbed by the old tar-
tar."

They approached a pretty petite brunette encircled by
a court of suitors. "You're in luck," Milhouse commented as they edged in. "The dragon's nowhere in evidence."

Oblivious to the protests of the gentlemen he shoul-
dered aside, Milhouse pushed his way to the center and
bowed to the girl. "Lady Barbara, may I have the honor
of presenting Lord Sandiford, lately Colonel in the Tenth
Hussars. Colonel, Lady Barbara Childress." With a wink
at Sinjin and another bow to the lady, Milhouse slipped
away.

"Tenth Hussars?" Lady Barbara exclaimed as Sinjin
bent to kiss the hand she offered. "Are you the colonel
of whom my friend Lieutenant Standish has spoken so
highly? Then I am indeed delighted to make your acquaintance."

"I was privileged to command Lieutenant Standish's
unit, my lady. A brave and skillful officer with whom I
was proud to serve."

The lady blushed. "I am not at all surprised to hear it.
But…does he not accompany you this evening? I have
not seen him, and he promised—that is, Lady Devonshire's ball being so notable, I was quite sure he would
attend."

"Would you stroll with me, my lady?" Sinjin bent
closer and lowered his voice. "I bear a message from
him."

Lady Barbara glanced about nervously—looking for

her mama, Sinjin surmised. It appeared the lady herself
stood in awe of her parent—a fact that did not augur well
for Alex. "I should be delighted, Colonel."

To her credit, Sinjin noted, Lady Barbara seemed totally unmoved by the cries of reproach uttered by the rest
of her court as he led her off.

"What is it, Colonel?" she asked as soon as they were
out of earshot. "He is not ill?"

"No, my lady. But he did suffer a trifling…accident.
Nothing grave, I assure you," he added as the lady
gasped. "Took a fall while riding, as we all do from time
to time, and put a neat cut over his eye. As he didn't
wish to alarm or," he added, thinking of her mother,
"embarrass you by appearing tonight tricked out in stick-
ing-plaster, he asked me to convey to you his deep disappointment, and beg your leave to call tomorrow."

"You are sure he was not…truly injured?" the lady
asked, her face anxious despite his reassurances. "You
are not making light of it? Please, I must know the truth."

"He will be wholly well by morning, I promise you,"
Sinjin replied, in spite of himself touched by Lady Barbara's concern. It appeared his lieutenant's affections
might be reciprocated. But if the family opposed the lovers, would this fragile-looking damsel have the strength
of mind to persevere?

Alex would, God help him. Though since Waterloo
Sinjin had not conversed with his Maker with quite the
regularity he ought, he now uttered a swift prayer that
the fine, brave lad he'd led would not get his heart broken.

"Thank Heaven," the lady sighed. "I am relieved he
took no serious harm. The evening will be sadly flat without him, though. Please tell him I shall expect him to-

morrow and no excuses! You will…see him again tonight?''

''Of course, ma'am. I must deliver your message.''

''Good. It's silly of me, perhaps, with him safely back in England, but still I…worry. I own I was not easy when he claimed he could not endure residing with his mama and all his sisters and insisted on taking rooms.''

Sinjin could well imagine his lieutenant eager to escape the cosseting of his mama and sisters. He also imagined Alex would find the solicitude of this particular lady much more pleasing. ''Truly, he is in no danger. You may rest easy, Lady Barbara.''

''Thank you, Colonel. For coming tonight—and for all you have done for him. I shall never forget it.''

From the corner of his eye Sinjin spotted an imposing dame with a headdress of ostrich plumes bearing down on them. By her rich display of jewels and disapproving air he concluded she must be the Countess of Wetherford, Lady Barbara's mother. Given the crowded room, it appeared Sinjin would not be able to shepherd the daughter back to her suitors quickly enough to escape.

His doom was sealed when the girl herself noticed the woman's approach. ''M-Mama,'' she faltered.

Her mother sniffed, setting the plumes in her headdress quivering. ''What do you mean, child, wandering off with this *stranger?*'' She subjected Sinjin to a glacial glare, as if he were a hair she'd just discovered in her blancmange.

Lady Barbara gave her mother an apologetic smile. ''Hardly a stranger, Mama. May I make known to you Colonel Lord Sandiford, formerly of the Tenth Hussars.''

The countess's sharp eyes assessed him. ''Sandiford, is it? Son of the late James Allen Sandiford?''

Sinjin bowed, realizing wryly this battleaxe had just branded him a fortune hunter. "I have that honor."

The countess dismissed his lineage with a wave. "A pleasure, I'm sure. Come along, Barbara. Your papa has a partner to present to you."

"Thank you, Colonel," the hapless young lady managed before her mother bore her away.

Alex must be besotted indeed to wish to ally himself to that family, Sinjin reflected as he set off to find Lord Englemere's party. A few minutes' polite chat and he would thankfully depart.

He spotted Sarah first, so serenely lovely in a gown of gold cloth that, for a moment, his breath caught. Then Englemere came to take her arm, bending his dark head to kiss her cheek. In his evening dress of midnight black, the marquess was a perfect foil for her pale blond beauty, his kiss in this most public assembly an unfashionable mark of devotion. The ache tightened Sinjin's chest again, and gritting his teeth, he damped it down.

Then Sarah spied him. "Sinjin! We'd about given up!"

He walked over to kiss her hand. "Sorry I'm late. My lieutenant, Alexander Standish, met with a bit of an accident. I had to attend him, then convince him to remain in his rooms, an even larger task, since there's a young lady here he particularly wanted to see."

"Clarissa was borne off by her admirers long ago," Englemere said. "Let me find Sarah a chair and I'll take you to hunt for her."

The tireless Sarah sitting? The idea amused him until he noticed she was looking unusually pale. "Are you ill?" he asked in some alarm.

"Just fatigued—'tis nothing. I agreed to let Nicholas convey me home once he's found Clarissa. You'll remember her, I expect. She's much too beautiful to forget.''

Sinjin vaguely recalled a tall girl with hair of auburn, skin of cream and all over diamonds. Possessing a flashy beauty not at all to his taste, he'd paid her small attention. ''No doubt,'' he returned noncommittally.

They reached a less crowded anteroom and found Sarah a sofa. ''Would you stay with her, Colonel?'' Englemere asked. ''It may take me a few moments to locate Clarissa.''

''I'd be delighted,'' Sinjin replied, surprised at Englemere's entrusting Sarah to him—and not sure he truly welcomed this opportunity for a tête-à-tête.

''Nicholas, I'm not about to faint,'' Sarah protested.

''Perhaps not, my dear, but these rooms are altogether too hot. The sooner we get you home, the better.'' He brushed her cheek with his fingers. ''I shall return as soon as possible.''

''Alexander Standish—is he not the Earl of Worth's son?'' Sarah asked as Sinjin drew up a chair.

''Yes,'' he replied, relieved she'd chosen so prosaic a topic. ''He joined the Tenth just before Waterloo.''

''And was badly wounded, was he not? He'd been courting Lady Barbara Childress. She was most anxious when she learned he was injured.''

''He's courting her again, though given the crowd of suitors I saw, I'm not sanguine about his chances.''

''The countess,'' Sarah said and rolled her eyes. ''Still, they are of equal birth and wealth, both possessed of unexceptional character. There can be no true impediment, if they desire it enough.''

Had fortune not mattered, such small obstacle as a parent's objection would not have stopped us, he thought, and knew by her expression Sarah was thinking the same.

"Which reminds me," she said, glancing away, "there was one other matter I wanted to speak to you about."

He groaned. "Such a preface usually means I'm about to be scolded. I didn't think I'd been in London long enough to incur your displeasure."

She shook her head. "'Twas not in London. Sinjin, how could you have stopped writing to your mama? I know you blame her in part for...what happened between us, but fate and time were equally at fault. Despite your differences, she does love you. When months passed after you returned to your regiment and she did not hear from you, she grew quite desperate for news." Sarah smiled faintly. "Desperate enough to visit me."

He looked up sharply. "She visited you?" he echoed. For his mother to have sought out a girl of whom she'd always been jealous, whose marriage to her son she'd been instrumental in preventing, was a major concession.

He shifted uncomfortably. "'Twas bad of me, I admit, but I...was at a very low point then. I simply could not bring myself to write her. But I did send notes to my solicitor—with instructions on how to handle the bills," he couldn't help the acrid note that crept into his tone. "I always instructed him to pass my regards on to Mama."

"Being a mama myself now, I can assure you how inadequate such messages would have been. And even those came rarely. You've...you've not seen her yet, then?"

He sighed. "No. I shall post down to Sandiford Court soon, I suppose. My batman handled things after Waterloo, but 'tis time I inspected the wreckage for myself. Both tasks, I must admit, I've been putting off."

"She's in London now. Indeed, I thought you might see her here tonight."

"London!" Anger flared. "How can she imagine I could support the expense of a London house?"

"She's staying with friends. Lord and Lady Avery, I believe." Sarah bent a reproving glance on him. "Really, Sinjin, you mustn't always be thinking the worst of her. She seems...much subdued of late."

"You're right, of course. You have her direction? I shall have to call on her, I suppose."

"Do it soon, please, Sinjin?" Sarah touched his sleeve, her eyes appealing. "She must have learned you've returned to London. It will grieve her mightily to know you are here and have not cared enough to see her."

He squeezed her fingers briefly, savoring the bittersweetness of that fleeting contact. "As you wish."

She nodded, then looked up. "Nicholas, you found Clarissa?"

"In the card room. Colonel, if you'll follow me? I'll return in an instant, Sarah."

"As Clarissa came with us, our departure will leave her stranded. You will escort her home, Sinjin? Number 10, Grosvenor Square," Sarah said.

"If she wishes, though I should think one of her usual suitors would sue for that honor."

"Perhaps, but if not, I trust you'll see her there." Sarah pressed his hand. "I'm sure Clare will introduce you to so many lovely ladies, your most difficult problem will be deciding which one you prefer."

When pigs fly, Sinjin thought, and bowed.

"In here," Englemere said as he ushered Sinjin into a crowded room. "Only three or four devoted suitors hanging about, so you should have an opportunity to converse."

"Before an audience of only three or four?"

Englemere chuckled. "Clare will send them to the

right-about if she so chooses. A lady of considerable spirit, is our Clare.''

Vain, spoiled, temperamental, Sinjin translated.

An assortment of small tables were set up, around which groups sat about playing cards. Sinjin repressed a shudder. *Gaming.* Yet another reason not to take an aristocratic wife.

Englemere led him across the room to where several fashionably attired young bucks leaned over a lady's chair. As they wove their way through the crowd, Sinjin got a glimpse of a satin-clad back, the sparkle of a jeweled clasp, and an artful arrangement of thick auburn curls. ''Ho, Clare!'' Englemere called. ''Here we are at last.''

They halted behind her. The young woman looked over her shoulder, fixing on him large, luminous and somehow familiar green eyes. Which then widened, her half smile fading even as the greeting Sinjin had been about to deliver withered on his lips.

''You!'' she exclaimed. And burst out laughing.

Chapter Five

Her laughter stinging his ears, Sinjin closed his eyes and fumbled for words. Before he could decide in what manner to address a lady to whom he'd recently been unpardonably rude, the said lady spoke.

"No need to stand on ceremony. As I expect you've surmised, I'm Clarissa Beaumont, Colonel. Delighted to meet you—officially. And please accept my apologies! No wonder you were so short with me."

"Miss Beaumont." Gritting his teeth, Sinjin bowed. How could he not have considered that a lady pausing before Sarah's house would doubtless be an acquaintance? True, Miss Beaumont's distinctive red hair had been concealed under a hat and veil, but surely he ought to have recognized Sarah's striking green-eyed friend. If he hadn't let his senseless fury master his sense.

Furious again at having made such a fool of himself, to avoid the acute eyes that undoubtedly were sizing up his considerably altered appearance, Sinjin glanced over to the marquess. And then away from the amused speculation on Englemere's face.

"You are already acquainted with Lord Sandiford?" that gentleman asked Clarissa.

"We, ah, met while riding."

Englemere lifted a quizzical brow at him.

"In a manner of speaking," Sinjin said shortly.

Meanwhile, Miss Beaumont addressed the men who had reluctantly risen when they arrived. Still flustered, Sinjin focused on them. Within a few moments he had been introduced, Miss Beaumont begged the other men's pardon, and then waved them away with the airy statement that Lord Englemere brought her a message from his wife.

"Neatly done, Clare. I'll let you two chat. I'm leaving with Sarah directly—no, don't be alarmed, she's merely tired. If you don't mind, I've asked Lord Sandiford to escort you home."

"If that will not be inconvenient, Colonel? Come sit beside me, then," she invited, gesturing him to a chair.

After bowing to the departing Lord Englemere, who walked off sporting a cat-in-the-cream-pot grin he longed to smack off that handsome face, Sinjin sat. Unable to avoid it any longer, he looked directly at Miss Beaumont.

He'd known by reputation and assorted glimpses of her that Sarah's friend was a striking woman. That intellectual concept did not prepare him for viewing, from the distance of a hand's touch, the lady he'd previously seen only glancingly. He gasped, then forgot to breathe.

Doggedly, his brain tried to remind him he scorned beauty and all its spendthrift frivolity. His body was having none of it.

The candles set gold flecks dancing in the flame of her hair, mesmerizing as the flicker of firelight. A scent of roses stole over him, conjuring up summer heat and the petal-soft touch of bare skin. Those remarkable emerald eyes flanked dainty earlobes and a lush lower lip that called out for a man's tasting. His dazzled gaze sank down a swan's sweep of neck to softly rounded shoulders and, Heaven forfend, such a temptingly lavish display of bosom that his temples grew moist and the hands at his sides cupped of their own accord, fingertips tingling. His tongue seemed swollen to the size of his neck cloth in a mouth gone too dry for words, while inevitable and unbidden reactions occurred in other parts of his anatomy.

After a struggle, his mind finally wrested back control. He jerked his gaze from contemplating what lay beneath the polished satin at her hips to her face.

To siren's eyes that gleamed in self-satisfied acknowledgment of the response she had just evoked in him.

Her knowing look tossed a welcome dash of cold water over his ardor. How many hapless men she must have tormented with that body, how many expensive trinkets wheedled out of besotted suitors. Or intended in future to wheedle out of a husband whose wits had descended to his nether regions.

Vain, he forced himself to whisper into the dizzy ringing in his ears. Obviously vain, unquestionably spoiled, and by all reports, exceedingly temperamental.

Though his sense of fairness tried to argue she had excellent cause for vanity, he managed to ignore it.

"So you've returned to England for good, Colonel?"

"Yes."

"You will be staying in London for the Season?"

"I expect."

"You must allow me to introduce you to several friends, then. Now that some of the regiments are returning from abroad I imagine you shall encounter fellow-officers, but 'tis always more comfortable to have a larger acquaintance, do you not think?"

"I suppose." Lud, where had his reason wandered?

Disgusted, he tried to dredge up some semblance of conversation and remembered it was unnecessary. He had no intention, however long he must remain in town, of frequenting such gatherings as this.

"That's kind of you, Miss Beaumont, but I shall not be mixing much in this society."

That caught her attention. She tilted her chin and inspected him, as if he were a specimen for study. "Indeed? I was under the impression that you were desirous of making the acquaintance of…eligible ladies. And I am quite certain such ladies will be most anxious to meet such a handsome and gallant officer."

"Former officer," he corrected. "I thank you again for the offer, ma'am, but I sincerely doubt in my…circumstances, of which you are undoubtedly aware, I would be of any interest to your friends whatsoever."

She raised an eyebrow. "You do wish to marry, do you not? Or was I misinformed?"

That was rather blunt, and he felt himself flushing. "It is my intention to seek a wife, yes. But I expect to look…elsewhere for her."

Her lip quirked in some amusement. "Elsewhere, my lord? Balls such as this may include guests not, ah, useful for your purposes, but they are, I guarantee, more comfortable than the gauntlet of hopeful mamas you will run at such a Marriage Mart as Almacks."

Once again she tilted her head and watched him. Wishing to bring the conversation to an end as expeditiously as possible, he said nothing.

When he remained silent she continued, "Given your wartime service, I would not have expected you to avoid beginning a task merely because you judge it…unpleasant. Indeed, the more undesirable it be, the better to accomplish it speedily.''

Her facile advice irritated him even more than her presumptuous assumption there existed no society other than the exclusive one she herself frequented. His answer was therefore blunter than he might have wished.

''I intend, Miss Beaumont, to seek a bride from among the merchant class.''

She was quick-witted, at least, for her reaction was more curiosity than confusion. ''Whatever for? Despite the current state of your finances, given your lineage and reputation you would still be accounted an eligible suitor for ladies of your own class. As you must know.''

Could she not simply say ''Indeed, my lord'' and leave it at that? 'Od's breath, intelligent as she appeared, surely his reticence clearly conveyed his desire not to pursue this matter further.

Annoyance sharpening, he said through clenched teeth, ''I do not think a lady of my—your—class would meet my requirements.''

''And what might those requirements be?''

Uncertain even a sharp set-down would curb Miss Beaumont's unladylike persistence, Sinjin grudgingly took the more polite path of answering. However, not having yet progressed in his own mind from what he *didn't* want to what he *did,* he had to grope for a reply.

''Modesty. Simplicity. Temperance in all things.''

''And ladies of breeding are not modest, simple, or temperate?'' she asked in a silky voice.

''You force me to be unchivalrous, but in my observation, generally not.''

''I see.'' Long lashes swept down, concealing her expression. She picked up a deck of cards and idly began to shuffle. ''Any other strictures?''

He eyed the cards with distaste. "An aversion to throwing away hard-won money at games of chance."

She looked up, a little smile playing at the corner of her lips. "Oh, but cards are so amusing. And we ladies normally play for chicken stakes. I can't recall ever losing more than four or five hundred pounds of an evening. But your list interests me, my lord. What else would you seek in a bride?"

He recalled her smug satisfaction at his reaction to her looks, the casual way she dismissed her court. "Beauty is a highly overrated attribute—a mere accident of birth, is it not? Of much greater value are lack of vanity and flirtatiousness. A lady content to remain at home of an evening, not forever gadding about vying for the attention of men. One educated enough to make pleasant conversation, perhaps possessing some skill at an instrument." Warming to the task now, he added, "Naturally, given my circumstances, she must be clever at household management, possess a cheerful disposition and be not so toplofty that she considers honest labor beneath her."

"Generous, wise, modest, and thrifty?" she summarized. "And, of course, innocent of all the vices of aristocracy."

Suspicious of her mild tone, he eyed her frostily. "Such attributes would not come amiss."

She shuffled the cards and cut them with a snap, then looked up, green eyes glittering. "My dear Colonel, you seek not a wife, but a saint."

The chit was mocking him. This rich, idle woman with the body of a temptress and the arrogance of a queen was mocking both his predicament and his expectations.

The very idea caused his simmering temper, uncertain all evening, to boil over.

"A modest woman of sense a saint? Perhaps. At any

rate, 'tis surely something you—and other ladies like you—will never be. I shall trouble you no further. Your servant, madam.'' Swiftly he rose to his feet and gave her an exaggerated bow.

For the second time in their renewed acquaintance Clarissa was left with her mouth agape while Colonel Lord Sandiford stalked off without a backward glance.

She took a deep, steadying breath and reined in her own temper. After a moment, he would realize how rag-mannered he'd been and return to apologize.

Knowing how his fortune had been lost, it was rather bad of her to tweak him about gambling. But the devil, she had apologized for mistaking him for a groom, hadn't she? Not that he'd shown the least appreciation for her admitting that quite understandable error. And she'd generously offered to assist him in his quest for a wife. She, a belle of the ton, had agreed to act as practically a...*duenna,* for Heaven's sake!

And what thanks had she gotten for her efforts? Her temper fraying further with each adjective, she mentally counted off the damning description of what he supposed she was not. Modest. Generous. Temperate. Intelligent. As for what she was—he'd all but called her an irresponsible gamester and a vain, shallow flirt!

Worst of all, she had felt his exploratory stare burn over every inch of skin he inspected. Though she was doubtless less experienced in the arts of love than the Colonel, she was no dewy-eyed innocent. She'd tasted kisses from a few select suitors, even a bit more, and thoroughly enjoyed the forbidden thrill of it. But this, tonight, had been far more than thrill.

His gaze set her smoldering with an unprecedented desire to take the hands he held so rigidly at his sides and

draw them to her breasts. To tease open with her tongue
that stern censorious mouth.

Heat scorched her face. She was accustomed to inspiring and controlling passion in men, not being singed
by it herself. Damn the bastard for looking so tall, hard,
muscled…delicious.

And rude. Unforgivably rude, she reminded herself,
fanning her warm cheeks. He had better be most eloquent
when he came to beg her pardon.

Praise Heaven, he was not indifferent to her. She
smiled slightly. When he did apologize, she was going
to make him grovel.

It occurred to her she'd been sitting there some few
moments and the colonel had yet to reappear. Thankful
the gamesters occupying the surrounding tables were too
engrossed to have noticed the unusual spectacle of Miss
Beaumont all alone, she slipped to the door.

Perhaps he'd been detained. He'd met one of his fellow
officers and been drawn into conversation. As she escaped into the hallway, she saw Grenville, Mountclare
and Lord Alastair walking toward her.

"Ah, our goddess is finally free!" Grenville exclaimed.

Lord Alastair took her arm. "Saw Englemere leave.
And that starched-up Colonel fellow, what's-his-name?"

"Sandiford," she replied absently before the meaning
of his comment jolted her alert. "Did you say Lord Sandiford left the ball?"

"Stiff as if he had a poker up his back. Greeted him
politely but the fellow just ignored me and walked out
the door." Alastair shook his head over such bad ton.
"Glad I never went into the Army, if it turns a fellow
into such a mannerless care-for-nobody."

Slowly her brain comprehended the reality. Lord Sandiford had departed. Without apologizing. Without even arranging her escort, he who had been entrusted with seeing her home!

The temper she'd just congratulated herself on managing rather well flared from spark to inferno.

The room went fuzzy in a red haze of rage beyond articulation. She scarcely felt Alastair patting her arm, did not hear the words exiting Mountclare's moving lips.

That pompous, rag-mannered, prudish military oaf! How dare—how *dare* he insult her, dismiss her as flighty and flawed with scarcely a second glance. He thought women feebleminded, yet he would judge her with no knowledge of her character whatsoever. Warm, generous, caring, Sarah had described him? Either war had changed him completely, or this precious Colonel Sandiford was an imposter.

She would give him the cut direct. No, that was too civilized. She would skewer him with the cleverest, most cutting words her tongue could summon. Then she recalled another use to which a few moments ago she'd felt moved to put her tongue and her rage refired.

She would murder him.

Gradually the faces around her refocused.

"I say, Miss Beaumont, are you feeling quite the thing? You look faint!" Grenville was saying.

"Let me assist you to a chair," Alastair urged.

She shook off his arm, unable at that moment, thinking of *him,* to bear another's touch. "Nonsense, I've never fainted in my life. I'm…I'm restless. I must walk."

"Let us come along. Wouldn't want you to—"

"—As you wish."

Her courtiers trotting alongside, mystified but docile, she marched down the hallway, breathing deeply and willing herself to calm. As she pivoted to return to the ballroom, a man walked out of an anteroom into her path.

"Miss Beaumont!" Lord John Weston halted abruptly. Apparently observing her now-flushed cheeks and air of agitation, he remarked in his unctuous voice, "You seem to be quite in a taking this evening."

Lovely. With her as furious as she could recall being in recent memory, who must she encounter but the one person in London she truly detested. "Lord John," she said coldly, wishing it were possible to squash this nasty, waspish man like the insect he was.

"Ah, but temper gives her such a vibrant air, does it not, gentleman? So fetching one almost forgets the rapier tongue and the occasional, shall we say, lapses in judgment such temper all too often provokes."

"Would that your rapier wit were as sharp as your malice," she shot back, too upset to ignore his barbed words as she normally would.

"Rapiers?" Mountclare interrupted. "Not here, surely, Weston. Bad ton to bring weapons to a ball."

Weston spared him a pitying look before replying to Clarissa. "A sadly dull blade there. But I am unkind, I fear. Being a lady, your...exuberance never leads you into doing anything too rash. Ladies are much too timid."

"Timid, Lord John? Or merely sensible?"

He laughed. "Timidity is often paraded as sense, my dear Miss Beaumont."

She threw him a withering glance. "I am neither timid, nor your 'dear', Lord John."

He bowed, unfazed. "Excuse me if I am too...familiar. Unlike other gentlemen, I, alas, cannot make that claim."

Was that detestable little worm implying she was free with her favors? "Have a care what you say, my lord.

Else I may give you ample cause not to doubt my timidity.''

His smile deepened. ''That sounds perfectly delectable, my—Miss Beaumont.''

Her less than needle-witted swains seemed not to have followed their rapid exchanges, but that remark was obvious enough even for them. ''Here now, Weston,'' Grenville frowned, ''Ain't no proper thing to say to a lady.''

''My apologies if I've offended.''

You do that by breathing, she thought, but merely nodded. ''My lord,'' she said, and started past.

He held out a hand, blocking her. ''Gentlemen, shall we see just how intrepid our brave Miss Beaumont can be? Let us challenge her to some feat even a gentleman would find adventuresome.''

''Challenge a lady?'' Grenville objected. ''Ain't done.''

''Ah, but Miss Beaumont is a most unusual lady. Even so, I expect you are right. The weaker sex shouldn't be tempted to exceed their limitations.''

Though prudence said to avoid discussing any proposal emanating from the snide mouth of Lord John, the man's condescending smile made her itch to get the better of him. ''What sort of challenge, Lord John?''

''Grenville is correct, Miss Beaumont. I should not have broached such a venture.''

''Was there no thought behind your suggestion?'' She exaggerated a sigh. ''An all-too-common fault among men.''

His smile faltered a moment, his eyes flashing. Then it revived, a curve of the lips as false as her own. ''If you think it proper, I shall be happy to elaborate.''

It wasn't proper, she knew, but fed by her smoldering

fury, the recklessness her mama had always deplored was seizing control. "I expect I am equal to any challenge *you* could envision."

"I doubt you have any idea what I envision—for us." He spoke the last words in a whisper for her ears alone.

Her anger abruptly redirected itself from Colonel Sandiford's veiled insults to this small man's presumption. Did that measly little muckworm imagine she'd ever accord him more than a disdainful glance? Reason drowning in wrath, she spat out, "Name your challenge, my lord."

"Miss Beaumont," Lord Alastair protested, "I think this whole discussion most ill-advised—"

"Indeed?" Mountclare chimed in. "I daresay Miss Beaumont is ripe for anything Lord John could devise."

"We shall see," Weston replied, directing a slow glance up and down her torso that made Clarissa's skin prickle with revulsion, as if a slug had just crawled over her.

"I still say it ain't fitting," Alastair persisted.

Lord John laughed. "Your champion," he gestured toward Alastair. "A wager then, Grenville?"

That gentleman's face brightened. One who'd been known to bet a hundred pounds on which of two raindrops would slide first to the bottom of a window, he could never resist a wager. "I'll give double odds on Miss Beaumont."

"This has gone far enough," Alastair insisted, but Clarissa stayed him with a touch.

Lord John had bandied innuendos before, but never quite as blatantly as tonight. Ah, to be a man, to be able to meet him at Jackson's where she might have the pleasure of pummeling his presumptuous face. Stymied of that pleasure, she'd do just about anything to wipe away that knowing leer.

"What do you suggest, Lord John?" she asked through fury-stiffened lips.

"Something unusual, daring. Ah...I have it. You're reputed to have a talent for theatricals, are you not, Miss Beaumont? How about a role totally unlike yourself—in a somewhat novel venue. Yes, that's the ticket."

His cunning smile broadened. "I propose that you en- act the part of a flower girl outside Covent Garden theatre tonight for an hour. And I've a hundred pounds that says you cannot do it."

Her mother would have palpitations; venturing into the darkness of Covent Garden unescorted might present un- known dangers, and if anyone with any pretense to gen- tility recognized her, her reputation would be in shreds. But she simply could not bring herself to let his challenge go unanswered.

Scornfully she looked him up and down. "Only a hun- dred pounds? But why should you risk much? When I can act the role of flower girl much more convincingly than you will ever play the part of a gentleman. Alastair, my cloak, if you please. It seems we have a rendezvous at Covent Garden."

Chapter Six

She'd really done it.

Garbed in the lower housemaid's cast-off Sunday dress and nervously clutching the posey of violets Grenville sent to complete her costume, an hour later Clarissa waited as her jarvey slowed to a halt in the night shadows of Covent Garden.

At the ball Alastair had argued the danger and impropriety of the mad venture, while Lord John countered that the gentlemen would loiter at the other side of the square to ensure her safety. He'd then turned to Clarissa and tauntingly asked if she wished to withdraw.

She'd rather have swallowed broken glass than back down.

And so she'd returned home to find a costume, thrown an evening cloak over the shabby gown, and with a disapproving Alastair glowering beside her, taken a hackney to their rendezvous.

Waiting until the square was empty of fashionable carriages, with a bravado she was far from feeling, Clarissa climbed down to assume her post at the corner and sent Alastair over to join Grenville, Mountclare and Weston.

Her gaze lingered a moment on Lord John and she

frowned. Though his extensive links with many prominent families gave him the entrée everywhere, she found
his innuendo increasingly discomfiting as well as detestable.

He desired her, of course—most men did. She recognized that fact without a trace of vanity, knowing she
was no more responsible for the generous curves that
drew men's eyes than she was for the trees growing in
the park. Generally she did not try to use her natural
assets to entice, except when directly challenged, as by
the pitiful Miss Glover, or when particularly annoyed or
intrigued.

She looked back to find Lord John staring at her and
a chill crawled up her spine. Prominent connections or
no, after tonight she would seriously consider giving him
the cut direct.

Having no wish to attract the notice of anyone in the
occasional crested carriage that passed in a clatter of
hoofs and harness, she stood in the shadows well back
from the street. The porch of St. Paul's looming in the
distance reassured her. How could anything distressing
happen within sight of Wren's spectacular church?

It not being part of the dare that she actually hawk the
flowers she carried, after a few moments she began to
relax. For the first time in her life, she had escaped the
restrictions imposed on a maiden of gentle birth and was
as free as a man to stroll about, unfettered by hovering
maids or trailing footman. Soon, she was caught up in
observing the goings-on in the square, for one of her
privileged existence as much a spectacle as those being
enacted in the neighborhood's grand theatres.

In the flickering light of a torch a few shopfronts down,
two barefoot, grubby boys played at dice, calling out to
each other in unintelligible language whose bantering

tone alone she could understand. A young woman, a maid by her dress, walked arm-in-arm with a strapping fellow who appeared to be a footman, their heads together, laughing softly. They passed a lump that turned out, when her eyes adjusted to the darkness, to be a ragged man, so motionless she feared he might be dead until the torchlight outlined the bottle he raised unsteadily to his lips. Castaway! she realized in scandalized amazement.

Quite a few pedestrians strolled about, though as she expected at this hour, the passersby were almost exclusively male. This one, with his long-tailed coat and glittering watch fob, might be a lawyer's clerk—perhaps, she thought with a thrill of titillation, going to visit a woman in the fancy-houses she knew bordered the ill-lit alleys nearby. Two young men arm-in-arm singing as they staggered along were obviously returning from a visit to some local tavern.

Apparently none of the walkers had either interest or blunt to waste on posies, for after a casual glance at her wilted blossoms and silent figure, they continued on.

Then Drury Lane must have let out, for from the direction of Russell Street the volume of carriage traffic increased. A moment later a party of well-dressed young bucks made a boisterous entry into the square. Glancing across the street to insure her ''protectors'' were still on guard, she eased herself farther back in the shadows. She didn't mean to ruin her splendid adventure by being recognized.

It appeared the revelers were known to Grenville, for after a moment he and her other ''guards'' walked over to speak with them. Drawing them away from her, she surmised, both amused and grateful.

Her attention distracted by the commotion opposite, at first she sensed rather than saw the hulking figure.

"Sell me some posies, dearie?" a rough voice asked.

A burly, broad-shouldered man in a shabby freize coat stood in front of her, weaving slightly. One tooth and two black eyes gleamed in the darkness of his face, and a sharp odor of spirits reached her nose. The hair on the back of her neck prickling, she glanced toward her protectors. They were still preoccupied.

"A shilling," she said, trying to mimic the accent of her London-born tweeny. "Yer lordship," she added, belatedly curtseying. Even with friends nearby, this hulk of a man made her uneasy. Being a flower girl seemed suddenly more hazardous than she'd anticipated.

"Shilling for them wilted blossoms?" the man jeered. "Buy me a woman fer that. Let's 'ave a look at ye, dearie, mebbe I'll take ye instead." He reached for her.

Alarmed but angered, she batted his hand away. "Buy me vi'lets, or get on with ye."

The man laughed, an unpleasant sound that sent shivers down her backbone. "Happen I'll jest get on with ye, eh?"

Before she could guess his intent, the stranger seized her with one beefy arm. "Come now, sweetings, give a feller a kiss 'n let 'im know what 'e's gettin'."

Truly frightened now, she tried to wriggle out of his grip, but in spite of her efforts he drew her closer to his foul-smelling face. Pushing him back as hard as she could, she dealt him a slap with her free hand. "Robert!" she screamed. "Gren—"

A callused hand tasting of dirt and sweat clamped over her mouth. "Feisty, ain't ye?" the big man snickered. "Don't be callin' none 'a yer fancy-men." He ripped back her cloak, then gasped as the shaft of streetlight caught on her face and hair. "By the saints, a fair angel ye've found yerself, Jack. Goin' to enjoy this penny's worth.''

She bit down hard on his thumb. Swearing, the man backed off a little, giving her room to bring up her knee, but hampered by her skirts and heavy cloak, her blow was did little more than infuriate the ruffian clutching her.

''Bitch!'' he swore, and slapped her.

Her head jerked back. By the time the ringing in her ears eased, he had dragged her into the adjacent alley. Hauling her close, he plastered his wet mouth on hers, one hand groping at her bottom as he sought to pull her lower torso against his. Trying not to gag at the tongue pushing against her firmly-closed teeth, she concentrated on working her hands loose. A few seconds later she managed to rake her nails down the sensitive skin beneath his ears.

He broke the kiss, gasping, and she struck him with all her might, then pulled free. No longer worried about discovery as long as she got away, she whirled and ran toward the square, screaming.

Again hampered by her skirts, she made it but three paces before her molester caught her, slamming her against him and once more clamping a hand over her mouth. ''Like games, bitch?'' he snarled, breathing gin fumes in her face as she kicked and struggled. ''Two kin play.'' At that, he pulled an object from his coat and brought it to her face.

A knife, its jagged blade silhouetted in the blackness of the alley by the torchlights of the square. With a mew of terror, she went still.

''’At's better.'' He touched his ear. ''Done made me bleed. Reckon I outter bleed you a little too.''

He forced her against the alley wall, then ran the knife

blade up her bare throat. "Only question is, afore or after?" With his free hand he pulled up her skirts.

He would not think about Miss Beaumont, Sinjin told himself as he exited the theater. If images of her had teased his mind all evening, it was doubtless because the play was mediocre and the farce that followed even worse.

Its chief merit consisted of the ravishing charms of its leading lady, whom Allensby impatiently awaited in the green room. Several of the frail sisterhood joined them there, all preening for the admiration of current or future lovers. Though their wares were undeniably attractive in a vulgar sort of way, Sinjin soon lost interest in the badinage backstage. Drawing Milhouse aside to plead the fatigue of his recent return, Sinjin excused himself from the Grenadiers' plans for the rest of the night.

To his annoyance, as he walked away from the theatre his thoughts drifted back to the beauteous Miss Beaumont. Despite their garish paint, the young actresses paled beside her vibrancy. Which was no wonder, his brain reminded his overappreciative body, considering the gown she wore was scarcely less revealing than those of the demi-reps from the stage. The figure thereby displayed had been, he grudgingly admitted, superior.

The whiff of roses and the whisper of emerald satin flashed in his mind, raising his temperature several degrees. Damn, but she was all too attractive. Still, he needn't berate himself over his reaction to Miss Beaumont, unwanted though it was. A man would have to be a saint made of stone not to be affected, and he was neither.

His acquaintance with the compliant ladies of the Bourbon court had lapsed some months previous, and as neither his purse nor his preference inclined him to pay for his pleasure, there had been none. Which made him particularly susceptible right now to such a display.

But when he recalled his parting words to Miss Beaumont, a flush of shame heated his face. Regardless of the provocation, to insult a lady was inexcusable, however subtlely the insult had been worded. In his irritation he'd allowed his prejudices to get the better of him and lost his temper. Again. He should write her an apology.

With a shock of dismay he then recalled he'd agreed to find her escort home, but too furious for rational thought, had left the ball without arranging it. Though with all the swains she had milling about there was little chance of her being stranded, it was still unprecedented for him to neglect a duty. He must apologize for that too.

Another set of apologies—too many to deliver by note. It appeared he would have to see her again. To his disgust, he felt an instinctive leap of anticipation.

He had to admit there was about her an aura of…energy, a crackling vitality that was nearly palpable. She seemed too feral for the civilized artificiality of a ballroom. Her air of barely-controlled passion recalled the wildness of a cavalry charge across hotly-contested ground, the clash of a worthy opponent's sword—or the intimate combat of the bedroom.

His breath caught before he could snuff out that glimmer of thought. He'd bet his spurs he wasn't the only one of Miss Beaumont's admirers to be ambushed by a vision of her acting the wanton. No man with blood in his veins could see her and not dream of being able to claim for a night what her lush body and vivid spirit promised. Though, he suspected, even one night with her could be dangerous. Should that tawny-haired tigress rake her claws over a man, she might leave scars to last a lifetime.

He had scars enough already. Firmly dismissing her this time, he was crossing the shadowed walk at the center of Covent Garden square when a muffled scream reached his ears. A feminine scream.

He halted, instantly on the alert, his hand going to where the sword normally hung at his side. When the sound came again, apparently from the alley he'd just passed, despite the lack of weapon he did not hesitate.

For a stunned instant, unable to accept this nightmare was occurring to *her,* Miss Beaumont the Belle of the ton, Clarissa remained motionless. The feel of the villain's rough hand sliding up the silk of her stocking shocked her to grim reality.

"Cor, what a beauty she is," her attacker breathed, stroking her bared leg.

With a strength fueled by terror and fury she slammed her knee against his fumbling fingers and struck with her fist the arm that held the knife. Clearly not expecting further resistance, her attacker stumbled sideways, losing his grip on her. Taking the burn of the knife on her shoulder, she rolled away from him and ran.

Two steps away she hurtled into a tall, solid figure. Screaming again, she clawed at him.

Iron hands captured her fists and muffled her mouth against a greatcoat. "Easy now, girl, I won't hurt you!"

"Find yer own bitch!" With a roar, her attacker launched himself at them.

The man pushed her behind him and turned to meet the charge. With his walking stick he deflected the raised knife as he sidestepped and delivered a hard punch to the attacker's kidney. Grunting, the villain whirled and grabbed her defender's arm, struggling to right his knife.

Running footsteps approached and another man dashed into the alley. "Rally here!" her defender called out. The newcomer struck a blow to the ruffian's back, and within a few more seconds the two had her attacker immobilized against the wall.

"Got 'is knife, governor," the second man said. "Tryin' to rob ye, was 'e?"

"No, attacking that lady. Is that rifleman green?"

"Aye, sir. Sergeant Brown, of the Ninety-fifth."

"Well done, Sergeant. Can you bundle this fellow off to a magistrate? I'll return to settle the charges as soon as I've seen to the lady's safety."

"I ain't done nuthin," her attacker whined. "Fancy-piece standin' about done asked fer it. I was goin' ta—"

"Shut him up, Sergeant."

She heard the sound of knuckle against bone and with a grunt, the ruffian slumped against the wall.

Her rescuer walked over. "Are you hurt, miss?"

Dread slammed Clarissa in the stomach as her still-racing mind suddenly identified the cultured voice of her rescuer. *Colonel Lord Sandiford.* Jerking her chin up, she saw his now-familiar features in the play of torchlight.

Consternation—and shame—rushed to replace her fear. She owed more than she could repay to the last man in London she would ever want to discover her in what she now recognized was the most ill-judged, reckless, idiotic stunt she had ever pulled.

"Quite well, thanks to you, sir." She clutched her hood to her face with trembling fingers, trying to muffle her voice.

"How came you to be standing alone in this place so

late at night?'' he asked as he walked her out of the alley. '''Tis much too dangerous.''

''My...my escort went to speak with friends, and—''

At that moment Alastair approached them at a run. ''Clare? Good God, Clare, what happened? When I glanced back a moment ago and you were not there—''

Colonel Sandiford halted as if suddenly cast to stone. Slowly he turned to look down at her. ''Miss Beaumont?'' he asked, his voice incredulous.

Her knees were going to jelly and she had a desperate desire to weep. What a horrific disaster her splendid adventure had become.

Sucking in a breath, she made herself straighten. She would not cap off her stupidity by turning into a helpless watering-pot. No matter how humiliating it was going to be to watch that handsome face twist in well-earned disgust.

''Colonel Sandiford, thank you again for your invaluable assistance. Now I should like to go h-home.''

Grenville, Mountclare and Weston joined the group. ''Aha!'' Lord John laughed and made a sweeping gesture. ''Did I not promise you, gentlemen, she would not last an hour?''

Colonel Sandiford turned to Lord John. With his face now fully illumed by a nearby streetlamp, she could see the contemptuous expression as he raked Weston from head to toe with a glance. ''Do you mean, sir, that you brought the lady here as some sort of—jest?''

''A wager, Sandiford,'' Grenville explained. '''Twas no harm in it, really. We were close by, just across the square, ready to protect—''

''A fat lot of protection you offered!'' The colonel's hand, still on her arm, went rigid. ''Are you all stupid as well as mad? Such scandalously unconscionable behavior could at the least ruin her reputation, and very nearly caused her serious physical harm!''

The others looked cowed, but Lord John thrust his chin up. ''What right have you, sir, to judge us?''

Colonel Sandiford said nothing, merely fixing on Weston a glare that made the other men step back. Lord John held his ground, though, and after a moment the colonel said softly, ''I shall call you to account later, *sir*. Right now I must escort Miss Beaumont home. You, boy—'' he called to one of the dicing urchins who'd scarcely looked up from their game. ''Summon a hackney.''

Weston stood motionless while Grenville and Mountclare shifted uncomfortably. Lord Alastair, his jaw working, approached the Colonel. ''You are right, Lord Sandiford,'' he said, his voice quivering with mortification, ''I knew from the very beginning this jest—''

''Enough,'' the colonel barked. ''Be gone, all of you. And should I hear the merest whisper about this evening's events anywhere in London, *gentlemen,* I will call each of you out. Though why any man would wish to reveal himself a party to so sorry an escapade I cannot imagine.''

Exchanging abashed glances, the others started to move away, but Weston stood fast. ''Dueling,'' he drawled with what Clarissa had to admit was remarkable sang-froid, ''is sadly unfashionable, Lord Sandiford. Not that I'd expect one in your…circumstances to know much of fashion.''

''Pugilistics, however, is all the rage,'' the colonel replied, apparently considering Weston's insult not worthy of answer. ''Correctly done, 'tis as effective as a bullet. If you value that scrawny neck of yours, I advise you to credit me with knowing *that*.''

Turning his back on Weston in clear dismissal, the

colonel looked to the alley where the rifleman staggered as he dragged her unconscious attacker toward the square.

"Are you injured, sergeant?"

"No, sir," the rifleman panted. "A bit…disguised."

"Best take yourself on home, then." The colonel's voice held a trace of amusement.

The sergeant grunted and let go his burden. "Ain't got me none. We was run off the land with the enclosures 'n' me mum got no way ta feed another mouth."

While the colonel inspected the sergeant's tattered, grimy figure, Clarissa suddenly recognized him as the silent tippler she'd seen earlier on the street.

"Still no excuse to disgrace that proud uniform by consoling yourself with blue ruin. The Ninety-fifth performed inestimable service—can't remember how many times a Baker rifle saved my neck. Can you read, Sergeant?" When the rifleman nodded, the colonel fished in his pocket and held out a hand. "Here's my card. Come by my rooms in the morning. I've a country estate much in need of work. If you know aught of farming, I could use your help."

The rifleman peered down at the pasteboard, then snapped to attention. "Aye, Colonel. I will indeed, sir!"

The jarvey arrived, and after returning the sergeant's salute, Colonel Sandiford helped her in.

"Your direction, Miss Beaumont?" he asked, his voice coolly impersonal.

He must be thinking her the most helpless, noodle-witted female ever to draw breath. Disgust with herself for blundering into this predicament warred with the mortification of having the colonel, of all the men in London, be the one to find her.

"Gr-Grosvenor Square," she replied unsteadily.

After instructing the driver, the colonel climbed in the cab and seated himself stiffly opposite her. The face illumed by the carriage lamp was grim, his jaw set, and he made no attempt at conversation.

How vain and ignorant she'd been, thinking that she, the peerless Miss Beaumont, might wander the city with impunity! For the first time she understood the reason behind some of the tiresome strictures that so often chaffed her. Though she'd read of citizens attacked on the streets and idly spoken herself of cutthroats and cutpurses, the reality of the London underworld had not until tonight penetrated her self-absorbed mind.

As the drive continued in silence, the enormity of what might have happened had the colonel not providentially appeared began to dawn. She owed to him not only her rescue, but likely her virtue and perhaps even her life.

Disgust and shame drained away, leaving her exhausted and once again near tears. A shivering began in her shoulders, progressed to her hands and the rest of her torso. Try as she might she couldn't make it stop.

The carriage slowed. "Which house, Miss Beaumont?"

She tried to form the number but her lips would not still long enough to answer. A dizziness grew, and for the first time in her life she thought she might faint.

"Miss Beaumont?" The colonel's body alerted. "'Od's blood, you're shaking all over. Are you all right?" When still she did not reply he seized her shoulder.

The sting of the knife fired to flame and she cried out. With an oath, Sandiford jerked the ties of her cape loose and flung it back. What he saw made him draw in a breath, strip off his gloves and pull a handkerchief from his pocket. Wadding it up, he held it to her shoulder.

"Why did you not tell me that villain had cut you?" he demanded, his voice furious. "I'll see him swing for this! Damn and bl—really, Miss Beaumont, a knife wound is no trifling matter. Though it does not appear deep, you must have that shoulder looked to at once! Let me help you inside and send for a physician."

The driver's face appeared at the window. "Which house, gov'nor?"

Clarissa imagined the scene: milling footmen, her little French maid succumbing to hysterics, her mama, roused from her slumber, following. The unpleasant and inevitable explanations.

Impossible. She must sneak in quietly, alone.

"N-n-no," she forced her lips to work. "M-M-Mama would have a-a-apoplexy. J-just l-let me out here."

She went to stand, but her knees seemed boneless. Furious at her weakness and desperate to escape the colonel's understandably disgusted glare, despite the gulping breath she took to try to forestall them, tears began leaking out. The detestable, cowardly shaking in her limbs intensified.

"Curzon Street, Number 34," Sandiford informed the driver. "Just do it," he snapped, cutting off question.

In one swift movement Sandiford pulled down the shade and sat beside her. Then gathered her in his arms.

Her body seeming deaf to her mind's direction, she could not pull away. The hard strength of the chest he held her against felt so warm, so comforting, so *safe* that in truth, she did not want to move. The degrading trickle of tears became a flood.

"Hush, hush now." He rocked her, stroking her hair, murmuring in a gentle tone she'd never heard from him before. "He can't hurt you. It's all over."

Not until the carriage slowed once more was she able

to marshall the strength to move away. He released her instantly.

"Excuse m-me again, colonel. I w-wish you might believe I am not always such an idiotic w-weakling. Though my behavior tonight gives no proof of it. Wh-where are—"

"I've brought you to Sarah's."

Alarm exceeded humiliation. "No, you mustn't. I'm…I'm recovered now, I promise. Ordinarily Sarah is game for anything, but just now I must not disturb her."

"Is Becky still her maid?"

"Yes, but—"

"Becky and I have been friends since my childhood. She's patched up many a wound, I promise you. I'll have the servants summon her without disturbing Sarah."

Before she could protest, Sandiford unlatched the door and left the carriage. In truth, it was a better solution. Ashamed as she was to have anyone learn of her wretched behavior, she'd rather it be Becky and Sarah than her own mama, who could—and often did—succumb to the vapors over the merest trifles. She shuddered to imagine Mama's reaction should she see Clarissa's bloody shoulder.

To her chagrin, her knees were still so rubbery when he returned to hand her down that she would have fallen had the colonel not caught her.

"Courage," he murmured.

"A quality, along with sense, of which I've displayed precious little tonight," she muttered, straightening once more by strength of will alone.

To place the final touch on what had been a disaster of an evening, she not only passed in the hallway a clearly astonished Glendenning, whose half-askew collar testified to how hurriedly he'd dressed to answer the colonel's summons, but when Sandiford led her into the parlor, Englemere himself awaited them.

"On the sofa, here," Englemere directed.

Clarissa closed her eyes, mortification burning her cheeks and prickling her eyes. Angrily she swiped at the trickle of tears and forced herself to face him.

But instead of the cold censure she expected, to her surprise, Englemere's expression, as he rapidly scanned her face and shoulder, contained only concern. "Chin up, my dear. Becky's on her way with the medicine box." He smiled reassuringly and squeezed Clarissa's hand. "She'll have you mended in a trice."

Englemere turned to Sandiford. "Thank you for bringing Clare to us, Colonel. Once more we stand in your debt. Becky can do all that is necessary."

At that moment the maid hurried in. "What's this— Master Sinjin!" She saw Clarissa then and gasped. "Miss Clare! What's about?"

"A knife-cut, Becky. If it were fitting, I'd tend it myself—I've far more experience, but... Wash it out well, preferably with brandy, and put on a paste to draw out infection. Yarrow works well, I've found." Sinjin shook his head. "No telling what might have been on that blade."

He looked at Clarissa, his face once again unreadable. "It shall burn like the devil, I'm afraid, Miss Beaumont."

"I expect I deserve it."

He smiled fleetingly—his expression holding wry amusement and a warmth that was unexpectedly compelling.

"It would probably be best for Miss Beaumont to rest the night, so you might check the bandage in the morning. Summon a physician if the wound's appearance worries you in any way. On my way home I'll leave a message at Grosvenor Square not to expect her until tomorrow.''

"Sounds wise, Master Sinjin. Don't you worry none, Miss Clare. I've doctored near about every cut and ailment a body could suffer, even if I've never been next or nigh a battlefield. I'll take good care of that shoulder.''

"I'm sure you will, Becky," Englemere said. "We'll leave you to your work. Good night, Clare. I'll break the news—gently—to Sarah in the morning. Colonel, would you like a glass of spirits before you depart?''

"Thank you, no, my lord. I'd best be alerting Miss Beaumont's household.''

Englemere walked out and with a short bow, the colonel prepared to follow him.

"Colonel," Clarissa forced herself to stop him. Much as it galled her to underline her folly this evening by acknowledging all he had done for her, both honor and courtesy compelled her to say it. "Once again, my thanks. I am fully conscious of—''

To her astonishment, he put a finger to her lips, stilling the apology. "No need to say more. If I had escorted you home as I pledged to do, none of this would have happened, so the blame is at least partly mine. Rest now, and sleep. Good night, Becky.''

He gave her another smile that braced her flagging spirits like brandy. Too weary to question its soothing effect, she watched him walk out.

If Colonel Sandiford hadn't already made his opinion of her all too clear earlier in the evening, this escapade would certainly seal it. She'd no need to worry about handling the embarrassment of meeting him again. He would undoubtedly avoid her.

It must be the aftershock of her unsettling experiences that caused the room to seem suddenly colder and made her chest ache with a curious sense of loss.

Chapter Seven

The next afternoon, Sinjin guided Valiant down the bustle of Berkeley Square toward Piccadilly. Before he left last night, Nicholas had thanked him once again for safeguarding Sarah's friend and invited him to meet at White's the following afternoon where they might discuss Sinjin's "requirements."

At the south end of the square he hesitated. A strong urge possessed him to stop by Curzon Street and check with Becky to make sure Miss Beaumont's wound was recovering. If the young lady were not still abed he might even be able to deliver the rest of his apology. Though his service to her last night had done much, he felt, to even the score he owed her for his earlier rudeness, he still could not dismiss a niggle of guilt that her injury would never have occurred had he seen her home as promised.

Stuff, he could not prevent the heedless chit from stumbling into harm's way if she were taffy-headed enough to follow the promptings of men witless as Grenville and venal as Weston. He pictured the latter man's narrow face with distaste. To persuade a gently-bred lady into so dangerous and disreputable a locale was unforgivable, regardless of the responsibility Miss Beaumont bore for falling in with the scheme. He still had a score to settle with Lord John.

The tawdry episode only underlined how wise he'd been to dismiss her whole class from consideration in his search for a wife. Though in fairness he had to admit that, much as he deplored the ignorance and conceit that had brought Miss Beaumont to the square in the first place, once the attack began, her response must command respect.

He thought of Alex's inamorata, the fragile Lady Barbara who shied at her own mama's approach. She would probably have fainted dead away at the ruffian's first touch. Miss Beaumont had both screamed and struggled, even managing somehow to pull herself free. And been wounded in the process. He had to admire her courage.

Her fortitude in enduring what must have been a painful knife-cut was equally admirable. Had he not chanced to place his hand on the wound, he wagered she'd have attempted to return home without revealing the injury.

As for her breaking down later, he thought no less of her for it. He'd seen hardened soldiers weep in the aftermath of battle. In fact, her reaction had been remarkably subdued, considering the terror she must have felt. He could think of only one other woman who wouldn't have emerged from that alley in screaming hysterics.

In spite of her failings, she was, he concluded, a plucky lass, someone he'd not have felt reluctant to have fight by his side—then chuckled at so ludicrous a thought.

That settled it. He turned his horse east toward Curzon Street. After an engagement, he always visited his wounded soldiers.

His grin faded, though, as Valiant approached Sarah's house. This was London, not the Peninsula, and Miss

Beaumont was certainly not, despite his momentary whimsy, a soldier. The only gentlemen who called on an unmarried lady were labeled "suitors."

Whickering in protest as Sinjin pulled him up hard, Valiant obediently responded to the knee that urged him back west. A note would sufficiently convey the remainder of the apology he owed her and Englemere could no doubt alleviate any lingering concern over her condition.

However, the first gentleman he encountered after handing over his hat and coat to White's majordomo was Lord Alastair.

Sinjin tried to pass by with a nod, but looking both shamefaced and earnest, in a low voice Alastair begged a moment of his time. Sure the man meant to entreat him with a caseshot of excuses for his participation in last night's folly, Sinjin tried to brush Alastair off.

"Please, sir." Alastair caught his sleeve. "Think what you will of me, I deserve it all and more, but I must not allow you to harbor an opinion of…a certain lady you might well have conceived upon finding her in such singular circumstances."

Aware that to have the man hang on his elbow would invite just the sort of speculation he was at pains to avoid on that same lady's behalf, he concluded with a flare of annoyance that 'twas best to let the man say his piece.

"Very well. But make short work of it."

He followed Alastair to the least-inhabited part of the reading room and impatiently took the seat indicated. "Say what you wish."

"First, thank you for your timely intervention last night. I could not sleep for reflecting upon the horror that might have befallen Miss…that might have occurred had you not happened by."

In truth, his lordship was pale, the skin beneath his

eyes shadowed. Sinjin felt a grudging sympathy. "I am thankful for it myself."

"As for how we all came to be there…you must understand the, ah, lady in question has great spirit and courage. For reasons of his own—and I intend to take him to account for them in the very near future—I now believe it was not mere whimsy that prompted Weston to propose the wager he did. No, he deliberately designed that particular 'challenge' in such terms that to refuse would have amounted to an admission of weakness and timidity such a person could never allow."

Sinjin's attention had been wandering, but Alastair caught it now. "You mean, Lord John set about from the first to entice this person into danger?"

"It's quite possible." The young man sighed heavily. "I also fear that in pointing out the risks and impropriety involved, I unknowingly abetted him. Even then, had the individual been in an equitable frame of mind, my cautions might have swayed her—normally she is able to ignore Weston's baiting—but something, I know not what, had occurred to put her in a rare temper."

Sinjin shifted uncomfortably, his parting words to Miss Beaumont echoing in his ears. He could not be sure they had set her off, for she'd seemed quite calm when he left her, but his insult must certainly have rattled her.

That unpleasant memory triggered another. Three years ago when he'd returned to London to find Sarah married, he'd discovered the malice her disappointed suitor, the late Sir James Findlay, harbored toward the new Lady Englemere. Lord John Weston had been Findlay's friend—and tool. Two villains cut from the same cloth?

"Has Weston any reason to wish this person harm?"

"He finds her attractive—who does not? Being too

honest to dissemble flirtation with a gentleman she cannot like, however, she has never hidden her disdain for him. I fear Weston, piqued by her disregard, may have intended for her to experience something uncomfortable or frightening. To…humble her, perhaps.''

"He might well have gotten her killed."

"Surely not! Ill-judged as his behavior was if such was his intent, I cannot imagine even Weston vile enough to have wished her real harm. Thank Heaven and your intervention there was none! I don't think I could live with myself had that villain actually hurt her.''

Sinjin thought of her bleeding shoulder and instantly decided to say nothing. For one, her young suitor already felt guilty enough. And if she had wished her injury to remain secret, who was he to reveal it?

Grimly his thoughts returned to Weston. "Lord John wished to teach her a lesson?''

"I very much fear so. Indeed, when we chanced to meet a party of friends, it was Weston who encouraged them to linger, allowing my—our—attention to be diverted for some moments longer than a simple greeting would have required.''

"Bastard,'' Sinjin muttered. "Thank you, Lord Alastair. What you've told me does alter my…impressions of what took place. I trust you'll continue your good offices by making sure no whisper of this gets out?''

"Of course. And I intend to watch Weston.''

Sinjin sat pensively after Alastair bowed and left, a grudging anger emerging. Though she was undoubtedly reckless and ignorant, perhaps Miss Beaumont wasn't entirely as witless as she'd first appeared. She *had* openly admitted her folly. Even more significant, although she'd had every opportunity to do so during their drive home, she'd not made any attempt to explain or excuse her behavior, despite the icy contempt he had displayed toward her. A forbearance he had to admire.

He'd never had much use for bullies, but a man who would deliberately lead a woman into danger was beneath contempt. Regardless of the provocation—and he had to admit Miss Beaumont could be very provoking—Weston needed more than watching. He needed a lesson. And, Sinjin thought, flexing his fists, he knew just the right teacher.

"Sorry I'm late, Sandiford," Englemere's voice interrupted his pleasant reverie of retribution. "You've wine already, I see. Good. Would you bring it and come along with me? There's a friend I'd like you to meet."

Englemere led him into a smaller room where groups of members sat conversing or reading the London papers. Sinjin had always considered himself tall, but the blond man who rose to greet them outstripped him by inches.

"Lord Sandiford, may I present Hal Waterman. Hal, this is the gentleman I spoke with you about."

Mr. Waterman bowed, then extended a hand that dwarfed Sinjin's long fingers. After an exchange of bows, the three men sat.

"Hal's papa helped me when I stood in much the situation you do now." At Sinjin's raised eyebrow, Englemere laughed. "We share more than you may think. I inherited a title barren of any assets save my name. Although initially I stayed afloat by gaming—" at Sinjin's involuntary grimace he waved a dismissive hand "—not that I would ever suggest that as a prudent course to anyone, but I happened to be lucky—"

"Englemere's Luck," Mr. Waterman inserted and nodded sagely, as if that explained all. "Byword. Still is."

Sinjin must have frowned as he tried to sort through

that response, for Englemere added, "Hal means I acquired, and have somehow managed to retain, this reputation for having the devil's own luck."

"Found Sarah, didn't he?"

Sinjin was beginning to appreciate the big man's logic. "True enough."

"Once I amassed sufficient funds to keep bread on the table, Mr. Waterman pressed me to invest some blunt on the 'change. Hal's father was one of the first aristocrats to have dealings there, and prospered accordingly. Hal's inherited his skill—and his contacts."

The big man shrugged. "Simple. Logic."

"Put that down to modesty, Sandiford. An astute trader possesses much more than logic. The play of financial numbers fascinates Hal, whereas investments are my particular fancy."

"Nose for gadgets, Nicky has," Waterman said. "Made 'im rich."

"Not half so rich as poor Hal. He's considered so eligible he has to take refuge at White's to avoid the matchmaking mamas."

Waterman shuddered and Englemere laughed out loud. Sinjin assumed this must be something of a running joke between them. Anxious to get to the point as soon as politely possible, though, he said, "My congratulations to you both on your successes, but as you well know, I've no blunt, either to invest or gamble."

"Patience, Colonel," Englemere said with a gleam of humor. "I asked Hal to meet you for several reasons. First, his contacts within the City are more extensive than mine. In fact, I took the liberty of confiding your intentions to him and asking him to come up with some potential...candidates. Second, if perhaps after next harvest you amass a small amount of capital to spare, Hal can recommend the most expeditious way to increase it. Lastly, should a bit of capital…assistance be required before your long-term plans can be accomplished, Hal can arrange it on the best terms, with absolute discretion.''

Sinjin felt his face warm. ''I assure you I—''

''Just keep the option in mind. Recall that I've sat where you're sitting and worse, half a desperate evening away from choosing a single bullet and a short trip to Hell.'' For a moment, his eyes glazed as he seemed to contemplate the past. ''But there's Richardson, I must speak with him.''

Englemere stood. ''I'll leave you to chat with Hal. If you're still set on wedding a middle-class heiress?''

Sinjin nodded. There seemed nothing to do but agree. Embarrassing as it was to know Englemere had discussed his situation with this stranger, soon enough his circumstances would be generally known. If Englemere, who had shown himself thus far a staunch ally, felt Mr. Waterman's advice would help him achieve his aims more speedily, he'd best swallow useless pride and get on with it.

''I must thank you for all your efforts, Englemere—''

''Nonsense.'' Englemere waved away his gratitude. ''As we both know, my debt to you is far greater. I trust Hal has several attractive possibilities to present.''

Feeling heat creep once more up his neck, Sinjin watched Englemere walk off. To discuss bartering himself in marriage was even more degrading than he'd anticipated.

He forced himself to face the man opposite. ''I must thank you as well, Mr. Water—''

''Hal. Marriage.'' He shook his head. ''Sorry business. Duty, though.''

Somehow, having his circumstances summarized in a few pithy words made the situation sting less. "I'm afraid so. Lord Englemere said you had some…prospects for me? You are amazingly kind to intervene, and I'm much obliged."

Waterman waved one large hand. "Best friend. Do anything for 'im. Sarah too."

A deeper understanding formed. "You…cared for Sarah?"

The big man sighed. "Went to a ball for 'er."

Given Englemere's humor over Mr. Waterman's unwelcome status as an extremely eligible gentlemen, Sinjin surmised that represented a major concession. But of course Sarah would have attracted him.

A bear of a man too large for fashion, his speech nearly unintelligible, Mr. Waterman would have been drawn as strongly by Sarah's innate kindness as by her serenity and pale blond beauty. Did Waterman, too, mourn losing her to his friend? Perhaps, as apparently he'd not yet been noosed into matrimony.

Mr. Waterman sighed again. "Nothing for it. Loved Nicky, y'see."

Sinjin could have sighed himself. "I do see."

"Sisters though. Wouldn't consider one of 'em?"

Sinjin shook himself, trying to follow the thread. "Marry one of Sarah's sisters?" To see on his wife's face a pale imitation of Sarah's features? To visit often with the intimacy of family, but with the wrong lady's hand on his arm?

The notion appalled, and in spite of himself he shuddered. "I—I must have a bride of some means."

"Wealthy now. Dowries from Nicky."

So her husband had dowered Sarah's sisters handsomely—a generous gesture. His respect for Englemere rose another notch.

"That was kind, but I still don't think—"

"No matter," Hal interrupted with a short nod. "Have to be the Cit then."

"If you have suggestions along that line, I would be most appreciative, Mr. Wa—Hal."

The marquess returned shortly afterward, and by the time they'd broached their second bottle, with Englemere's help in translating some of Hal's less intelligible utterings, they had a list of three wealthy businessmen with daughters of appropriate age for whom, Hal guessed, it might be assumed their proud papas cherished the highest of ambitions. That none of these gentlemen were known to be hanging out for an aristocratic son-in-law was, Englemere affirmed, a decided plus, and another benefit of having access to Hal's knowledge of the City.

"Should I...contact the gentlemen?" Sinjin asked, suddenly appalled at the prospect of approaching a stranger, hat in hand, and bargaining his title for settlement money, like haggling over beef at market.

As he'd rather have stood through another Waterloo cannonade than do so, he was relieved when Waterman shook his head. "Nicky'll chat 'em up. Eloquent."

"Hal's right, 'tis best to approach this through a neutral third party. Once I've screened the prospects, would you be willing to meet with any who seem interested? For lunch or dinner at his home, perhaps. Hal and I could go with you, so the initial contact takes place under the guise of a business meeting."

Sinjin caught his breath in surprise. "You would do that? 'Tis wonderous generous of you both."

Hal grinned. "I eat. Nicky talks. Set a good table."

"I'm sure they do," Sinjin replied, finding it easier now to follow the leaps in Waterman's conversation.

"It's settled, then. I'll send you a note when I've arranged something, in a day or so, I should guess."

Sinjin stood and bowed, still awed and a little humbled by their open, unqualified support. It seemed Englemere meant his pledge to do whatever he could to assist his former rival. "I am much in your debt."

Hal shook his head. "Soldier. Fought for England. Our debt." He offered Sinjin his hand.

"Thank you." Sinjin shook it, feeling as if he were the unworthy recipient of accolades earned by the sacrifices of all the soldiers who had battled and bled and died—he who had joined the army on a whim to escape a future he could not then face.

The same future he faced now. He'd best prove equal to their trust. Inhaling a sharp breath, he took the first step. "Let me know when all's arranged."

Three mornings later Clarissa drank tea with Sarah in her sitting room. She'd easily convinced her mama that, with Sarah once again in an "interesting condition," her friend had need of her help for a few days.

At least as long as it took for her shoulder to heal completely. She had much more trust in Becky's discretion than in that of her own volatile maid.

Though she might well no longer need the Frenchwoman's innate sense of style. If despite Sandiford's warning, any specific details of her escapade circulated through the ton, she was likely to be the one receiving the cut direct.

A prospect she greeted with more indifference than she'd have credited possible just four years ago, dizzy with the heady sensation of finding herself, as she'd long dreamed, the most celebrated Beauty of the ton. The only significant drawback of being ostracized, she decided, would be finding it even more difficult to fill up the idleness of her days.

Oh, for a challenge, for a task of worth and significance to pursue. Oh, for a way to stop being envious of the avenues open to men, to content herself with the few straight and simple lanes permitted a woman.

She thought of Aubrey. Given the enticement of motherhood, the only traditional role that appealed to her, perhaps she should seriously reconsider marriage. If, after Sir John finished dropping the veiled innuendos she felt certain, despite Sandiford's warning, he would spread, she had any suitors left.

Sarah asked Englemere to visit his clubs and listen for any reaction. Clarissa hadn't been sure whether to be relieved or disappointed when after two days he reported all he'd heard was the intrepid Miss Beaumont had engaged in some sort of daring wager, the lack of detail inviting speculation that caused her reputation to augment rather than diminish.

To check for rumors among the feminine contingent, Sarah accepted Lady Cowper's invitation to tea. After that Almack's patroness stopped trying to pry details of Clarissa's escapade from her, to which Sarah blandly replied she knew nothing, the society leader merely shook her head and remarked how adventuresome their Clare was.

It seemed scandal and ignominy were not to be hers, at least not yet. Still, Clarissa had determined to go out on this, the third evening after the attack, her shoulder discreetly bandaged under the least revealing of her evening gowns. Best not to give the gossip mills too much grist for speculation.

Sarah, to whom Clarissa had confided in full the wretched details of her adventure, listened without comment. "My, Clare, you were mad for diversion," was the only criticism she uttered.

Too mild a criticism for Clarissa's awakened conscience. "I was an idiot. I should have realized any scheme of Weston's had to be tawdry and ill-advised, but then I was so furious..." Recalling her fury brought to mind the face of the man who had inspired it, and she lost track of the thought.

"What happened to put you in such a taking?"

"Your precious Sinjin! First he informed me he had no need of the help I offered in finding a wife. Because, you understand, ladies of the upper classes are too vain, mindless, immoral, spendthrift and lazy to be worth considering," Clarissa finished hotly.

"Oh, Clare! Surely he didn't phrase it like that."

"It was words very like," she replied defensively.

Sarah caught her breath on a chuckle. "Oh, dear. I expect I should have warned you. Sinjin fought a running battle with his mama's extravagance for years, and she was initially instrumental in parting us. Though she and I have since made peace, I fear Sinjin still bitterly resents her. I had no idea his disdain extended to our entire class."

"Believe it. He informed me quite frostily he will have none but a merchant's daughter for wife."

"If that isn't just like a man!" Sarah shook her head. "Summarily choosing that course when I'd be willing to wager he hasn't the least notion what a wealthy middle-class maiden is like. If all are raised like those we encountered at school, I expect he'll find they possess every bit as much vanity, vacuousness, and extravagance as their aristocratic sisters."

"If not more," Clarissa agreed.

"Still, given his battles with his mama, I must allow Sinjin has more than earned his moment of pique. Once he discovers the truth, I expect he'll abandon the plan unless he first stumbles upon a simple, modest, accomplished lady he can admire and love. Which is what I most desire for him, regardless from which class she springs."

Clarissa couldn't suppress a pang of envy for the girl who eventually succeeded in winning the colonel's admiration—the right to those endearing smiles and that strong shoulder to lean on the rest of her days.

It would never be her, that was certain, she thought, grimacing at the memory of his face going rigid with disgust when Alastair identified her in that squalid alley.

Who said she wanted it to be? He'd insulted her even before she'd given him cause.

Whomever the former Colonel Lord Sandiford decided to wed, it was nothing to her. She might stand in his debt, but he'd absolved her of any obligation to assist him in settling his matrimonial business.

The breath of anger sighed out. How revolting that the only intriguing man she'd met in years was also a hopelessly opinionated autocrat who thought her a fool. She'd dismiss him from her thoughts this instant, regardless of whether or not he ever returned to the bosom of the ton.

She had even less success in squelching the wistful hope that someday soon he might.

Chapter Eight

Having taken the first step toward his future and mindful of Sarah's reprimand, the next afternoon Sinjin dressed in the best of his new coats and walked the short distance to a handsome townhouse on Upper Brook Street.

Ushered by the butler to a small salon, he sat tapping a finger on the sofa as the servant carried his card up to the Dowager Vicountess Sandiford. His mother.

He'd stopped by his solicitor earlier and verified, somewhat to his surprise, the information Sarah had given. His mama had traveled to town in her hostess's barouche and had placed no demands upon the estate since arriving there a month previous, apparently not even shopping for new gowns. That was so unlike his mama he wondered, with a combination of cynicism and concern, if she were unwell.

At a rustle of skirts he turned to see her enter. After so long an absence, he was struck by how lovely she remained, despite being now well into her middle years. Scarcely a line creased the fine skin at corners of her eyes and mouth; the turquoise-blue eyes she'd bequeathed him were as clear and brilliant as his own and her golden hair held no trace of gray.

"Madam." He rose and made her a bow.

"S-Sinjin," she said, a slight quaver in her voice. "Please, do sit." She walked to the sofa, hesitated, then took the wing chair nearby.

He watched her, both bitter and amused by the stiff formality of their reunion. He might be a tradesman come to inquire about an overdue bill.

Having rung for tea, she at last looked at him—not so much looked as devoured, her eyes inspecting every inch of his countenance and frame. The hunger of her glance recalled to him Sarah's words about her worry at his silence, and a touch of shame heated his face.

"You look wonderful, Sinjin. Older, a bit—fierce. Oh, it is good to see you! Thank you so much for calling."

He shifted uncomfortably. "You are lovely as ever, Mama. And of course I called. I should have come earlier had I known you were in town."

She smiled, the slightest curve of her lips. "I did write you of my plans. When word reached England that some of the regiments would be returning, I asked Lady Englemere to have her husband discover when the Tenth was expected. I...I longed to see for myself that you really had survived. The reports of Waterloo were dreadful."

The flash of an echo filled his ears—cannons, rifle fire, the howls of charging men and screams of the wounded. He shuddered, forcing the memory back into its tightly-guarded cell. "A bloody business, but I am, as you see, quite safe. You are...established here in London?"

"You must not worry that I've incurred any extra expense! Lady Avery—you will remember my old friend Amelia—insisted on bringing me, and I've been living very quietly. No evening engagements. Indeed, one reason I agreed to come was with me gone, Mrs. Hawkins could shut up Sandiford and let two housemaids go. We save on coal and victuals as well.'' She smiled. ''You see, I *am* trying.''

His shame deepened at the thought of his mother, with her love of luxurious finery, denying herself even basic necessities. ''You think I begrudge you food and shelter?''

''Of course not. But I did have another purpose for wishing to see you as soon as possible.''

With the arrival of the tea tray conversation halted and Sinjin was left to wonder just what his mama wanted from him. Though physically she appeared unchanged, the grave, quiet woman before him seemed so unlike the gay, frivolous, spendthrift Beauty he remembered he scarce recognized her. That she was even conscious of the need for, much less had made, economies rattled him, loosening the stranglehold of his angry resentment.

After the footman withdrew, Sinjin set down his cup. ''How may I be of service, Madam?''

Did she wince, or was it a trick of the light? ''I discussed our...circumstances with the solicitor. Is it true that, should you be able to rent Sandiford, we might meet our expenses until the next corn harvest?''

His mother—his mother!—initiating a discussion of their financial condition? He'd have sworn she had no idea whether their fields grew flax or turnips. For a moment he was too stunned to reply.

''Perhaps,'' he found his voice, his mind trying to accommodate the incredible vision of his mama as a thrifty household manager. ''If the house is in as bad a repair as Jeffers indicated when he rejoined me in Paris, though, I doubt anyone could be induced to rent it. Besides, as you've long urged, I now intend to choose a bride with sufficient dowry that you have no need to worry any longer about the roof falling in—or the price of coal.''

"But if Sandiford could be rented, you would have no need to marry immediately. Is that correct?''

He waved a hand impatiently. "We might stave off disaster another year, but to truly restore the estate, I see no alternative to making a—'' he gritted his teeth over the word, "—*suitable* marriage.''

That detestable necessity—and his mama's part in bringing him to it—still stung too much for him to be able to discuss the prospect with equanimity. "Why, after all this time, do you suddenly counsel delay?''

"I would not have you make a hasty marriage and be as unhappy the rest of your life as you have been these last few years. No, I must say it!'' she waved him to silence. "I was wrong, Sinjin. At the time I thought I was doing the right thing for us both, but I was wrong. I should not have come between you and Sarah. I should not have harangued you about 'duty' until you saw no honorable escape but the Army.''

She was admitting guilt over Sarah? He sat, jaw rigid, unable to credit what he was hearing, utterly incapable of response.

"Oh, Sinjin, you'd grown up with Sarah! You knew nothing of the world. I thought your passion a young man's fancy that would fade once you'd mingled with Society, met other girls. I gave Sarah too little credit and my worldly wisdom too much.'' Her voice softened. "It's too late to matter now, but I'm dreadfully sorry, Sinjin.''

He stunned mind was still trying to make sense of it. That his mama had made her peace with Sarah he knew. But to admit she'd misjudged both Sarah's worth and the strength of their love? He sighed. "I'm sorry too, Mama."

She inhaled sharply and her eyes grew moist. "If it's any consolation, I've suffered, too. To have my only surviving child, flesh of my flesh, view me with such a-abhorrence he would not trouble to let me know whether he lived or d-died. During the last campaigns, I think I should have gone mad had Sarah not been kind enough to bring me news. But," she brushed her hand impatiently at her eyes, "the experience forced me to confront the truth I might otherwise have continued to deny. And I've learned things too, useful things. Like mending sheets and turning hems and how to make do with peat fires instead of coal. So you see, if it is at all possible to get by, we can do it. Anything but have you choose hastily. Not this time."

His imagination failed at conjuring a vision of his impeccably gowned mama bent over a needle. "I cannot imagine you mending sheets."

She chuckled. "Oh, I've become a capital housewife. I discovered there are things of much greater importance than gowns and jewels and the adulation of the ton. My son's life. His safe return. The s-sweet pleasure of once again gazing upon his face."

Suddenly he remembered the mother of his youth, a gay, charming, impossibly beautiful creature who, heedless of her maid's protests, caught the grubby boy who raced into her chamber and lifted him to her immaculate lap, feeding him sweetmeats and exclaiming over his adventures. A fairy-tale princess he'd adored, as had his father, who'd spared no expense before his death to give her anything her fancy desired. Cosseted by her wealthy parents and indulged by her doting husband, 'twas small wonder she'd been ill-equipped to handle sudden poverty and the loneliness of becoming too young a widow.

"I should have written. I'm sorry, Mama." He took her trembling fingers.

She clutched his hand, brought it to her lips and kissed it. "Forgive me," she whispered, moisture welling at the corners of her turquoise eyes.

The hard resentment he had harbored so long began to soften. She *had* suffered—he could see the truth of it in those glassy eyes. Suffered for doing, in error, what she'd truly felt would be best for both of them. How could he continue to fault her for that?

"Forgive me, too, Mama. I've not been such a paragon of a son."

"Nonsense! I'm so proud of all you've accomplished. Were I never to see you again, I should still count myself the most fortunate of women to be able to call you my son."

If it were time to put away the dreams of the past, it was also past time to conquer his anger. Not that six years' bitterness would dissolve in a moment, but suddenly he too wished to rejoin the family circle he'd turned his back on when he lost Sarah to Englemere. "I must hope that brave aura doesn't fade upon better acquaintance, since I expect to see much more of you in future. We should establish a home somewhere, Mama, here or at Sandiford. Together."

"Then you do forgive me?" she asked, tremulous hope dawning in her face.

"Let's forgive each other." Affection bubbling out like a long-dammed stream, he smiled at her.

"Welcome home, my dearest son." With a breath that was half gasp, half sob, she came into his outstretched arms.

* * *

Having received a note from Englemere inviting him to dinner, a few hours later Sinjin once again returned to White's. The interview with his mama intensified the disorientation that had afflicted him since he gave up his uniform and the familiar world it represented.

One of the few unchanging tenets of his existence had been his struggle with his mother's extravagance and his bitter resentment of the part she'd played in Sarah's loss. It annoyed, angered and shamed him to admit that, much as their rapprochement warmed him, still he almost—regretted—having that comfortable certainty stripped away.

He handed over his coat, hat, and cane, and settled in to wait, a little uncomfortable to be dining here once more as Englemere's guest. The marquess was certainly fulfilling his pledge of help, exerting his influence to acquaint Sinjin with the most influential men in London—and guaranteeing a prospective father-in-law found nothing lacking in the social standing he was purchasing for his daughter.

Raucous laughter interrupted his thoughts. Annoyed, he glanced over to see a party of fashionables entering the room. Their loud, slightly slurred voices and immoderate mirth suggested they were already three parts cast-away.

"*You* entering the lists, Markham?" said the one sporting a waistcoat striped in vibrant crimson and gold. "Unlikely! You ain't nearly lively enough for the Vixen's taste. Make you a wager on it. Where's the betting book?"

"If it's the Virtuous Vixen he's got in his sights, I'll offer another wager," a thin man in a puce coat exclaimed. "Stake my blunt, if he does get her wed, he won't be the first to bed our delectable Miss Beaumont."

Another volley of laughter met that remark, but galvanized by the mention of Miss Beaumont's name, Sinjin scarcely heard it. Indignant that they would discuss a lady of quality in such coarse terms, he was halfway out of his chair before it occurred to him the worst turn he could do her would be to intervene—thereby inferring her reputation needed defense.

"You doubt her virtue?" Markham said, his round face troubled.

"Haven't you heard, man? Up to another start just the other day. Some escapade, I was assured, no *lady* would attempt. Not surprising—she's always been mad to go. Usually on Grenville's arm, and everyone knows he's as wild as he is witless. Maxwell courted her last Season. Though she refused him, he said she gave him something *sweet* to remember." The man wagged his eyebrows suggestively.

"She'll warm your bed nicely enough." A man in a bilious green waistcoat punched Markham's arm. "Get her to pop out an heir or two, and afterward you'll have all that money to compensate for any worries over her virtue!"

By now incensed, Sinjin rose with teeth gritted. He was a pace away from planting his fist into Green Coat's face when a footman blocked his path.

"Lord Sandiford? Lord Englemere desires your presence, if you please."

The interruption served to revive prudence. Denying himself the pleasure of pummeling Green Coat's leering face, he followed the servant. To accost these louts would only add fuel to the speculation over Miss Beaumont.

Much as he deplored the conversation, he had to admit

there was a germ of truth in the remarks. Miss Beaumont's behavior *was* reckless, if the fix he'd recently discovered her in was at all typical. Couple her volatile nature with a tantalizing body displayed in gowns that flaunted her attractions and the result, given the nature of the male mind, was more than enough to incite salacious gossip.

Wherever were the gentlemen of her own family? Someone ought to take her to task, warn her that if she didn't restrain her behavior and modify her dress, she ran the risk of forfeiting her reputation.

Still mulling over the matter when he arrived at the dining room, Sinjin found to his surprise not Englemere, but the broad hulk of Hal Waterman awaiting him.

The tall man rose at his approach and extended a hand. "'Evening, Sandiford. Delayed. Tuck in without him?''

Sinjin surmised Sarah's husband would be late. "Of course, if you are ready.''

Waterman motioned a footman to pour wine and grinned. "Always ready. Can't you tell?''

Though Waterman's frame was massive and his shoulders approached an oxbow's width, Sinjin saw no superfluous weight on him. "You look fit enough. I'd say 'tis a pity you can't enter the ring. I'd back you in an instant.''

"Right handy with m'fives,'' Waterman allowed, looking pleased. "Too big to match, though. Not fair.''

The first course arrived. "Eat,'' Englemere's friend invited. "No good at conversation,'' he added, his tone apologetic. "You won't mind?''

"Not at all. Please, let us proceed.''

Waterman nodded and the meal commenced. Sinjin found Waterman's calm, unpretentious manner relaxing and the silence refreshing rather than intimidating.

After the dessert was served, Waterman cleared his throat, obviously gearing up to speech. "Silas Motrum. Lunch tomorrow. If you agree?"

"Your…prospect?" Sinjin asked, startled out of mellow enjoyment back to unpleasant reality.

"Banker. Father a tailor. Made his fortune himself. Fair. Shrewd. Like him. Nicky approves," he added, as if that were the clinching argument.

"Of—of course," he fumbled, trying to school his features from distaste to approval. "I…appreciate your quick action on this."

"Nicky's coach. Motrum's house. Meet the gel after, if you're both willing."

Englemere meant to collect him and proceed to the banker's house for luncheon, he deduced. Tomorrow.

He took a deep breath and willed the sickness gathering in his gut to dispel. His plan for securing the future had always been distasteful but mercifully vague. Meeting a banker tomorrow was much too definite.

"Will you be…joining us?"

"Course. Friend. Good table."

Sinjin wasn't sure whether Waterman accompanied them out of friendship for Englemere, the banker, or both, but the notion of having Hal's solid presence at this unnerving event was somehow comforting.

"Good," he said fervently and could think of nothing to add. Perhaps Mr. Waterman's brevity was catching.

"Chit's name is Anne. Blonde. China-blue eyes, papa says. Blonde acceptable?"

Because he'd expressed reservations about Sarah's blond sisters? "Fine," he said with more assurance than he felt. As acceptable as any candidate, which was not at all, were he free to follow his own inclinations.

He couldn't, he reminded himself with a flash of irritation. No sense having a fit of nerves now, like a raw recruit blanching at the first volley of the guns.

"Good man. Young tradesman hanging about. Won't leave her in the lurch, whatever you decide. Brandy?"

Numbly Sinjin nodded, wondering whether the "good man" meant him, Englemere, the tradesman, or Miss Motrum's papa. And then was touched to notice that Waterman's longest sentence yet had doubtless been meant to reassure him.

Hal raised his glass. "Duty. Friendship."

"Thank you for both."

They were draining their brandy when Sinjin spied Alex passing by in the hallway, looking distracted and vaguely discontent. His troubled gaze fell on Sinjin and he halted, his thin face brightening. "'Evening, Colonel!"

"Join us?" Waterman invited.

For a moment Alex hesitated. "Yes, thank you."

While introductions were made, Sinjin watched the lieutenant in some concern. Although Alex did not appear to be suffering any ill effects from his fall, his spirits were definitely in sad frame. Had his interview with Lady Barbara not gone well?

"Will you gentlemen be attending the Maxwell ball tonight?" Alex asked.

Hal shook his head in an emphatic negative. "No balls. Bang-up affair, though. All London."

"If it's that renowned, I imagine Lady Barbara will be there," Sinjin said. "You'll go too, I expect?"

Despite the light that leapt in Alex's eyes at the mention of Lady Barbara, he didn't smile. "I'm not sure of her plans. With the throng in the drawing room when I called, we never exchanged a private word." He grimaced. "The Countess made sure of that. Perhaps I shall

retire to the country for a time, as Mama keeps urging.''
A sigh shook his emaciated frame. ''Heaven knows I'm
not fully fit yet, and it appears I waste my time here.''

The bleakness of his tone fired Sinjin with righteous
anger. Damn Lady Barbara, her officious patronizing per-
fectionist of a mama, and women in general! Unreliable,
troublesome creatures, they seemed unable to distinguish
sterling worth from the dross of appearance.

''I believe I shall attend the ball,'' Sinjin announced,
deciding on the spot. ''If you'll accompany me, Alex?
Mustn't appear to be abandoning the field in full retreat.''

Alex smiled grimly. ''I suppose not. Even if it happens
to be the truth.''

''Nonsense,'' Sinjin said bracingly. ''Attend a few
more functions with every appearance of enjoyment, call
upon Lady Barbara or not as you choose, then retire to
the country. If Lady Barbara has the wit you believe her
to possess, she will miss you—and eagerly await your
return.''

Alex's shadowed eyes lightened. ''You believe so? I
own, I still think she feels a bond between us. I doubt
the Countess can prevail upon her to marry someone she
does not love, but for Lady Barbara to continue resisting
a woman as determined as her mama…'' Alex looked
down at his useless hand as if willing it to flex, and Sinjin
knew he was trying to maintain hope of an eventual re-
covery. ''Perhaps giving the matter time would be best.''

''Shall I meet you in an hour?''

Alex nodded. ''Very good. And—thank you, Colonel.''

Waving away his gratitude, Sinjin rose. ''If I'm to
change I must also take my leave. Until tomorrow, Hal.''

As he made his way out, Sinjin's thoughts advanced
to the ball he'd just pledged to attend. It would doubtless

be a tedious affair. He'd stay only long enough to make sure Alex was at ease.

Though should Miss Beaumont chance to be present, he could be assured her injury was healing. Perhaps he'd even take it upon himself to deliver a warning. Her courage certainly deserved that she be made aware of the vicious comments circulating about her. *Cowardly buffoons,* he recalled with contempt.

Aside from assisting Alex, of course, attending the ball would be a cursed waste of time. Which was why, as he strode down the steps to summon a hackney, it was deuced odd he should feel this definite stirring of excitement.

Chapter Nine

Pleased their late entrance spared them going through a receiving line, Sinjin ushered Alex into the tightly-packed ballroom. Despite the crowd, his height allowed him to speedily locate a slender brunette in white surrounded by a milling group of courtiers. Bedecked in regal purple satin and a plumed headdress, her mama stood guard nearby.

As if conscious of his scrutiny, the countess glanced over. For a shocked instant he thought she would cut him, but then she nodded, setting her ostrich plumes aquiver.

Lady Barbara turned and saw them. A brilliant smile sprang to her lips—until the countess bent to whisper in her ear. The smile died and Lady Barbara looked away.

All Sinjin's fighting instincts went on alert. The men of the Tenth, who'd not broken under attack by Napoleon's famed Imperial Guard, were not about to let one imperious countess halt them. "Shall we approach?"

But Alex's mouth set in a grim line and his dark eyes hardened to flint. "I'll not force my way in to be rebuffed, nor will I linger at the edges of her court like a supplicant. If she wishes to speak, she knows I am here."

"That's the spirit." With mingled anger and sadness,

Sinjin watched the lines around Alex's mouth and eyes deepen, revealing how much that show of nonchalance cost him. "Who shall we look for, then?"

Alex shrugged. "Perhaps I shouldn't have bothered to come." He waved a hand, forestalling Sinjin's reply. "Yes, I recall your advice. I'll remain for a decent interval and endeavor to look entertained. But as I don't dance and my recent memories don't lend themselves to witty conversation, I'm not of much use to anyone present."

Before he could reply, the lieutenant's sister Caroline emerged from the throng. "Alex, I thought you'd never arrive! And Colonel, good evening. Brothers!" She shook her head at Sinjin, the concern in her eyes belying her light tone. "If I waited upon Alex's escort I should scarce leave home!" Though she laughed, the darkling glance she threw toward Lady Barbara told Sinjin she too was aware of her brother's heartache.

"Come along, Alex, Colonel." She linked an arm with each man. "My friends are waiting. Oh, Alex, your old Oxford mate Brice Peirson's just arrived in town, and most anxious to chat with you."

Ushered along perforce, Sinjin inserted an obligatory word as needed into Caroline's spirited commentary. She led them to a gaggle of young people, all of whom Alex seemed to know well. After a few moments Alex's shoulders began to relax and the pinched look left his face. When the promised Oxford friend appeared, bringing a genuine enthusiasm to Alex's eyes, Sinjin slipped away.

And spotted Miss Beaumont across the ballroom. Anticipation made his breath catch and all his senses heighten.

It must be the dress. A form-hugging concoction of turquoise satin that gleamed in the candlelight as she moved, it made her sparkle like a central stone set in the jewel-bright broach of swirling dancers.

As he approached he noted with surprise that she'd topped the gown with a wisp of a Belgian lace fichu. In taunting mockery of its normal use, however, the lacy scrap did not modestly cover her bosom. Instead, it veiled her shoulders and then was pinned in narrow outline along the plunging depth of her décolletage, leading the eye straight to the generous breasts half-revealed there.

A spectacle sure to rivet the attention of every male over eight and under eighty who came within eyeshot of her.

And, he admitted grudgingly as a surge of heat engulfed him, he was as susceptible as any other man.

Firmly he detached his gaze from her chest and commanded his body to react no further. His body ignored him, and it required several minutes' struggle to get himself under control.

Damn and blast, he swore under his breath, sweating. No wonder men called her wanton. Surely she realized the effect she caused. She probably deserved all the comments the White's Club oafs had made, and more.

Not fair, his stubborn intellect replied. Her décolletage wasn't lower than that of many other ladies present. It wasn't her fault she had more to display.

Was she a wanton?

His memory flicked back to that solitary ride in the hackney. He'd been furious, and she'd known it. But not only had she not spouted a litany of excuses, she'd made no attempt to use her beauty to soften his anger. Of course, with her shoulder dripping blood and wrapped in a grimy cloak that smelled of onions, she hadn't presented quite the seductive picture she did tonight. Or perhaps he didn't appeal to her?

The sharp edge of male pique he felt at that prospect irritated him even more than his unwanted response.

Wanton or not was immaterial. Would that he'd had more green subordinates who'd reacted to a dangerous situation or a painful wound with the cool-headed initiative and considerable courage she'd displayed.

Unfortunately her common sense didn't appear to reach a similarly elevated plane. Since she didn't seem to possess an advisor with the fortitude and candor to inform her of the damage her dress and manners were leading her into, he would. He'd do as much for any friend.

She'd likely not thank him for it, so 'twas just as well he wasn't courting her good opinion. He'd deliver the warning he felt honor bound to give and depart.

Nonetheless, prickles of anticipation such as he'd felt before battle needled his gut as he walked over. A few steps away, she saw him approaching, and smiled.

He sucked in a breath, momentarily dazzled by that smile and her remarkable emerald eyes. His initial reaction in the game room hadn't been an aberration, apparently. From a distance she attracted, but up close she was nothing short of stunning. No wonder men fell at her feet in droves.

"Colonel, how nice to see you."

"Miss Beaumont. Would y-you…" Something tingled along his nerves as he raised her hand to his lips and he lost track of his sentence. *Damn and blast.*

He cleared his throat. "Walk with me, please?"

She raised an eyebrow. "If you wish."

As she raised her hand to place it on his arm, she made a small grimace. Under the lace at her shoulder he could just make out the line of a bandage.

How could he have forgotten her injury? Concern overcame annoyance. "You are recovered, ma'am?"

"Yes, thank you. A little stiff, merely."

"You should take care. Such…events can turn nasty."

He'd deliberately chosen words to obscure, should anyone nearby chance to overhear, but she placed another meaning on his comment.

"A singularly ill-judged escapade, which might have ended very badly. I am mortified you were obliged to assist me, but I thank you again for it." She smiled wryly. "And for refraining from giving me the dressing-down I deserved. If it is any reward for your forbearance, I shall endeavor never to be so foolish again."

"I am glad of it." Her frank avowal of fault once again impressed him, and he found himself returning her smile. "You are certainly looking…recovered."

She laughed outright. "An awkward contrivance. However, it does…direct attention from my shoulder."

"Most effectively," he agreed with a grin. So she had deliberately chosen the effect as an odd sort of camouflage. No coquetry there.

The need for a warning recurred, and his grin faded. How to begin? "It does, uh, draw a man's eye," he said, groping his way.

She sighed. "Colonel, I've been the focus of male eyes since I turned twelve. As it matters little whether I wear sackcloth or silk—I have experimented, I assure you—I give the subject little thought." She raised her chin, as if expecting criticism. "I wear what I like."

"Including sackcloth?"

"Seldom that," she allowed. "Though after Covent Garden, I expect you believe I should."

"I wouldn't say something so unhandsome. However…"

She inclined her head toward him, her green eyes assessing. "'However'?"

Steeling himself to seize the opening, he plunged forward. "I do think it would be prudent for you to...take somewhat more care in your appearance and behavior."

As he'd expected, the warmth in her eyes chilled. "And what do you suggest?"

"Before I explain, please understand I speak only out of genuine concern. You may have exhibited a lamentable lack of judgment the other night, but your reactions once the unfortunate encounter began showed laudable good sense. I hope I may persuade you of the need to extend that prudence to your behavior in general. Otherwise I fear you stand in some danger."

She tilted her head up, locking her green eyes on his, and raised an eyebrow. "Danger?"

"I chanced to overhear a conversation at a gentleman's club. Normally I should not listen to gossip, but the name being bandied about was yours."

"In danger from gossip?" She made a scornful noise. "I recommend you ignore it. I always do."

"In this case perhaps it's wiser to pay attention. I had never before heard such...comments made in reference to a gently-born lady. Not an unmarried one, at least."

"And what was it that so injured your sensibilities?"

There wasn't a kind way to phrase it, so having come this far, better to just state it baldly. "They expressed doubts about your virtue. One went so far as to assert that he knew a gentlemen who claimed to have received such...testaments to your, um, spirited nature that your eventual husband must discover you no longer a maid."

She said nothing for so long, he wondered if she'd understood his rather tortuous language. Sweating once more, he wished he'd never broached the wretched business.

Then the hand on his arm trembled. "I'm a whore, then? And odds are being laid in the betting books against the possibility that I come to wedlock still a virgin?"

He flinched. Stripped of the polite euphemisms in which he'd tried to cloak them, the vulgar accusations sounded even coarser.

"The gossip hasn't gone that far, nor will it, if you could but be a bit more…circumspect. Men expect a virtuous maiden to act in a certain fashion, and are, I'm afraid, quite censorious of those who do not."

"And do you, too, believe me a wanton?"

"If I did, would I have troubled to warn you?"

Her face had gone white, then pink again, and she seemed to struggle before at last she spoke. "It appears I am once again in your debt. Since I assume the gallant gentlemen who made these illuminating remarks would never have dared do so to my face."

He bowed, glad she was taking this in so reasonable a light. "I only did what I felt was right."

"How *kind* of you, Colonel."

He was about to assure her to think nothing of it when fury flashed in her eyes, so abrupt and intense he instinctively stepped back a pace.

Before he could stammer out a word, she rounded on him. "You may take yourself and your warning back to the cowardly curs at your club. *I* should modify *my* behavior? Curry the good opinion of a passel of lecherous fools who have nothing better to do than play cards, drink themselves senseless and slander the innocent? As if being a 'virtuous maiden' did not already crib and confine me enough! I am who I am, and not a jot of it shall I change. Go add that codicil to your betting book!''

Appalled that she seemed to be including him among the wretches who'd made the comments, he opened his mouth to protest, then shut it with a snap. He owed her no explanations. After he'd gone out of his way to warn her, how dared she insult him by equating him with those half-witted society wastrels?

Incensed, he withdrew his arm. ''You must suit yourself, of course. I only felt it fair that you be warned.'' With a stiff bow, he prepared to walk away.

Until he looked at her face.

Disbelief and hurt were painted in emerald eyes glassy with unshed tears. The hurt of finding herself betrayed by men of her own class who doubtless flattered and cajoled to her face and then, she'd just discovered, spread foul rumors behind her back.

The opening strains of a waltz sounded. Though he'd opened his lips with the intention of bidding her goodbye, he found himself saying instead, ''Would you like to dance?''

She stared at him as if the words made no sense.

''Could I have this waltz, Miss Beaumont?'' he repeated.

He wasn't sure she ever responded, but when he took her arm, she docilely followed him onto the dance floor.

Captured, as he had been the night of the Covent Garden episode, by a perverse protectiveness, he pulled her close and swept her into the waltz.

Miss Beaumont remained silent and he didn't attempt to force a conversation. Her stormy eyes still reflected anger and hurt, and he couldn't really blame her. She was right—the men who slandered her conducted themselves much less honorably, yet as men they were unlikely ever to be subjected to reproach. Her lowliest servants were freer to come and go than she. How the petty restrictions of their society must chafe someone of her tempestuous nature.

As London's narcissistic idleness chafed him. He felt a curious sense of connection, as if they shared a bond. Ridiculous, of course.

This time as he held her close she was neither bleeding nor grubby. The rose-scented curls tickling his chin, the softness of her breasts brushing his chest, the warmth of her waist under his hand were producing the inevitable consequences, swamping his sympathy for her plight in impulses of quite another sort. Breathing harder, and not from the dance, he stepped away.

No wonder the waltz was considered scandalous.

Mercifully the music reached a final chord. As they walked off the floor, he tried to order his thoughts. "I must take my leave now, Miss Beaumont. I hope you will consider the…news I brought and act upon it prudently."

Her chin snapped up and she eyed him frostily. "Yes, *I* must act prudently. Do not let me detain you, Colonel. An upright man like yourself cannot wish to partner a woman whom gossip proclaims practically a demi-rep. Indeed, should you not be out trolling for virtuous virgins in the seas of the middle-class righteous?"

Her attack once again caught him unawares, and anger evaporated his sympathy. Viper-tongued virago!

"How kind you are to remind me. My apologies for intruding upon your presence with a matter you find of no consequence. Your servant, Miss Beaumont." Swallowing his anger with an effort, he bowed and walked away.

* * *

Cursing her unruly tongue, Clarissa watched the colonel stalk out. After having the decency—and courage, for he must have realized the bearer of bad news risked arousing her infamous temper—to bring the despicable rumors to her attention, he deserved better than having her use him to blunt her anger. And she really must stop twitting him about his quest for a rich wife.

Still, what did he expect after honesty forced her to practically grovel before him, acknowledging shortcomings he'd been only too happy to point out?

Besides, before he started lecturing again, in the intimacy of a waltz's embrace she found him entirely too attractive. She had no business growing breathless and faint over the touch of his large strong hands or the brush of his whipcord-lean body. The man thought her a bird-witted twit and despised her whole class.

Damn his eyes. This soldier whose handsome face still bore a French lance's scar had done difficult and dangerous service while most of the men she knew slept past noon and gambled all night. Returning to poverty and heartache, he wasn't bewailing his fate over strong drink, but facing it squarely and taking prudent steps to repair the situation. Here was a man to admire, honorable and courageous, persistent and resolute. The sort of man on whom a person—a woman—could depend.

Reviewing her large acquaintance, she couldn't think of another man whose good opinion she'd rather have. Or, after the Covent Garden episode and her behavior tonight, one whose good opinion she was less likely ever to earn.

Angrily she brought herself up short. She'd been accused of being reckless and wanton—no need to add maudlin to the mix. Blinking, she found herself in the hallway near the ladies' withdrawing room and realized she'd marched out of the ballroom, oblivious to all in her anger.

Returning there meant running a gauntlet of gentlemen seeking dances—and wondering which of the honey-tongued courtiers had been responsible for the rumor.

Once again she felt the sting of betrayal and caught her breath at the pain. No, she couldn't face that just yet. She pushed into the crowded withdrawing room.

Taking an unoccupied seat, she made a show of adjusting the pins in her thick hair, letting the chatter flow unheeded around her.

She scarcely noticed the three young women beside her until one of them, combing through the blond curls of her taller friend, bumped Clarissa's arm. "Oh Miss Beaumont, pray excuse us!" the short blonde exclaimed.

Clarissa waved one pin-laden hand. "No harm done."

"So gracious of you," the girl replied, while the third friend, a rather plain brunette, smiled shyly.

Straight out of the schoolroom, Clarissa thought.

"I wouldn't even consider him," the tall blonde said, recapturing her friends' attention.

"Why not, Deidre? I think he's quite handsome, even if he is rather thin," the brunette said.

"Of course he's thin, Maryanne," Deidre said to the brunette. "He was wounded at Waterloo and only just got out of hospital, Mama says."

Clarissa's attention snagged at that. Who were they discussing?

"He will inherit the title one day, and he's quite rich," the short blonde said. "Even if Lady Barbara won't have him, I'd not dismiss him out of hand."

Not the colonel. Clarissa released the breath she'd been holding, but curious now, continued to listen.

Deidre tittered. "My dear Arabella, that's the point—his hand! He cannot use it at all, you know. However handsome he may be in that Hussar's coat, the idea of his touching one with those lifeless fingers…" She shuddered. "It makes me positively ill."

The short blonde shuddered as well and the plain brunette looked thoughtful. "It would be…unpleasant. Still, Lady Jersey told my mama he fought most valiantly. One must make certain allowances for a hero, I think."

"What does that matter here in England?" Deidre reached over to pat Maryanne's hand. "You're not likely to need someone to lead you a cavalry charge across Hyde Park."

As the two blondes went off into giggles, Clarissa's fingers stilled on her pins in disbelief. Having read every account of that dreadful battle printed in the London papers, augmented by details drawn from Englemere's private sources, she could not believe even a giddy chit from the schoolroom would dismiss a man cited for valor there.

"Only imagine—he cannot *dance*," Deidre continued. "And I heard the other day he took a fall from his horse. On *Bond* Street. Can you imagine anything more ridiculous?"

Clarissa gave up any pretense of pinning her hair. All her turbulent emotion focused into outrage, and she had to bite her tongue to keep from lashing out at the girls.

"How humiliating!" the short blonde agreed.

"I couldn't abide a husband who embarrassed me," Deidre declared. "Add to that his revolting hand and, well, you must see he's totally out of the question."

"But—"

"Oh, Maryanne," Deidre cut off the brunette with a laugh. "You've too soft a heart. If you fancy a husband in uniform, there are enough other handsome and well-born candidates. You mustn't even consider throwing yourself away on a *cripple*. Are you quite finished, Arabella? Bixby bespoke a waltz, and I shouldn't wish to keep him waiting.'' She winked at her friends. ''*Ten thousand* a year, Mama says, and a lovely townhouse on Portman Square. Much better than a withered hand and a coat hung with medals, Maryanne.''

Not trusting herself to speak civilly, Clarissa acknowledged the girls' goodbyes with a nod. As the little brunette made to follow them, Clarissa snagged her elbow.

The girl's eyes rounded in surprise. ''Miss Beaumont?''

''Miss Maryanne—Bennett, is it not? Lady Arundel's granddaughter? If you please, who is the soldier you were just discussing?''

The girl seemed to sense Clarissa's anger. ''L-Lieutenant Alexander Standish of the Tenth Hussars. Is he a…kinsman of yours? Please, Miss Beaumont, we meant no—''

''Not a kinsman,'' Clarissa cut her off. ''But every Englishman must hold dear the soldiers who fought and bled in their country's service. I'm relieved you, at least, seem to agree.''

''Y-yes, of course! But you must not think—''

''You may go now. Your friends will be missing you.'' Clarissa waved the girl away.

Her face distressed, the brunette glanced toward the door and back, apparently uncertain whether to obey the command of a lady whom she held in obvious awe or to stay and defend her friends. Swallowing hard, she curtseyed again, whispered, ''I'm sorry, Miss Beaumont,'' and fled.

Bixby! The man was an ass with groping hands. So the finicky Miss Deidre prized that rotund, floor-capering London macaroni-merchant over a soldier who'd survived the hell of battle to return with a wound's badge of honor?

As did one Lady Barbara. Clarissa scanned her memory of the misses currently on the Marriage Mart and came up with Lady Barbara Childress. A soft, pretty brunette who'd been pining over a young soldier, Clarissa recalled. The chit's mother, the imperious Countess of Wetherford, she remembered with distaste.

So her lover had returned with a crippled hand that rendered him no longer eligible, according to the vastly discriminating countess?

Men might whisper she was a reckless wanton, but as a leader of the ton for the past four years, Clarissa knew to a fine point the power she wielded. The styles she wore, the mantua-makers she employed, the hostesses whose parties she graced with her presence all were, or soon became, London's most favored. In short, Miss Clarissa Beaumont could bring something—or someone—into fashion.

Clarissa rose, delighted to channel her irritation and outrage into action. If she had anything to do with it— and she intended to have a great deal—Miss Deidre and Lady Barbara were about to see the man they so cavalierly dismissed become the most sought-after party in London.

Chapter Ten

Clarissa was fortunate to encounter Lord Alastair coming out of the card room. After enduring his obligatory compliments with barely-repressed impatience, she broke in, "Robert, do you know Lieutenant Alexander Standish?"

"The Earl of Worth's cub? He's a member of my club, I believe."

Squelching the associations that word conjured up, she continued, "I understand he is something of a Waterloo hero, and just returned from hospital in Brussels."

"Yes. Acquitted himself well indeed, I've heard."

"Excellent. If he is present tonight, could you introduce me? I should like to extend my thanks."

Looking startled and none too pleased, Lord Alastair smiled gamely. "Ah, certainly, Miss Beaumont. You do so admire our valiant ˈsoldiers. Very—patriotic. Of course, Standish is hardly more than a stripling. Not that the fact diminishes the gallantry of his service—"

"Quite." She put her hand on Alastair's arm and smiled warmly. "I should be most appreciative were you to find him for me."

Alastair clasped her gloved fingers. "You know I am

honored to render any service you desire. Excuse me but a moment, and I shall determine it.''

"Thank you," she murmured, and watched him walk away with a tweak of guilt. She feared Robert would be making her another offer soon, although she'd already turned him down twice. He was nice enough, and sometimes she wished he inspired in her a more fervent response. But he didn't.

Unlike a certain Hussar who came to mind.

A group of gentleman hailed her loudly, distracting her from that unwelcome observation, and bore her off to the refreshment room. When Alastair reappeared some time later with a soldier whose fur-pelissed coat hung about his thin frame, the crowd around her was thick enough that she had liberty to observe him as they approached.

Clarissa noted the slightly halting gait and the arm held stiffly at his side. Her eyes lingered a moment on his left hand—the one whose touch Miss Deidre so abhorred. Renewed outrage, and simple curiosity, stirred.

As he drew nearer, compassion colored her anger. Lieutenant Standish was entirely too thin. His eyes and mouth were bracketed by lines that, she knew from watching her mama develop similar ones during a severe attack of dropsy, represented considerable suffering. In spite of his emaciated frame and the lingering pain his limp revealed, he held himself proudly erect.

"Miss Beaumont," Alastair said when they reached her, "allow me to present Lieutenant Lord Alexander Standish."

"Miss Beaumont, an honor." His voice pleasantly deep, with his right hand he lifted her fingers to his lips. Though his hazel eyes registered admiration of her beauty, he refrained from the fawning compliments so often heaped upon her by men meeting her for the first time. Indeed, he remained coolly self-possessed, his slightly quizzical smile indicating his puzzlement over why an acknowledged Diamond whose suitors included men of greater wealth and stature than he had chosen to single him out.

Clarissa decided she liked him. "The honor is mine, to make the acquaintance of such a valiant officer."

He waved his right hand. "Please, Miss Beaumont, you flatter me. I trust I did my duty, but no more so than every other soldier." His hazel eyes clouded. "Including many not fortunate enough to return to bask in the praise of so lovely a lady."

"Then we must treasure those of you who did."

His eyes veered briefly to a young brunette dancing the quadrille. "It is kind of you to think so. How may I be of service, ma'am?"

The veiled longing in that stolen glance deepened her resolve. "Would you stroll with me, Lieutenant?"

He bowed and extended his right arm. Placing her gloved hand on it, she walked him toward the corner of the room. "Tenth Hussars, is it not? Were you wounded during Lord Uxbridge's charge?"

He turned to look her in the face, obviously surprised. "Why, yes! You've heard of it?"

"I'm a great admirer of our 'Infamous Army.' I've read all the *Gazette* accounts, including Lord Uxbridge and the Duke's full descriptions. Is it true French cuirassiers nearly captured Old Hookey the first day?"

"Quite true, ma'am. The Duke was, as usual, riding forward to encourage the men. Some frog lancers broke through suddenly and nearly surrounded him. He only escaped by ordering the Fifty-second Foot to lie down and jumping Challenger clean over them!"

"Like a box hedge?"

He chuckled. "Quite. Lucky for us he's such a good horseman. I daresay the battle might have had quite a different outcome, had he not been there to direct us."

By now they'd reached the corner. Instead of turning, Clarissa maneuvered the lieutenant to about-face. Obligingly he shifted direction, but when he again offered his right arm, she waved it away.

"I should like to remain on the side toward the dancers. Your left hand, sir?" She tapped it lightly.

Lieutenant Standish halted. Color rose in his thin cheeks. "I'm sorry, Miss Beaumont," he said after a moment. "I...I have no feeling in that hand."

His strained tone revealed just how much he detested admitting that weakness, and for a moment she regretted forcing him to it. But, she comforted herself, the result would be well worth this fleeting embarrassment.

"Ah, but the lady does." Resting her hand on his left wrist, she clasped her gloved fingers around his motionless ones. Though he did not—could not—return the pressure, his hand was quite warm—not at all cold or repulsive.

His eyes riveted on their intertwined fingers, he said nothing as she nudged them forward.

For the next few moments Clarissa guided them around the ballroom, making sure the newly-returned Lieutenant chatted with the most prominent political and society guests. Most of them were acquainted with the young soldier's father, and greeted him pleasantly, often with compliments about his gallant service.

Occasionally in the intervals between guests she caught his quizzical glance on her. Nor, Clarissa was pleased to acknowledge, was his gaze the only one she attracted. Clarissa's courtiers, who'd protested her abandoning them for yet another soldier, watched with vary-

ing degrees of puzzlement or mild indignation. Young
ladies who copied her fashions and manners, and the mamas of hopeful daughters, cast openly assessing looks at
her and the well-born, wealthy young man at her side. A
virtual hum of speculation followed them.

Her last visit—the pièce de résistance, she considered
it—was with Lady Arundel and her granddaughter.
Clutching the maligned left hand tighter, she greeted both
ladies, introduced the lieutenant to the blushing Miss
Maryanne, and after a bare nod to Miss Deidre and Miss
Anabelle who stood gawking at Maryanne's elbow,
walked away.

She was delighted to note that Lady Barbara Childress's gaze was among those which followed them
across the floor when, like Moses through the Red Sea,
they parted the dancers before making a very public exit
out the French doors onto the terrace.

Having reached the relative privacy of the moonlit balcony, Lieutenant Standish stood for a moment silently
staring at her fingers still gripping his left hand. Then he
threw back his head and laughed. "Did Colonel Sandiford set you to that?"

A tingle of shock drove all other thoughts from her
head. "Colonel Sandiford?"

"My commanding officer. You are acquainted?"

Only as opponents, she thought. Still, it wasn't fair to
hold that against this thoroughly charming young man.
"A little acquainted," she allowed. "Why do you ask?"

"A similarity of tactics. He's been recommending I
not allow my...disability to make me reticent. When
you—an influential lady upon whom I'd never have imposed in such fashion—made it a point to parade me
about, I thought surely 'twas he who incited you to it.
He did not?"

"No. I wasn't even aware he was your commander."

While he pondered that, she tried to reconcile Sandiford's evident concern for the lieutenant with her impressions of the stiff-necked Colonel who despised Society. It appeared he respected at least some of his own class. Just not the ladies.

With a start, she realized Lieutenant Standish stood staring at her, his expression perplexed. "Then why...?"

She squeezed his unresponsive fingers. "Let's just say I have a fondness for returning soldiers."

Once more he cast a glance of wistful longing toward the dancers beyond the balcony's French doors. "I still don't understand, but 'twas very kind of you."

"Would you go driving with me tomorrow?"

His head snapped back toward her. "Driving?" Once again, his cheeks flushed. "I'm afraid I don't yet—"

"As a cavalry officer you must be a notable horseman. I'd like your opinion of the new pair I just purchased for my phaeton." She smiled at him. "I'm accounted a tolerable whip. I shan't land you in a ditch, I promise."

"Of course. I should be honored to drive with you."

"Meet me at Grosvenor Square at five?"

That took him aback. "You mean to drive in Hyde Park?"

"Have you any objection?"

He laughed. "Why would I? Driving with the peerless Miss Beaumont during the promenade is a signal honor to which I'd never have aspired." He studied her, as if trying to ascertain her motives. "You seem quite determined to bring one obscure lieutenant into fashion. You are sure Colonel Sandiford didn't speak to you?"

"Of Lady Barbara?" The mingled surprise and pain on his face, before he once again schooled his expression to neutrality, confirmed her guess. "My...information came from a different source. You mustn't worry that I know your secret. I'm quite discreet.''

He laughed without humor. '''Tis not much of a secret. We had…at least I thought we had, an understanding. But that was long ago, before—'' he gestured toward his left side. "Obviously I was mistaken.''

Her suspicions confirmed now, Clarissa knew just how to proceed. If Lady Barbara harbored any feelings whatsoever for the lieutenant, she was about to find herself awash in remorse, regret, and with a modicum of cooperation from the lieutenant, raging jealousy.

"Perhaps. But the lady is just out, and very lovely. 'Tis not unusual all the flattering attention may have turned her head. Perhaps she merely needs a bit of…encouragement to help her decide what she really wants.''

He sighed. "She *is* lovely, is she not? A sweet, gentle girl who deserves the very best. Apparently her mama no longer includes me in that category, and I can't say I blame her. Why should she not want better than a…cripple for a son-in-law? Nor would I wish to cause Lady Barbara the distress of going against her mama's wishes.''

"Crippled because your leg and hand carry the scars of battle? Nonsense! And I must disagree. If Lady Barbara does not value the man she loves above her mama's approval, *she* doesn't deserve *him*. In any event, seeing you pining away gives her no incentive to ponder the depth of her feelings. Should we not make a push to help her discover that? I should think you would rather know sooner than later whether your hopes are futile.''

He shook his head in bemusement. "You certainly sound like the colonel.''

Lord forfend, she thought. "The Park tomorrow, then?"

He took a deep breath. "The Park tomorrow. Whatever your reasons, whatever the outcome—thank you. Your beauty is exceeded only by your kindness. Now, I should take you back before 'tis your reputation the ton is buzzing about."

Clarissa repressed a shudder. Still gripping his numb left hand, she let him lead her inside. She could almost feel the eyes of the crowd focus on them as they walked to the dance floor's edge. Satisfied, she leaned close.

"Can you lift your left hand with mine resting on it?"

He raised an eyebrow quizzically. "Y-yes. But—"

"Kiss my hand, please."

She knew the moment he realized Lady Barbara stood behind her. A grin blossomed on his face, obscuring the pain lines and making him look young and light-hearted again. "You," he murmured as he touched her fingers to his lips, "are a minx."

"I should be delighted to drive with you in the Park tomorrow," she said in a carrying voice. As a scowling Lord Alastair hastened to claim the hand the lieutenant relinquished, she gave him a quick wink.

He acknowledged it with a nod, then bowed. "Until tomorrow, Miss Beaumont." Without a sideways glance—as if no one else in the room was of any importance—the lieutenant crossed the dance floor and exited the ballroom.

She watched his theatrical departure with an approval that intensified as she stole a glimpse at the surprise—and dismay—on Lady Barbara's sweet young face.

Several of her swains looked no better pleased. She singled out Lord Alastair and gave him her most captivating smile. "I feel…flushed, Robert. Could you escort me to the refreshments? I should love a glass of champagne.''

Looking somewhat mollified, Alastair led her away. Miss Deidre and Miss Anabelle, she noted as she passed, stood with mouths agape.

Helping Lieutenant Standish, she thought with great satisfaction, was going to be quite amusing.

Having touched little of the substantial luncheon laid out for them, Sinjin rose to follow Hal, Englemere and his host out of the classically appointed dining room and down the marble hallway. Like Daniel going into the lion's den, in a very few moments he would enter the parlor to make the acquaintance of Mr. Motrum's daughter. Mercifully Englemere and Hal would remain for the introductions.

He'd come to the luncheon alive with trepidation, some of which had been speedily allayed. A trim man of middle age with a quiet air of authority, as might be expected of one who oversaw a financial empire stretching from England to the Indies, Mr. Motrum had a blunt but refreshingly honest manner and displayed not a trace of nouveau-riche vulgarity. His home, decorated in neutral tones with classical detailing, was equally elegant and well-run. If the young lady was anything like her sire, Sinjin might well be able to end his quest at its beginning.

If only they might conclude this as a business deal and meet for the first time at the altar, as often happened in weddings of state. But understandably, though frankly acknowledging the nature of the negotiations Englemere had undertaken on Sinjin's behalf—and indicating his own investigation of the potential bridegroom reassured him Sinjin was an honorable man to whom he'd feel confident turning over his beloved daughter—Mr. Motrum stated his blessing on the union would be given only if his pet found the young aristocrat to her liking.

As they turned a corner and entered the front hallway, Sinjin found it increasingly hard to move forward. By the time they reached the Adamesque archway outside the parlor door, his neck cloth had grown uncomfortably tight and his palms inside the kid gloves were damp.

As favorably impressed as he'd been by his prospective father-in-law and as often as he'd steeled himself to the inevitability of it, Sinjin was discovering that actually presenting himself to Miss Motrum as a matrimonial offering was infinitely more degrading than he'd ever imagined.

He reminded himself this was the fastest, most honorable way to fulfill his familial duty. He reassured himself there was no subterfuge—the young lady would not be expecting sham declarations of affection. He tried to convince himself the lady must meet *his* standards as well.

He still couldn't stop feeling like a high-priced stud about to be put on the block.

Only ingrained duty and iron self-discipline kept him in place, his best attempt at a smile plastered on his face. He'd never abandoned his post, no matter how desperate or hopeless his position, and he didn't intend to start now.

He jumped, however, when Hal touched his elbow. "Steady," the big man whispered. "Worst be over soon."

Grateful for the support, Sinjin took a deep breath, squared his shoulders, and feeling for all the world as if he were about to face a firing squad, followed Mr. Motrum into the parlor.

Chapter Eleven

With a sense of unreality Sinjin murmured the correct greeting to Miss Motrum and her chaperone, then focused his attention on the young lady.

Her lace-trimmed jonquil gown of expensive cut and costly material would have won the instant approval of his discriminating mama. Hair a shade more golden than Sarah's, eyes of a deeper blue, and pleasant, regular features gave her a quiet beauty that was quite lovely.

Neither vulgar nor an antidote. He was conscious of a sharp relief—and then anxiety. She looked...she looked just like a young lady of quality.

Well, what had he expected—homespun? Her enormously wealthy papa, he'd been told, had her educated at one of England's premier schools for young ladies and could well afford as many gowns and fripperies as she fancied.

He bowed over her gloved hand, uncomfortably conscious of her nearness and a faint scent of violets.

"A great pleasure, Miss Motrum."

"An even greater pleasure for us, dear Lord Sandiford," her duenna enthused before Miss Motrum could reply. "You're of the Hampshire Sandifords?"

"Yes, madam."

"Such a lovely county. I was just yesterday telling Anne it would be of all things agreeable to spend one's summer in the country."

"It is indeed pleasant, ma'am."

Sinjin slid a glance at Miss Motrum. The young lady sat serenely, apparently quite content to let Mrs. Cartwright manage the conversation.

Gritting his teeth, he made himself follow through on the plan he'd devised. "I understand the weather tomorrow will be fine, and hoped you two ladies might join me for a walk about Hyde Park. You do enjoy walking?"

"Oh, Anne is excessively fond of walking. Though our own garden is quite pleasant, 'tis ever so much more...space in the Park."

"I like to walk," Miss Motrum affirmed, reassuring him she possessed faculties of speech.

"Very good, then, I shall call for you. Would eleven be convenient? 'Tis more pleasant when it is not crowded."

The duenna gave him a sharp look, as if suspecting he thought himself too high in the instep to be seen with them at the fashionable promenade hour. But Sinjin had no intention of doing something designed to draw down on them the speculation of the gossips. Not until he'd determined what action he meant to take regarding Miss Motrum—if then.

At Mr. Motrum's nod, Mrs. Cartwright turned her frown into a smile. "Yes, 'twill be easier for us all to get better acquainted without the discomforts of a milling crowd. 'Tis settled, then?"

"Yes, ma'am."

Mercifully, as Sinjin's panicky brain could come up with nothing further to say—though in truth, Mrs. Cartwright appeared well able to carry on both sides of the conversation—Englemere smoothly intervened. "Ladies, we must not trespass too long upon your time."

."No, indeed," Sinjin affirmed with alacrity.

"Mr. Motrum, thank you for an informative meeting and delicious lunch. Ladies, an honor to have met you." Englemere bowed.

"Honored," Hal echoed.

"Until tomorrow," Sinjin said. And with infinite relief, he bowed and followed his friends from the room.

"Not so bad," Hal said, clapping him on the shoulder as they descended the entry stairs. "Pretty gel."

"Yes. Pleasing manners, too," Englemere said. "A bit...quiet, perhaps, but you might consider silence an admirable trait in a wife."

If it comes to that, Sinjin thought. "She is lovely. Gentlemen, my thanks for...smoothing the way."

"You are under no obligation to proceed," Englemere added. "Mr. Motrum understands, and has assured me he has conveyed the understanding to his daughter, that a link between you will be pursued only if both parties agree to it. You have complete freedom of action."

Given his financial state, that wasn't precisely true, but still he owed Englemere a debt for negotiating the business so delicately. "I appreciate your arranging it."

"Enough," Hal pronounced. "Thirsty business. Have a drink?"

In the aftermath of the meeting, he found himself too edgy to sit bending an elbow, even in Hal's genial company. "Not now, thank you. I...I promised to ride with Alex."

True enough, if not prearranged for this afternoon. He thought longingly of a hard gallop across the open Spanish plain or the sweet earth of a Hampshire pasture. The Park would have to do.

Turning down Englemere's offer of a lift, Sinjin bid the men goodbye at their carriage. Relieved to be at last alone with his turbulent thoughts, he set off walking.

Despite her expensive dress, Miss Motrum appeared in other respects to be an eminently proper candidate for his bride. She was attractive, her manners pretty, and better that she be reticent than bold. Once they became better acquainted, the bad taste in his mouth and the tension in his gut would disappear. They'd made a favorable beginning, he told himself firmly.

Not until he'd hailed a jarvey and given the driver Alex's direction did the odd thought occur. At the touch of his lips to Miss Motrum's hand, he'd felt…nothing.

Well, one didn't need to fall on one's wife like a mongrel in heat. Given his dislike of the whole business, at this awkward early juncture he could hardly expect to drum up warmer feelings. The lady was lovely enough, and surely as he came to know his future bride better the idea of performing a husband's duties would generate more excitement. A necessity, if he wanted heirs.

The image of Sarah's son suddenly recurred and something wrenched in his chest. Sons to teach to fish and shoot, daughters to dote on and tease and spoil. Yes, children would go a long way to reconciling him to a suitable but loveless match.

Should he and Miss Motrum decide to proceed, affection would doubtless come in time. Respect and affection would be enough. It would have to be.

Damn and blast, he was turning mawkish again. A stiff drink and hard gallop would set him to rights, and Alex was just the fellow with whom to share them.

He reached his friend's rooms to be met by the disquieting intelligence that Lieutenant Standish had gone out—driving. Incredulous, for Alex's weak leg made balancing in a carriage a precarious business, Sinjin questioned him further, but the valet continued to insist his master meant to take a phaeton to the Park.

Sinjin's uncertain mix of emotions seethed into anxiety. Whatever possessed Alex to attempt something so bacon-brained? If that spill from his horse on Bond Street had embarrassed as well as injured him, how much more humiliating it would be to take a tumble before the entire ton, massed together at promenade hour and hawk-eyed for the latest scrap of gossip?

Damn Lady Barbara and women in general, he swore, memory of a certain red-haired termagant adding vehemence to his oath.

But as he awaited a hackney, he realized the idea of Alex driving Lady Barbara made no sense. For one, he doubted the countess would entrust her precious daughter to his "damaged" lieutenant. Second, as far as he knew Alex had no carriage in London, and wouldn't be able to impress a gnat with the well-worn vehicles obtainable for hire.

Puzzlement and worry intensified during the interminable drive to the Park. As soon as practical, he sprang down, tossing the fare in the driver's general direction as his eyes scanned the crowd for coats of the Tenth's distinctive blue hue. His temper shortening with every pace, he forced his way along a path thronged with vehicles and horsemen, wishing he'd thought to return to his lodgings for Valiant.

When he finally spotted the back of Alex's dark head over a familiar, silver-laced blue coat, his heart nearly stopped. Not only was the gudgeon fool enough to drive the lady in green beside him, they sat some six feet off the ground in a high-perch phaeton, a dangerously unstable vehicle under the best of circumstances.

Eyeing the green-clad damsel with murder on his mind, Sinjin fought his way toward the vehicle. He hadn't ridden miles over a bloody battlefield, his unconscious lieutenant's shattered body draped across his saddle, to let the cloth-headed fool pitch himself out of that accident waiting to happen and ruin the field surgeon's hard and painful work.

He'd come up with some excuse to force Alex down, then drive the blasted chit home himself. Mercifully, since the press of the crowd slowed Sinjin's progress to a crawl, Alex's carriage had stopped while the lady conversed with some friends on horseback.

Panting slightly, he rounded the front of the equippage and prepared to offer a greeting. But instead of Lady Barbara's heart-shaped face and cornflower eyes, he glanced up at an all-too-familiar profile. His words of welcome caught in his throat.

It couldn't be Miss Beaumont! As far as he knew, the lieutenant wasn't even acquainted with her. And whatever was she doing, laughing up at Alex so coyly, one gloved hand clasped cozily over his, her other holding the reins?

Before he could dredge up coherent speech, Alex spotted him. "Hallo, Colonel! Lovely day for a drive, is it not? You are acquainted with Miss Beaumont?"

Sinjin bowed, trying to reshape his grimace into a smile. "Ma'am."

"Colonel." She accorded him a cool nod.

"Miss Beaumont wished me to evaluate the action of this fine new pair she just purchased. 'Twas an even greater privilege, though, to witness how skillfully she handles them. I must say, when I first saw the carriage I

had my doubts a lady could control it, but you're quite
a whipster, ma'am. Bore me here as gently as if I'd been
rocking in a cradle.''

Fortunately the lieutenant's words were addressed to
the lady, since Sinjin was still too flabbergasted to speak.

A cradle indeed, he thought, fuming. Of course this
highly unstable, highly unsuitable carriage would be
hers—and of course she would confound modesty and
tradition by driving it herself. 'Twas all of a piece with
her earlier actions—reckless, thoughtless, impulsive.
Well, she may have dazzled poor heartsick Alex, who
was evidently too confused and vulnerable now to be
thinking clearly, into believing this conveyance safe—
with a female at the reins, no less!—but Sinjin knew
better.

''Should you like to take a turn, Colonel, if Miss Beaumont permits?'' Alex turned to the lady. ''The colonel's
a fine judge of horseflesh, ma'am. I think the beasts a
superior pair, but if he agrees, you can rest assured you
have the very best.''

''I'm sure I can rely on your opinion, Lieutenant,''
Miss Beaumont said, ignoring Sinjin.

Of course the last thing he wished was to put himself
back into proximity of the unmanageable redhead's acid
tongue—but having been offered a perfect avenue to detach Alex from his perilous perch, Sinjin nobly put aside
personal inclination. ''I should like that very much, Miss
Beaumont. I've never been driven by a lady.''

Skeptical green eyes fixed on his. ''I'm quite sure you
haven't.'' Then, after a pause so long Sinjin felt heat rise
to his face, she finally shrugged. ''Since you think it
amusing, Colonel, by all means join me for a circuit.''

While Sinjin held his breath, Alex managed to lower

Do You Have the Lucky Key?

PLAY THE
Lucky Key Game

If you do, you can get

FREE BOOKS
and a
FREE GIFT!

Turn the page & find out if you have the LUCKY KEY!

PLAY THE
Lucky Key Game
and get

HOW TO PLAY:

1. With a coin, carefully scratch off gold area at the right. Then check the claim chart to see what we have for you —**2 FREE BOOKS** and a **FREE GIFT** — **ALL YOURS FREE!**

2. Send back the card and you'll receive two brand-new Harlequin Historicals® novels. These books have a cover price of $4.99 each in the U.S. and $5.99 each in Canada, but they are yours to keep absolutely free.

3. There's no catch. You're under no obligation to buy anything. We charge nothing —ZERO — for your first shipment. And you don't have to make any minimum number of purchases — not even one!

4. The fact is, thousands of readers enjoy receiving books by mail from the Harlequin Reader Service®. They enjoy the convenience of home delivery...they like getting the best new novels at discount prices, BEFORE they're available in stores...and they love their *Heart to Heart* subscriber newsletter featuring author news, horoscopes, recipes, book reviews and much more!

5. We hope that after receiving your free books you'll want to remain a subscriber. But the choice is yours — to continue or cancel, any time at all! So why not take us up on our invitation, with no risk of any kind. You'll be glad you did!

YOURS FREE!
A SURPRISE MYSTERY GIFT

We can't tell you what it is...but we're sure you'll like it! A
FREE GIFT—
just for playing the LUCKY KEY game!

Visit us online at
www.eHarlequin.com

The Harlequin Reader Service® — Here's how it works:

Accepting your 2 free books and gift places you under no obligation to buy anything. You may keep the books and gift and return the shipping statement marked "cancel." If you do not cancel, about a month later we'll send you 6 additional novels and bill you just $4.05 each in the U.S., or $4.46 each in Canada, plus 25¢ shipping & handling per book and applicable taxes if any.* That's the complete price and — compared to cover prices of $4.99 each in the U.S. and $5.99 each in Canada — it's quite a bargain! You may cancel at any time, but if you choose to continue, every month we'll send you 6 more books, which you may either purchase at the discount price or return to us and cancel your subscription.

*Terms and prices subject to change without notice. Sales tax applicable in N.Y. Canadian residents will be charged applicable provincial taxes and GST.

himself to the ground without incident, even clapping Sinjin on the shoulder and abjuring him to enjoy his ride.

Perversely annoyed by the lieutenant's cheerfulness, Sinjin hauled himself up to the ridiculously high seat and tried not to glower at its driver.

"You'll wait for us?" he asked Alex. "I've a matter of some urgency to discuss. If you are ready, Miss Beaumont?"

With a flick of the reins, she set the carriage in motion. Sinjin braced himself beside her, trying to withdraw from his murderous thoughts snippets polite enough for conversation.

Her proximity wasn't helping. He had trouble arranging coherent sentences with her insidiously seductive body a mere handspan away.

Damn and blast! What sort of rig was she running with Alex, driving him in the Park in full view of the assembled ton? With his bruised heart and damaged ego, he was much too vulnerable to one of her dangerous attraction. Given a little encouragement, the poor sot might well imagine himself in love with her—or at least in lust, no more comfortable a condition, as he knew all too well.

With the crowd of suitors already hanging about her, she had no need to feed her vanity by adding his lieutenant to the number. And so he'd tell her.

"Well, Colonel? Are you satisfied yet that I won't overturn us? Or is terror still tying your tongue?"

The despicable chit was laughing at him. Again. Stifling an urge to snap at her, he said through gritted teeth, "I must admit you drive rather well. For a woman."

She laughed then in truth. "*Almost* a handsome admission. Come, Colonel, you look as if you'd lunched upon cannonballs. What have I done now to incur your displeasure?"

He wouldn't pass up such an opening. "You've been driving my lieutenant in this infernal contraption. Da— Good Heavens, Miss Beaumont, can you not tell how weak his left leg is? Should the carriage jolt in that direction, with his bad hand he cannot even grip the rail to brace himself. One sharp curve, and he'd be out on the pavement, lucky if humiliation were the only harm he suffered!"

"And cannot you, of all people, look past his injury and see a man who wishes to display his strengths, not his weaknesses? Not only have I driven at a pace that would put an infant to sleep, you may notice I stationed Lieutenant Standish to my right. He'd have to crash through me to fall out of the carriage."

"Having borne his deadweight a time or two, I have no doubt he could do just that."

"With me handling the ribbons," she returned sweetly, "he'd have no occasion to. Surely you believe I would never do anything to injure the lieutenant."

In full dudgeon now, he was delighted at this chance to speak his mind. "Not knowingly, perhaps. But there are matters at stake here of which you may be unaware. Alex is currently enduring a…disappointment of the heart and would be, I fear, all too vulnerable to a woman of such surpassing charm as yourself."

She looked at him then, surprise in the green depths of her eyes. "Is that a backhanded compliment of sorts?"

"I doubt you have any need to be reminded how attractive you are. Your large court of sycophants, I am sure, do a fair job of that daily."

"And you think I mean to add Lieutenant Standish to that number?"

He reined in his temper with an effort. No sense affronting her such that she proceeded to do precisely what he warned against, merely to spite him. "I believe you might attach him without conscious effort. Few men could resist the heady gift of your company, and once close, 'twould be all too easy to fall under your spell. For one who is vulnerable, that is."

"And I'm the sort of mindless, shallow flirt who delights in collecting men's hearts as trophies?"

While he hesitated, trying to turn that blunt indictment—which he tended to believe—into words polite enough to agree with, she cut the phaeton neatly out of the line of plodding carriages, inched the pair past the two vehicles in front of them, and sprang the horses.

The sudden forward motion slammed him into his seat. He grabbed the rail, his protest lost in the rush of wind past the phaeton. To his consternation—and grudging admiration—Miss Beaumont urged the team on, neatly catching the thong of her whip as she kept the pair at a ground-eating gallop, then guided them into a sharp turn onto the trail leading toward Kensington. Not until they'd reached the far limits of the park did she finally slow the horses.

Despite his temper, the drive left him breathless and exhilarated. Miss Beaumont appeared to be breathing rather heavily as well, he noticed as his gaze strayed to the rise and fall of that deliciously rounded chest. He jerked his eyes away.

"Was that little exhibition meant to chide me for lack of faith in your driving, or terrify me anew?" he asked when he caught his breath.

She turned an innocent gaze upon him. "You were to observe the action of my horses, I thought."

In spite of himself he had to grin. Damn, but she had a quick wit. "So I was. A good purchase—they're well matched." Fairness forced him to add, "And your driving is most competent. If a bit reckless, to race such a powerful pair in the crowded confines of the Park.''

''I knew you could not bring yourself to deliver a barb-less compliment.'' Fisting the reins in one hand, she turned to him, eyebrow raised. ''You might observe,'' she made a sweeping gesture with her free hand, ''be-yond the carriage road there are no crowds.''

Indeed, given the tall stand of trees at the park's bor-der, one could no longer see fashionable London prom-enading on Rotten Row far behind. They were, in fact, nearly alone, their only observers the warbling birds, a small herd of cows, and at some distance, a few farm laborers toiling in the fields.

His gaze fell to her full lips, slightly pursed in irony. A sudden, terrifying impulse came over him to lean past the small space that separated them and kiss her, capture for an instant her passionate contradiction of recklessness and courage.

Her eyes widened with something like alarm. Abruptly she moved away and flicked the reins. Once again the motion threw him back against the seat.

Barely conscious of the pounding hooves and swaying carriage, he retreated to the far edge of the phaeton. He'd been without a woman far too long, that was all, he as-sured himself, trying to minimize the intensity of his re-sponse to her.

'Twas base need that inflamed his admiration for her wit and daring into this spurious sense of…kinship. A discreet, willing widow would tame these misguided im-pulses, and he should seek one. *Soon.*

Before he got himself in hand enough to dredge up some thread of conversation, they'd reached the crowded carriage way.

With, he noted unwillingly, consummate skill she insinuated the vehicle back to the spot where Alex stood. A small group appeared to be waiting with him, in which Sinjin recognized a cluster of Miss Beaumont's usual admirers—and two carriages containing eligible young ladies and their mamas. Looking more at ease than Sinjin had yet seen him since returning to London, Alex was conversing with a pair of dark-haired girls, eliciting a peal of laughter from one and a blush from the other.

"Excellent animals indeed, and a most…interesting drive, Miss Beaumont." Intent on drawing Alex away before he could attempt to retake his seat in the phaeton, Sinjin added hastily, "There's that matter of import I must discuss with you. Now. Miss Beaumont, my apologies for stealing your escort, but if you would be so gracious as to excuse him? I shall return myself in a moment to see you home."

"No need for that."

Leading a tall gray, Lord Alastair emerged from behind a carriage. His tense, aggrieved look told Sinjin he must have watched their reckless drive across the park— and into the woodlands beyond. "I'd be delighted to accompany Miss Beaumont. Grenville, you'll mind my horse, won't you?"

Sinjin need not even see her home. Feeling a pang that must be relief, he swung down to allow Alastair to replace him on the high perch beside her.

"Rather play groom than risk my neck in that demmed phaeton," Grenville said as he walked over to take Alastair's reins. "Notable whip you may be, Clare, but nothing would induce me to ride in that rig. Even if I drove."

"If you drove she'd end in a ditch for sure," Alastair returned. "Whenever you're ready, Miss Beaumont."

Sinjin felt the heat of her green-eyed gaze upon him, the sizzling flash of sensation between them nearly palpable. "You shouldn't judge so harshly...Lord Alastair," she said.

Before Sinjin realized her remarks were not addressed to him, she'd turned to smile at Alex. "I have no qualms at all driving the phaeton, particularly when accompanied by so accomplished a cavalryman as Lieutenant Standish. Had we encountered the least difficulty, I am quite certain he could have controlled the horses in a trice."

As her tribute was clearly audible to the young ladies in the nearby carriages, Alex's lean cheeks reddened. "Miss Beaumont, you are too kind."

"The truth merely, Lieutenant. I shall release you to military *necessity*," her stress on the word told Sinjin she found his excuse for detaching Alex all too transparent, "but only if you promise to meet me again very soon. Indeed, as it happens I'm planning to attend Covent Garden this evening. Would you be free to join me?"

"I should be honored."

"Excellent. I shall expect you at my house tonight, then." She offered her hand.

Alex limped over to take it. "It will be," he touched his lips to her fingers, "a great pleasure, Miss Beaumont."

But instead of allowing Alex to release her hand, she clasped his fingers in hers and leaned closer. Positively batting her indecently long lashes at him, she murmured, "I shall endeavor to see that it is, Lieutenant Standish."

The purring intimacy of her voice made every hair on the back of Sinjin's neck stand on end. Uninterested in enticing Alex, ha! Not even the glare on Lord Alastair's face could match the outrage swelling Sinjin's chest as he witnessed that blatant display.

With an arch—nay, challenging!—upsweep of lashes,

Miss Beaumont glanced at Sinjin, then straightened and gathered the reins in hand. "Shall we be off, Robert?"

As the phaeton moved away, the understandably be-dazzled Alex remained motionless, hand still outstretched where Miss Beaumont had released it. "Come along, Alex," Sinjin growled, pulling the lieutenant's arm.

Like a wooden puppet, Alex followed him. Not until some moments later did the lieutenant find his voice. "What an entrancing woman," he said in tones of awe.

"Just remember what kind of women cast spells," Sinjin spat out, still seething.

Alex gave him a startled look, as if not sure he'd heard correctly, then burst out laughing. "How very unhand-some of you, Colonel!"

"Perhaps," Sinjin admitted, a little shamefaced, "but you'd do well to consider the crowd of men at her feet and beware. A siren indeed is the beauteous Miss Beau-mont. Don't forget what happens to mariners who sail past."

"Am I to be lured onto the rocks of destruction?" Alex asked, his tone amused. "Colonel, I think you mis-take Miss Beaumont. She's very kind."

The undisguised admiration in Alex's comment made Sinjin wince. "Kind? That fall you took last week must have rattled your wits."

"You are entirely too cynical."

Sinjin snorted. "She's dazzling, I'll grant you. Just don't let your loins take the place of your brain."

Alex turned to give him a measuring look. "I've never heard you so anxious to disparage the charms of any lady. Are you sure you've no aspirations there?"

Sinjin recoiled. "Me? Certainly not! I'd rather mate with a scorpion! If you've not yet felt the sting of that lady's tongue, you are fortunate, I assure you! Miss

Beaumont is a sterling example of why I insist on a sensible middle-class bride. No idiocies of high-perch phaetons and dashes through a crowded park for my wife.''

''If you say.''

Sinjin didn't much like the grin that appeared on Alex's face in the wake of that innocuous reply. Before he could think of a suitable retort, however, Alex shrugged. ''Suit yourself,'' he said, a disquieting twinkle in his eye, ''but for me, I find the prospect of spending time in company of a stunning creature who drives like a Valkyrie and rides like the wind not the least bit disagreeable.''

With an upsurge of alarm Sinjin recalled the big black stallion careening to a halt in front of Sarah's door. ''You're not riding with her?''

''I haven't been invited…yet.''

''Well, if you are and don't have the sense to refuse, at least don't attempt to match her exploits,'' Sinjin grumbled.

Gazing into the distance, Alex sighed. ''You must admit, when she turns the full force of those emerald eyes on one and smiles to rival an angel, 'tis blasted difficult to retain one's sense of perspective.''

Sinjin sighed as well. *Indeed it is,* he thought, and realized with a shock he'd come perilously close to uttering the admission aloud. Swallowing the words, he growled instead, ''Exactly what I've been warning you about. Alex, you're…upset over Lady Barbara. You may not be thinking too clearly now. Just be cautious. I wouldn't wish you to take another fall. Of any sort.''

The smile Sinjin mistrusted returned to Alex's lips. ''Ah, but such a fall!''

The arrival of the hackney forestalled a reply, and Sinjin decided to give the matter a rest. Best not to be too insistent, lest he inadvertently push the gallant lieutenant closer to the lady by inspiring Alex to take up the cudgels in her defense.

But the whole afternoon left him strangely dissatisfied, and once he'd dropped the lieutenant off at the Albany, the events surrounding Alex and Miss Beaumont returned to buzz about in his head.

What was it about the image of his lieutenant and That Woman together that so aroused his ire? Alex had survived his drive intact. Though Sinjin couldn't be easy on that score, Alex didn't as yet seem to have fallen victim to Miss Beaumont's considerable allure. For the first time since returning to London the lieutenant had engaged him in a conversation in which Alex's every thought and word had not been of Lady Barbara and the progress of his suit. Wasn't that the very result Sinjin had hoped for?

Indeed, he'd not seen Alex as relaxed as he'd appeared this afternoon since…since before his injuries.

Alex's highly public circuit of the park with a ton leader like Miss Beaumont could only improve his credit among the beau monde, as the admiring glances of those young ladies—and their mamas—had eloquently testified. Though Alex had blushed at Miss Beaumont's praise of his horseman's skill, he'd basked in the compliment as well.

Was he too protective of Alex, ever focused on his lieutenant's disabilities rather than his gradually returning strength, as Miss Beaumont accused? Sinjin tried to consider the matter dispassionately, rather than as one who'd watched the young man struggle through a long, painful convalescence.

Another thought occurred, even more discomforting. Was he also, as Alex claimed, letting his prejudice against her whole class bias his opinion of Miss Beaumont's actions? Surely she knew what influence she wielded in the ton…and how her approval could raise an obscure young lieutenant to prominence. He recalled the cluster of young ladies hanging on Alex's words after their turn about the Park—and the approving looks of their attendant mamas. Could Miss Beaumont have meant this excursion to display the recovering young lieutenant at his best?

There was that business of her flirting outrageously when she bid Alex farewell, then tossing Sinjin down a gauntlet of a look, as if to prove she could ensorcel the lieutenant if she so wished, in spite of Sinjin's disapproval.

Kind, as Alex claimed—or calculating? Siren—or savior?

Damn and blast! The hot-tempered vixen had nearly thrown him out of that poor excuse of a carriage, flirted blatantly with his susceptible lieutenant minutes after he implored her to refrain from doing so, and worst yet, had seen through all his attempts to cloak his rather negative opinion of her in kinder words.

He had problems enough without becoming caught up in the puzzle of the fascinating but volatile Miss Beaumont. And therefore, he vowed as he sprang down from the jarvey and stomped up the stairs to his rooms, he would dismiss the lady from his thoughts *now* and for *good*.

Chapter Twelve

For the first part of the drive back to Grosvenor Square, Clarissa occupied herself with soothing Lord Alastair's ruffled sensibilities. Distressed already by her neglecting him to drive with not one but two military gentlemen, he'd been nearly beside himself, she could tell, when she cavalierly invited the lieutenant to what had initially been their private theatre party.

Having the lieutenant attend the event as one of her group would forward their designs on Lady Barbara's peace of mind—but not nearly as well as if Lieutenant Standish were her sole escort. So of course, he must be. Listening to Alastair with one ear, Clarissa contemplated how best to inform her erstwhile suitor that she'd just decided to replace him as her evening's primary escort.

"Robert, thank you for stepping in to bring me home. I know it inconvenienced you, and—"

"Nonsense. No service I could do you would ever be an inconvenience. Especially not one that allows me to stand here so close beside you. Clare, you know I'd—"

That sounding dangerously like the lead-in to another proposal, she hastily interrupted, "I know. Which is why it is beastly to ask you for another favor."

Cut off in mid-oratory, he groped for words. "F-favor? What sort of favor?"

"Nothing arduous, but my asking it at this late juncture is rather rude. Robert, I'd like you to let Lieutenant Standish escort me to the theatre tonight in your stead. Only Lieutenant Standish."

She saw surprise in his eyes—and then a pain that smote her conscience. "You no longer wish my company?" he asked quietly.

"It isn't that! I've undertaken a sort of—mission to help Lieutenant Standish, but 'tis a rather delicate matter. You will divulge nothing of what I tell you, I trust?"

Still looking stricken, he nodded a little stiffly. "Of course not."

"Lieutenant Standish is enamored of a certain young lady who, though she once gave evidence of returning his regard, has been rather fickle of late. I convinced the lieutenant a bit of jealousy might help her discover her true feelings, so for a few days I'm making a show of being seen with him as frequently and publicly as possible. So you can understand 'twould advance my purposes better if he alone escorted me. Will you assist in the plan?"

"Is it just show?"

"Of course. He's charming, but as you noted, rather young, and in any event he's in love with another lady."

Alastair was silent a moment, long enough to make Clarissa feel guilty for asking. Finally, with a sigh he nodded. "If you wish it, of course I shall do my possible to assist. Though I consider giving up an evening in your company a great sacrifice."

"Then I shall have to see you are amply rewarded."

"I shall hold you to that."

Uneasy with the warmth her jesting comment brought

to Alastair's eyes, Clarissa noted with relief that they'd reached Grosvenor Square. "Ah, home at last. Would you hand me down?"

Too impatient by now to fend off the amorous advances she suspected Robert would make, could he get her alone in the parlor, she excused herself from inviting him in, pleading the need to spend some time with her mama. With rather ill grace, he allowed her to summon him a hackney. After pressing a fervent kiss on her hand, he left her.

Sighing, she mounted the stairs to her room and rang for Lizette to set out her dinner dress. Why couldn't she feel for this kind, handsome man who adored her at least a particle of the attraction that consumed her for one disapproving colonel?

On a happier note, the results of her drive with Lieutenant Standish, she decided as she stripped off her habit, were quite promising. As she'd anticipated, he was an amusing and straightforward young man with a great deal of unpretentious charm. She'd had the pleasure of watching him relax, even become rather animated as he conversed with the awestruck Miss Maryanne. And when they'd passed the carriage containing Lady Barbara and her mother, the reaction was all she could have hoped.

The countess gave them a brief nod, but the distress in Lady Barbara's blue eyes belied the calm cordiality of her greeting. After they passed, that young lady turned back twice to gaze after them, a fact, Clarissa recalled with satisfaction, that Lieutenant Standish duly noted, though he was too much the gentleman to comment upon it. With any luck, the attention she and the lieutenant had attracted, added to the reports Miss Maryanne's party, would certainly circulate should give one dark-haired beauty much to think about.

Lieutenant Standish was truly a charming man, she concluded warmly. Should Lady Barbara not come to her senses, perhaps she ought to encourage him. She did have such a weak spot for a valiant soldier.

Prickly unease coursed through her as she recalled her drive with that *other* soldier. Lucifer's eyebrow, but Colonel Lord Sandiford could inflame her temper in an instant. Initially admiring his obvious concern for his lieutenant's welfare, her kind thoughts withered when he proceeded to accuse her, first of recklessly endangering the young man, then of trying to beguile him into losing his already-beaten heart.

Entice him! She felt anger flush her face anew. Was the man so presumptuously prejudiced he could not give her credit for any unselfish impulses at all? Had his pompous accusations not made her so furious—she smiled again at how she'd nearly unseated him when she whipped her team to a gallop—she might have explained her sudden attentions to Lieutenant Standish. No, she'd let the lieutenant enlighten his mother-hen of a colonel if he chose—*she* would not do so.

A wistful sadness dissolved some of the anger. Could the colonel not give her credit for possessing some unselfish impulses? She'd best stop thinking about him and master this foolishly persistent hope that they might one day become friends.

Friends. She recalled that little episode on the Kensington lane when he'd almost kissed her, and a shudder rippled through her, heating her to her toes. The really awful thing was, had he in fact kissed her she was fairly certain she'd not have wanted him to stop.

Drat the man! She hated that he elucidated so powerful a response in her, one she seemed unable to suppress or control. Thank Heaven he was also arrogant, managing and prejudiced. Were that much too attractive person coupled to a character composed solely of admirable traits, the colonel might pose a serious threat to her peace.

Realizing she was still thinking of the man after having just commanded herself to cease, she gave a scornful laugh, causing Lizette, who was helping her into her dinner gown, to glance up in surprise. Assuring her maid that nothing was amiss, she dismissed her and walked the short distance to her mama's apartments.

As always, seeing her once gay, giddy mama sitting so pale and still, a lap robe thrown over her legs, caused Clarissa a pang of grief. Ever since the attack that nearly killed her, Lady Beaumont had become a virtual recluse, convinced she was too frail to drive out, to entertain but rarely or to leave the small kingdom of her rooms, much as her daughter urged her otherwise. Clarissa went over to kiss the soft cheek.

"Did you have a nice drive, darling?"

"Yes, Mama. The weather was fine, and I'm quite pleased with the new team."

Her mama frowned. "I do wish you wouldn't take that shocking vehicle. To be sure, you're a capital driver, but it is dangerous, and if anything were to happen—"

"Nothing will." Though she knew the endeavor a hopeless one, still Clarissa could not help trying to coax her mama out of her self-imposed exile. "Can I not persuade you to accompany me to the theatre this evening? Many of your friends will be there, as the play is said to be quite amusing. And," Clarissa added what she knew would be the most telling argument, "a very charming young man shall escort us—a lieutenant newly returned from Belgium."

As she expected, her mother's vacant gaze focused sharply. Having buried a husband and two infant sons,

Lady Beaumont's one remaining goal in life was to see her only surviving child safely wed. "Indeed. Do you like him, dear, this new young man?"

"He's quite charming. And a hero no less. Englemere tells me he was part of Lord Uxbridge's gallant charge, the one that broke the back of Napoleon's Imperial Guard."

Her mama smiled with real enthusiasm. "You must bring him to call on me."

"You could become acquainted tonight at the theatre."

Lady Beaumont shook her head. "I'm afraid I'm not feeling up to it just yet. Perhaps later in the Season."

Clarissa hadn't really expected her mama to agree, but with that lady distracted by news of a new suitor who might finally be The One to sweep her finicky daughter to the altar, said daughter could press the advantage. "You must let Wapping help you into the garden after breakfast, then. Mornings there are so lovely, with the flowers budding out. I should like to have Lieutenant Standish greet my mother with a blush of sunshine on her cheeks."

"Aye, the fresh air will do her good," Wapping, her mama's maid and dresser, said as she entered. "And so I've been telling her. You listen to Miss Clare, Madam, and we'll have you dancing again by summer. Now, let's get you down to dinner."

Having planted the suggestion, Clarissa followed as Wapping handed her mama a cane and helped her toward the dining room. Silly and frivolous as she'd often thought her mama back in the days when Lady Beaumont was one of society's gayest hostesses, Clarissa would give much to have her mama restored to health.

Later, having seen Lady Beaumont tucked back up into bed, Clarissa joined Lieutenant Standish in the coach that would take them to Covent Garden. For a brief, unsettling moment she wondered what plans Colonel Sandiford had made for this evening. Would he too attend the play all London was discussing—or would he be seated in a Cit's drawing room, courting his middle-class heiress?

Irritated that she'd again fallen into musing about him, she shook her head, as if that motion could shake him free. Thanks heavens tonight, instead of the empty flattery of her usual court, she'd have Lieutenant Standish's witty, attentive company to blot out any further thought of his maddeningly attractive, absolutely unattainable colonel.

The carriage clattered past the portico of St. Paul's and into Covent Garden Square. As they passed the alley where she'd been attacked, Clarissa couldn't prevent a reminiscent shiver. How lucky she'd been that night. And no wonder the colonel despised her.

She'd just determined to drag her mind from the dismals and make a better attempt to entertain her escort when the carriage suddenly jerked to a halt, throwing her back against the squabs.

In that moment, she heard the protesting squeal of the horses—and a girl's high, piercing scream.

Chapter Thirteen

"Miss Beaumont, are you all right?"

Lieutenant Standish's inquiry came over the sounds of stomping horses, the shouts of her coachman and a woman's strident tones. "Yes, of course. I must discover what—"

"Allow me." With surprising swiftness, the lieutenant levered himself out of the carriage.

Clarissa caught the door before it shut and leaned out. Craning her neck, she tried to discern in the darkness what had occurred at the front of the carriage. She could see little, hear only the lieutenant's low tones interspersed with the increasing volume of other voices. Though no further screams rent the night, she soon grew too anxious to remain cooped up in the carriage.

She clambered out to find her coachman exchanging insults with a heavyset, heavily-rouged woman while both of them tried to pull a thin girl, garbed only in a scandalously brief gown, out of a tangle of reins at the center of the traces. A footman held the team's leads, trying to calm the restive, stamping beasts that threatened at any moment to trample the slight girl under their iron-shod hooves. Lieutenant Standish was attempting both to coax the girl out and mediate the argument between the rouged woman and the coachman.

"Whatever is going on?" Clarissa demanded.

"Crazy girl done leaped outta nowheres and clamped herself onta the horses, ma'am." John Coachman sent Clarissa a quick look of apology. "Soon's we get this beldam outta the way and pry the lass free, we'll be off. Sorry for the delay, Miss Clarissa."

"Outta the way?" the rouged woman shrieked. "'Tis my runaway apprentice yer talkin' of peeling free, ya lunk o'lard, and nowheres she'll be goin' but back to my shop."

"Ain't no wonder she don't wanna go back to no harpy like you!" the coachman returned.

"Best return to the carriage, Miss Beaumont. I'll settle this and rejoin you in a trice," Lieutenant Standish said and gestured to the footman. "You, sir, give me the reins and help Miss Beaumont up."

Clarissa waved the footman off, her attention captured by the look of absolute desperation on the grimy face of the struggling girl. "Whatever were you about, miss? You could have been killed!"

"Don't pay 'er no mind, ma'am," the woman abandoned her hostilities with the coachman to make Clarissa a quick curtsey. "Right willful she is, but I promised her dear ma afore she died I'd train her up right, and so I shall."

"Train me up right?" the girl suddenly spoke up, her tone near-hysterical. "To be a baud like ye? How dare the likes of ye speak of a godly woman like me ma? No!" she screamed, kicking at the coachman as he attempted to grab her. "Leave me be! Better to be trampled than go back!"

The painted woman darted past the coachman to deal

the girl a stinging slap. "Dontcha lissen to her ravin', missie," she told Clarissa as she retreated again out of John Coachman's reach. "Girl don't know enough not to bother 'er betters. You jest git yer coachman to let me 'ave 'er and you can be on yer way."

The dark square, the tattered, sleazy dress and the girl's anguish called up disturbing memories of Clarissa's own struggle in the alley not far from this very spot. A shudder went through her and the fine hair at the back of her neck raised. "John Coachman, stand aside."

"Really, Miss Beaumont, I must insist you return—"

"If you would do something useful, Lieutenant, restrain that…woman. I will speak to the girl."

Aiming a triumphant look at the painted woman, who shrilled her disapproval of the proceedings, the coachman stepped away. The lieutenant looked as if he meant to protest as well, but obligingly moved to guard the girl.

After a sweeping glance at the lieutenant's height and impressive uniform, the painted woman, still protesting loudly, gave ground.

"Are you a runaway apprentice?" Clarissa asked.

"No, ma'am. I'm just a country lass, come to work in the city. I never seen that woman afore the postin' house where the Mail put in. She seemed so nice-like, offerin' me tea and askin' if I needed a ride somewheres. Next thing I knows I wake up in a strange house, all me things gone and me wearin' a gown me ma would flay me alive for ever puttin' on. And then a man come…" The girl's eyes widened until the whites shone in the darkness. She choked on a sob and shook her head violently. "I won't go back, I won't! I'll die first."

A small crowd was beginning to gather, their faces condemning as they looked at the girl in the tawdry dress.

"Send 'er back, I say," one man called.

"Whore's argument," another offered. "Let the bauds settle it out of sight of decent folk."

"That's right, listen to 'im," the painted woman told Clarissa, then snarled, "snotfaced weasel" at the man.

Would such people have condemned her, ignored her cries for help that night, had they come upon her unescorted and struggling with a man who proclaimed her a whore? Revulsion and sympathy coursed through Clarissa, then coalesced into firm purpose.

"Would you come with me?" she asked the girl.

For a moment silence fell, even the rouged woman looking at Clarissa with mouth agape.

"No one shall hurt you, I promise. And I will take you wherever you want to go."

The girl glanced up, her frantic eyes searching Clarissa's. After a moment, she whispered, "Aye."

"Here now, ye can't be stealin' me apprentice—"

"Take it up with the magistrate," Clarissa snapped.

The painted woman continued to object, the bystanders voiced loud and conflicting opinions, her coachman remonstrated. Even the lieutenant, his voice incredulous, asked "Miss Beaumont, are you sure you want to do this?"

"With—or without your help, Lieutenant."

He lifted an eyebrow, but snapped her a salute. "Then I'm at your service, ma'am."

Grateful for his support, Clarissa gave him a brilliant smile. "See her settled in the carriage, if you please. Then John Coachman, I should like to proceed."

"To the theatre?" the coachman gasped.

"Of course not. Back home. Miss—"

"Maddie, ma'am. Maddie Gray." Still clutching the reins, the girl bobbed a curtsey.

"Will you release my horses and come with me, Maddie?"

For another moment the girl clung to the leather wrapped around her hands, as if it were her lifeline out of perdition. Then she nodded and slowly loosened her grip. As the girl unraveled the reins, Clarissa saw red dripping from the deep grooves the straps had cut into her hands.

The lieutenant shook his head at Clarissa as he waved the girl to the carriage. "In with you now, Maddie Gray."

The footman, who'd gone still as stone, finally recovered himself and sprang to open the door. A few moments later, leaving the baud's outraged shouts and the exclamations of the crowd behind, Clarissa, Lieutenant Standish and their unusual passenger set off.

With a dazed look in eyes that stared, unfocused, into the distance, Maddie huddled at the edge of the seat, thin arms wrapped around herself to conceal the plunging bodice of the gown. She was shivering, Clarissa realized. When she put a hand to the girl's shoulder to offer her cloak, the lass started violently and recoiled. Clarissa drew in her breath, a sharp ache of compassion in her chest.

Had I not been rich Miss Beaumont of Grosvenor Square, had I been a poor girl from the country that night in the square, this might be me.

"Here," Clarissa said, unlacing the ties of her evening cloak. "You are freezing. Wear this."

Lieutenant Standish stayed her hand. "Allow me." Quickly he pulled off his wool jacket, stripping it down over his useless hand with surprising speed. "Would you take this, Maddie?"

It seemed to take a moment for his words to penetrate.

Then dismay registered in Maddie's eyes. "Oh no, sir, I couldn't! I'm...I'm so dirty, I'll muss yer fine coat."

"Nonsense." Waving off her protests, the lieutenant draped the garment over her shoulders. "It's seen a good deal worse than dirt, I assure you. Now, would you tell us what happened? You're not a runaway apprentice, are you?"

The girl laid her cheek against the thick wool and closed her eyes, as if grateful for the simple gift of its warmth. Clarissa's chest contracted again. Maddie sighed and a single tear tracked down the dirt of her cheek.

"Nay. 'Twas as I said. Pa's a farmer on a freehold next to Lord Willoughby's in Hampshire and me ma is a housekeeper there. She trained me up to be a maid, but I wanted—" her voice trailed off and she swallowed "—I wanted somethin' more. Me cousin's a maid here in the city, and I figured if'n I could get a start here, and worked hard, I might be a lady's maid someday."

"Perhaps you shall," Clarissa said.

Maddie turned toward her eyes dull with the loss of hope. "Not likely now."

As Clarissa had no ready answer to that, she was grateful when Lieutenant Standish intervened. "Where would you like us to take you? To your cousin?"

Maddie simply stared straight ahead, as if she had not heard. The lieutenant started to repeat the question when she finally said, "I don't know. I can't go to Ginnie's— look at me! No respectable house would have me now. And I can't go back home. It would kill Ma, and Pa would—" She choked back a sob. "Reckon you might leave me at Lunnon Bridge. 'Tis naught but the river for such as m-me."

After those words, the last of them uttered in a bare

whisper, Maddie laid her face on her hands and began to weep, her thin shoulders shaking.

Clarissa felt her heart contract. The girl was hardly more than a child. To think of her tricked, abducted, ruined, and in such despair that she contemplated ending her own life filled Clarissa with outraged fury.

Heedless of the girl's grimy condition, Clarissa gathered her close. "There now, you mustn't give up! We shall think of something."

Though she made no attempt to pull herself from Clarissa's grasp, Maddie's weeping continued unabated. Patting her back and making soothing sounds, Clarissa held the sobbing girl.

"What will you do with her?" the lieutenant asked.

"Take her home with me, I suppose. I cannot leave her wandering about the streets for that baud or," with a shudder she recalled the hulking man in the freize coat, "someone even worse to discover."

"And then? Though one could hardly blame her for what happened, I doubt your household staff will be any better disposed to accept her than the one that employs her cousin. Surely there are institutions for such folk."

"None that I know of, save the workhouse. Would you have me send this frail scrap of a girl to such a place?" she asked with a flash of anger.

"I suppose not," he admitted.

It was so unfair, that though Maddie wasn't at fault, the simple fact of what she had been forced to do would forever taint her.

But that wasn't the lieutenant's fault either, and she shouldn't have lashed out at him. "I'm sorry, Lieutenant, I didn't mean to be sharp. I appreciate your assistance more than I can say. And you're right, my own staff will probably disdain her as well. However, they know better than to disobey a direct order, so disapprove or not, tend Maddie they shall. Which will likely result in a domestic scene you can't wish to witness. Shall I have John Coachman drop you by your rooms?''

"Can I be of no further service?''

She smiled at him. He really was an engaging gentleman. "Can you mount a cavalry charge against prejudice? No? Then I suppose there is nothing else."

"Very well, but I'll see you home first. And if I might make a suggestion? Try enlisting your staff's sympathy on Maddie's behalf, rather than simply commanding them. A man will do as he's ordered, but he'll put his heart into a cause in which he believes.'' The lieutenant glanced down at the weeping girl, whose sobs were at last beginning to diminish. "The end result may be the same, but I believe the difference to Maddie would be marked."

"You're right, of course. Win their hearts?'' She thought of her butler Timms and Mrs. Woburn, her housekeeper, their exacting standards and the firm hold they maintained over the staff. "Well," she sighed, not at all sure her persuasive abilities were up to the task, "I shall give it a go.''

As Maddie's sobs dissipated to hiccupping shudders, she seemed at last to recall herself, and pushed out of Clarissa's arms. "Excuse me, ma'am! I b-be so s-sorry…''

"Rest easy, Maddie. I'm taking you to my home, where we'll get you some proper clothes and something to eat. Everything will look much brighter once you're comfortable,'' Clarissa reassured the girl to forestall the fresh bout of tears that threatened. The remainder of the short ride took place in near silence.

The lieutenant insisted upon helping her assist Maddie

into the warm kitchen, where in front of the curious staff he treated the girl with conspicuous solicitude.

Having instructed her already-frowning housekeeper to find Maddie some decent clothes and the cook to rustle up some meat and bread, Clarissa left the kitchen to walk Lieutenant Standish out.

"I'm sorry our evening was disrupted. We must make up another theatre party, soon."

"With the greatest pleasure." Lieutenant Standish took her hand and kissed it. "You are a remarkable lady, Miss Beaumont. Most people would have had their coachman pull the girl free and drive on. Had I not been with you, I'm ashamed to admit, I should probably have done so myself. I am proud to claim your acquaintance."

And so should I have done, a month ago. It pricked her conscience to accept a compliment of which she knew herself to be entirely unworthy, but though she trusted his discretion, the fewer who knew of the escapade that had elicited this night's compassion, the better. "Thank you, Lieutenant. Though I suspect if our 'good deed' becomes public knowledge, we shall both be subjected more to ridicule than praise."

The image of one hard, disapproving face sprang immediately to mind, and she sighed. "Thank you again for your help, and good night."

When she returned to the kitchen, Maddie was in the storeroom changing clothes. Most of the staff, expressions ranging from surprise to dismay to disgust, idled about, clearly still discussing the precipitous arrival of this outsider in baud's attire. "One of Miss Clarissa's latest starts," Clare overheard before that member of the group noticed her and fell silent.

Mrs. Woburn, her face set in disapproving lines, came forward.

"Begging your pardon, Miss, but the staff have asked that I speak with you about that...Young Person."

"Please accompany me to the bookroom, Mrs. Woburn. I am most anxious to talk with you as well."

As the housekeeper followed her down the hall to the room that stored the household account books, Clarissa rapidly reviewed what she knew about Mrs. Woburn, searching for a link that would lead from condemnation to compassion.

"Were you able to find Maddie suitable garments?" Clarissa asked once they were behind the closed door.

"Yes, miss. The under housemaid had an old dress I thought might fit. And what should you be wishful to do with her, once she's decently dressed?"

"That's what we must discuss. Molly, the upstairs maid, is your niece, is she not? Sent to you from your sister in the country?"

"Yes, Miss." A look of alarm crossed Woburn's face. "Do you find some fault with her—"

"No, of course not! Since you had the training of her, how could she be less than superior? I'm sure you and your sister are very proud of her."

The housekeeper bobbed a curtsey. "We are, and thank you, Miss."

"Which brings me to Maddie. She is not at all what her appearance might have led you to believe."

Woburn's warmth rapidly chilled. "Indeed?"

"Truly. She, too, came from the country a few weeks ago, intending to go into service at her cousin's household. But she never arrived there. Being country-bred yourself, you can imagine how noisy and confusing London must have seemed to a young girl straight out of Hampshire. At the posting inn where the stage put in, she was offered tea by what she took to be a kindly older woman. Only to awake later in a brothel. Now you may think 'tis a Banbury tale,'' Clarissa waved a hand to counter Mrs. Woburn's raised eyebrows, ''but I believe it the truth. Somehow she managed to escape tonight, and threw herself under our passing carriage. Aye, and you may ask John Coachman yourself, 'tis a miracle she wasn't trampled outright. She told us, when the procuress chasing her tried to wrest her free, that she'd rather die than go back. She begged us to take her to London Bridge, that she might end her life, believing no decent soul would ever again befriend a girl who'd been disgraced and ruined.''

Clarissa fell silent, watching the progression from disbelief, to horror, to grudging sympathy on the housekeeper's face. ''If she's truly an innocent, why don't she find her kin here, or return to the country?''

''Can you imagine how Molly would feel if such had befallen her? Do you think she would have dared seek you out? Or be able to bear returning home to tell her mama what happened to her in London?''

Once again she allowed the housekeeper to mull over her words. ''No, I expect she'd be too ashamed,'' Mrs. Woburn admitted at last.

''Ashamed enough to die of it. But that isn't right, is it, Mrs. Woburn? What happened was not her fault. She's a good, honest, upright young girl who wanted to better herself and be a credit to her family. 'Tis only fair she have such a chance, don't you think?''

The housekeeper gave her a shrewd look. ''Here, you mean, Miss?''

''Here, Mrs. Woburn. But her situation is, as you well know, especially delicate. The staff received a rather negative first impression of Maddie.'' Pleased with her progress so far, Clarissa proceeded to deliver her final salvo.

"I might have confided her story to Timms, but your influence with the staff is considerable, and I felt there are some things only another woman could best understand."

Since the two household giants who ruled the staff were in constant, subtle rivalry, her approach produced exactly the results Clarissa had hoped. "Menfolk seldom understand anything," Mrs. Woburn said with a sniff.

Cautiously Clarissa pressed her advantage. "You agree to take her in service, then?"

"I expect I can train one more maid," Mrs. Woburn allowed.

"And you will ensure she is treated fairly?"

"If *I* treat her so, the others will also."

"Excellent. Make no mistake, she is to mind and do her work, just like any other maid. If she does not, she'll be turned off, regardless of the misfortune of her circumstances. But I suspect she will work twice as hard."

"Can't say as I like having such as her here hangin' about the footmen, but I'll train her proper."

Clarissa felt a surge of satisfaction. With Mrs. Woburn an ally, Maddie need not fear her reception by the rest of the staff. Lieutenant Standish was right—persuasion had worked much better than a flat order.

"After she's been clothed and fed, send Maddie to my chambers, Mrs. Woburn. I should like to ascertain more of what happened when she was abducted."

Some half hour later, a knock sounded at her sitting room door and Maddie entered, garbed now in a sober gray gown and crisply starched apron. She'd scrubbed herself from top to toe, revealing under the grime and desperation a cream-skinned, fresh-faced country girl whose obvious innocence was so at odds with the circumstances under which they'd found her that Clarissa's rage stirred again.

This tender young maid should be looking forward to walking out with a handsome young footman, to courtship and weddings and babes. A future that, even if the staff finally accepted her, would now probably never be hers.

She tried to set aside the ache in her heart. "You're looking much refreshed, Maddie."

After sinking into a curtsey deep enough to have honored a Royal, the girl rose to fix on Clarissa adoring eyes glassy with unshed tears.

"Oh, Miss, how can I ever thank ye? Mrs. Woburn says ye've offered me a place here in yer own household. 'Twas mercy enough to save me from that—but to do this too, and for one such as me..." the girl's voice broke. "Why, ye be a blessed saint."

"Nonsense," Clarissa said, uncomfortable with the novelty of being worshiped. "I simply thought you an honest maid who will be an excellent addition to my staff."

"Aye, Miss, ye'll never regret takin' me on, I swear it! I'll work for ye twenty hours a day, I will, doin' whatever ye wish of me."

"Following Mrs. Woburn's orders and learning your job well is more than enough. But I would try to do something else for you. If you can describe to me the place where...that woman kept you, I will see if we cannot at least recover your belongings."

Maddie's joyous look faded. "Thank ye kindly, Miss, but I dunno about that. There was two other girls she done tricked into coming there and they said likely she sold all me things immediate. So's we had nuthin' to run off in but...such as what I was wearin.'"

Cunning logic, Clarissa knew, having observed the results firsthand. Dressed as Maddie was in whore's garments, none of the crowd had believed the girl's story. Nor, had Clarissa not chanced by, would any have helped Maddie escape. Once again Clarissa recalled her attacker in the freize coat. He'd likely have haggled with the baud over price and then pulled the girl free to use himself.

Clarissa was mulling over that when the first of Maddie's words finally struck her. "Did you say there were two other girls abducted in the same manner as you?"

"Aye, Miss. Jest like me, they'd come down to Lunnon to find work, and met…her…at the postin' inn, acting so kind and helpful. Next thing they knows, they wake up at…her house. They're good girls, Miss, I swear to ye! But neither of 'em had any kin here, and no money to get 'em nowheres else, so what good would it do for 'em to try escaping? Anyone what found 'em wouldda jest sent 'em back to Maisie's, like that gent tonight wanted to do with me."

"But that's abduction, kidnapping, and entrapment into vice! Surely the law can do something to stop it!"

Maddie shrugged with the fatalism of the powerless. "Dunno, Miss. But sure as sure, Maisie'd swear the girls come into it willin.' Who'd believe otherwise from the likes of us, or even care?"

"Still, something should be done. I shall look into it immediately. But it's late now, and you must be weary. You're safe now, Maddie. Mrs. Woburn will show you where to sleep and begin your training tomorrow."

"Yes'm." Once again Maddie curtseyed and walked to the door. She hesitated on the threshold and then, to Clarissa's surprise, ran back, seized Clarissa's hand and kissed it. "Thank ye, Miss. I'll never fergit yer kindness.

If the Lord truly does reward them what cares fer the meek, ye've earned yerself a crown in Heaven.''

Though she knew she in no way merited the accolade, Clarissa was still touched. ''I shall call on you when I meet St. Peter! Sleep well, Maddie.''

After the girl withdrew, Clarissa donned her night rail and let her maid braid her hair. But the horror of Maddie's ruin, so painfully close to her own experience, kept her from sleep.

She stood at her window overlooking the London night and thought of the heavyset baud, the glimmer of the knife in her attacker's beefy hands, the river that beckoned in Maddie's despair. A glass of wine later, she'd not yet figured out how to right the wrong done Maddie and the other two girls in Maisie's bawdy house, but she had formulated the beginnings of a plan that might prevent the ruin of other innocents.

Though doubtless *some* would call her ''reckless'' to intrude upon a dangerous world whose workings she little understood, she simply couldn't let the outrage done to Maddie go unchecked. Early tomorrow morning, she would visit Bow Street.

Chapter Fourteen

Sinjin sat stiffly on the well-padded squabs of Mr. Motrum's luxurious carriage and told himself everything was going perfectly. The day was cool but fine, with bright sun and just the hint of a breeze. During their walk in the park he'd be able to detach Miss Motrum from her chatty chaperone, who'd not ceased talking since the equipage left Mr. Motrum's townhouse, and get to know better the young woman who very probably would become his wife. An idea with which, he told himself firmly, he was becoming increasingly comfortable.

Well, if not comfortable, at least resigned.

After reaching the park, the necessities of handing out Miss Motrum and her duenna caused a merciful if momentary lull in that lady's conversation. Then, with suitable comments on the beauty of the morning, the freshness of the air and the pleasing arrangement of the shrubbery, the threesome set off down one of the pathways.

This is your chance, so use it. Abandoning the protection of silence, Sinjin forced himself to converse.

"The arrangement of park is very like the one at my

home, Sandiford Court. You enjoy the country, Miss Motrum?''

The young lady opened her lips, but before she could answer, Mrs. Cartwright said, ''Oh, Anne delights in the country! She fair rhapsodizes over it every time we visit. Though to be sure, she's town-bred, and the country can be a bit…savage for one of such delicate sensibilities.''

Sinjin wondered with wry amusement what would, from this quiet girl, be considered ''rhapsodizing.'' Producing two complete sentences together, perhaps?

''You attended school in the country, Miss Motrum?''

''Oh no, Anne's papa couldn't have borne having her so far away,'' the duenna once again answered. ''She's quite the apple of his eye, aren't you, my pet?'' Mrs. Cartwright patted her charge's hand. ''Anne attended a select ladies' academy here in London.''

Irritated, Sinjin cast a glance at Miss Motrum, but she seemed unperturbed at having her part of the conversation usurped. Turning pointedly toward the young lady, he asked, ''And what did you find of most interest during your studies, Miss Motrum?''

''Dear Anne is quite accomplished! Not a bluestocking, of course, but excessively skilled in all the ladylike arts. She sings like a lark, plays the pianoforte splendidly and her embroidery—ah, such fine, tiny stitches she makes!''

Gritting his teeth, Sinjin hung on to his patience, refraining with some difficulty from giving Mrs. Cartwright the set-down hovering on his tongue. When the lady finally paused for breath, he once again addressed her charge.

''I admire a skilled needlewoman, Miss Motrum. On several occasions in the Peninsula, my lieutenant's wife,

Mrs. Fitzwilliam, saved me on parade day by reattaching a button or stitching up a tear.''

''Indeed.'' Mrs. Cartwright gave him a sharp look, as if affronted. ''Dear Anne does fine work only. We have maids to handle the mending.''

So simple stitchery was beneath her? Though disconcerted, he persevered. ''I'm sure your fine work is, um, fine. Are you skilled in the kitchen, Miss Motrum?''

''Anne handles all her papa's entertainments, though of course she wouldn't stoop to actually preparing food her—''

''Mrs. Cartwright,'' Sinjin interrupted, his patience finally exhausted, ''I should like to hear Miss Motrum's reply from her own charming lips, if you please.''

Halted in midsentence, the older woman gaped at him, mouth open like a beached trout. In the silence that ensued, Miss Motrum at last spoke.

''Mrs. Cartwright, I fear I left my muff in the coach. Would you be so kind as to fetch it?''

Sinjin could see in the expressions crossing the duenna's face a battle between her desire to succor her charge and a dislike of losing control of the conversation. After a short struggle, protection won. ''Yes of course, Anne dear. I shan't be but a minute.''

Once the woman was out of earshot, Miss Motrum turned to Sinjin. ''You must forgive her. She's very nervous.''

''That makes two of us,'' Sinjin said with feeling.

Miss Motrum smiled. ''Three. We've never entertained an aristocrat before.''

''I'm just another man of your father's acquaintance. Please, treat me as you would any other of his friends.''

That wasn't precisely the case and they both knew it. Reflecting upon how silent Miss Motrum had been at both their meetings, Sinjin felt a pang of unease. "You did consent to receive me, did you not? You were not…coerced."

"Oh, no, Papa would never do that! Of course, he thinks me fit to become a princess royal, though I do not aspire to such heights."

"To what do you aspire?" he asked, genuinely curious.

"To wed a kind husband who values me," she replied. "I fear I have no skills at mending or cooking, nor am I clever about finances. Papa has always taken care of that. And I regret I know nothing whatsoever about farms."

His cherished image of a hardworking, skillful helpmeet like Mrs. Trapper was beginning to crack. A hitherto suppressed doubt about the wisdom of this whole enterprise struggled to emerge. Could his plan be mistaken?

Before he could reassemble his rattled thoughts, Mrs. Cartwright approached, her face set in rigid lines as a young man marched determinedly after her.

"Jeremy, what are you doing in the park?" Miss Motrum exclaimed. "Oh, forgive me. Lord Sandiford, this is Jeremy Wickham, from my father's London office. Colonel Lord Sandiford is a…friend of Papa's, Jeremy."

"Lord Sandiford." Though they exchanged cordial bows, the look Mr. Wickham directed at Sinjin was most unfriendly.

"We're charmed to see you, of course," Mrs. Cartwright said, "but busy as the office is, we mustn't detain you."

The young man's face reddened. "I've got Randall checking accounts and Phillips processing the new orders, so there's naught demanding my attention just now. Thought I could use a breath of fresh air."

"Did Mr. Motrum approve this sudden desire for exercise?" Mrs. Cartwright asked pointedly.

Mr. Wickham's flush deepened. "He's...he's down at the shipyards today."

"Surely Papa wouldn't mind Mr. Wickham taking a walk, Mrs. Cartwright. It's such a lovely day." Miss Motrum smiled at the young man in a charming display of dimples.

"It is now." The warmth in Mr. Wickham's eyes as he gazed at his employer's daughter left little doubt as to the tenor of his feelings. "Besides, if you require escort," he directed a belligerent look at Sinjin, "you know you can always count on me."

Sinjin had to hide a grin, amused for the first time since this uncomfortable encounter had begun. Mr. Wickham must be the "young tradesman" Hal had mentioned, and Mrs. Cartwright was clearly eager to do whatever was necessary to sweep Sinjin's social inferior from the courtship field.

Miss Motrum laughed, a clear bell-like sound. "Haven't I always counted on you, Jeremy?"

"Since you were a scrubby brat in short skirts," he said gruffly.

"Jeremy is Papa's right-hand man," Miss Motrum explained. "Indeed, he's at the house so often he's practically like one of the family."

"I ain't family yet." Mr. Wickham sidled another hostile glance at Sinjin. "But someday I hope to be."

"Surely you must be needed back at the office," Mrs. Cartwright interposed. "After all, *working men* haven't the leisure to stroll about the park."

Having had little experience gauging the emotions of females, Sinjin couldn't determine from Miss Motrum's friendly responses whether or not she returned Mr. Wickham's regard. He ought, therefore, to speedily eliminate this potential check to his suit.

A few words in his most imperious aristocratic manner would have done it. Perversely, in part to spite the managing Mrs. Cartwright, he said instead, "I daresay Mr. Wickham could be spared long enough to stroll back to the carriage with us. Miss Motrum, if you are ready?" He offered his arm.

With a murmur of assent from Miss Motrum, a warily puzzled glance from Mr. Wickham, and an angry glare that Mrs. Cartwright quickly refashioned into a smile when she caught Sinjin's gaze upon her, the ill-assorted foursome set off down the path.

He really shouldn't be maneuvering the Motrum party like actors in a Kabuki play. But—and he found the notion curiously depressing—should he choose to offer for Miss Motrum, he knew beyond doubt the weight of his title and lineage alone would be enough to crush any aspirations the smitten Mr. Wickham might harbor.

Since this outing had brought him no closer to deciding whether he would in fact offer for her, the walk back was rather strained. Miss Motrum and Mr. Wickham said nothing, the lady blushing as the young man gazed at her adoringly, while he and Mrs. Cartwright exchanged stilted conversation.

As they were taking their leave of Mr. Wickham, Sinjin spotted a rider mounted sidesaddle on a big black stallion, sunlight striking sparks off the fire of her hair as she cantered toward them. His stomach contracted and a dizzy excitement tingled down his limbs.

"What a striking lady!" Miss Motrum exclaimed. "And that horse—I should be terrified to ride so large a beast."

Before Sinjin could gather his disordered senses, Miss

Beaumont drew near. Though he wasn't at all sure he wished to speak with her, particularly in Miss Motrum's presence, simple courtesy required it.

"Miss Beaumont, good day," he said.

"Colonel Sandiford." Smiling, she reined in.

If she'd ridden past, he might have been able to leave it at that, but now that she'd halted, courtesy demanded he make his party known to her. Grudgingly he performed the introductions, receiving for his pains the dubious satisfaction of watching Mr. Wickham reduced to stammering incoherency after his first good look at Miss Beaumont.

Jaw clenched, Sinjin waited. Any minute now her clever brain was going to figure out the status of his companions. He braced himself for the worst.

Disturbed and angry by all she'd learned from Maddie and the Bow Street runner she'd just consulted, Clarissa guided her mount into Hyde Park. She wanted Sarah's opinion on what she intended to do next, but first, in the relatively deserted midmorning park, she'd have a quick gallop to help settle her nerves.

Murmuring encouragement, she bent low over Diablo's head and spurred him to a gallop. As always, the sheer speed of his run and the whistle of the wind rushing past soothed her.

This morning it also managed to work her hat loose from its pins and send it sailing. She couldn't bring herself to check Diablo, who reveled in the gallop as much as she, to go in search. Shaking her head with delight at the glorious and unaccustomed warmth of the sun in her hair, she let him run on.

Not until the black's sides were heaving and foam-flecked did she finally command him to slow. Crooning her approval of his prowess, she guided him on a gentle circuit of the park while they both caught their breath.

She was just about to go in search of her hat when she spotted a party on the path ahead of her. Even at a distance, one unmistakable figure held her eye.

Now there's a man who could help Maddie.

Her next reaction, though, was dismay. Breath catching in her throat, for a panicked moment she didn't know whether to proceed or wheel Diablo and flee. Once again she'd encountered the exacting Colonel Sandiford while looking like a hoyden, her habit mud-spattered, her bare head haloed by wisps of windblown hair, both her hat and her groom left somewhere far behind.

She saw his body alert and knew he'd recognized her. Realizing she'd look a complete fool if she turned tail now, she swallowed a ridiculous nervousness and made herself proceed.

What difference would his current disapproval make? she asked herself mutinously as she pasted a bright smile on her face. He already thoroughly disapproved of her. Unless she returned to the streets from which he'd once ignominiously rescued her, she doubted she could drop any lower in his opinion.

Nonetheless, she was so flustered upon joining him that it wasn't until he was halfway through the introductions that she realized who made up the rest of his party. This lovely pale blond creature must be his virtuous middle-class virgin, the older woman her chaperone, and the young man some sort of acquaintance.

Her hands and voice automatically performed the rituals of civility, shaking the young woman's hand, calming the awestruck young man and replying to the rather intrusive and vulgar questioning of the chaperone. But her attention remained riveted on the blond beauty who hung on the Colonel's arm as if she belonged there.

Lovely but not strikingly beautiful, the Virgin smiled demurely, said little, and deferred to those around her. No doubt she could total sums in a twink, sew and knit handily, prepare a meal herself as skillfully as she could direct her staff to do so, and took alms to the poor every Saturday. She was, in short, everything the colonel professed to seek in a wife.

A nearly irresistible urge boiled up from some ugly place deep within her to leap down from the saddle, slap the Virgin's hand off the colonel's sleeve and rip every perfectly arranged hair from that artfully coifed head.

But of course, even a hoyden couldn't attack another lady in the Park. Her facial muscles aching with the effort of keeping a smile in place, her fingers clenched on the reins as she envisioned raking her nails down the Virgin's placid, smiling face.

Had the colonel been any other man, she would have known just what flutter of lash and purr of tone would draw him to her side. Having pried him away from the Virgin, she would have him help her down from the saddle, allowing his hands to linger a few moments longer than necessary at her waist. Standing together chest to chest a mere hand's breadth apart, she'd let him breathe in her subtle rose scent, watch the play of her lips raised tantalizingly close to his while she teased and flattered him.

With a deep sense of despair she knew without even attempting it that all the tricks and stratagems she'd used so successfully before would never work on this man. Though desire her he did, Colonel Sandiford had told her himself he thought beauty a paltry allure. Without a doubt

he'd see through her every move, resisting the pull between them even as he rebuffed her attempts.

No, what he prized was that silent, placid cow of perfection hanging on his arm. Doubtless the Virgin had
never spoken a word in anger, never wrinkled her gown
nor succumbed to a spontaneous impulse in her expensively sheltered life.

How Clarissa managed to end their short conversation
without her face cracking she couldn't imagine, but mercifully soon she was able to say her goodbyes. The only
positive note about the whole dreadful episode was she'd
brushed through it without having to utter more than two
sentences to the colonel.

What could she have said? Certainly not what she felt.
That seeing him courting another lady had been like a
blow to the stomach, a shock that robbed her of breath.

Back straight, head high, she rode away, resisting the
impulse to look back until she knew the party must be
safely ensconced in their carriage. Not until she heard the
crack of the coachman's whip did she turn in the saddle
and watch the vehicle drive away, her chest tightening
with an absurd sense of...abandonment.

'Twas ridiculous to react so, she chided herself as she
spurred Diablo to pick up the pace. What matter to her
if the colonel married his middle-class heiress, as he'd
told her from the very outset he intended. She could have
any other man in London she wanted, couldn't she? Alastair was going to propose again any day, forestall him
though she try, and she couldn't think of any other eligible bachelor she couldn't bring up to scratch if she truly
desired him.

Though she was not nearly as capricious as she'd once
been—the need to run the household during her mama's
illness had been a most sobering experience—still, she

had to admit, she *was* used to getting what she desired. This feeling of—no, despair was too strong a word—resulted simply from encountering, for the first time, a man she wanted but could not control.

Such a thing was bound to happen eventually. She should shake it off and go on. Perhaps after consulting with Sarah about the problem with Maddie, she would take her friend shopping.

Even as she conceived of it, the idea fell sadly flat, and with irritation she dismissed it. She was already riding, but that didn't seem to be helping much either. A rapid inventory of the other activities that normally cheered her revealed not one that sounded appealing.

Not that she begrudged the colonel his wealthy bride. He might be judgmental and prejudiced, but he was also honest, honorable, courageous and in most ways wholly admirable. He ought to have the capable wife he wanted.

If the possessiveness of the Virgin's clinging hand were any indication, it appeared he had found one.

Clarissa was happy for him, truly she was. Even though now the colonel could never be her friend. The two of them were ill-suited for friendship anyway, always striking sparks off one another. Despite the strong desire that flared between them like heat lightning on a June night, any relationship lasting longer than a conversation—or a kiss—would turn to disaster. Indeed, she'd give herself a thorough scold for even entertaining the ridiculous hope that they might have built a friendship—if it weren't for this awful desire to burst into tears.

Impatiently she brushed moisture from the corners of her watering eyes, an aftereffect of her gallop, no doubt. *Get hold,* she admonished. Surely she wasn't so vain that she must turn into a watering pot simply because she couldn't make every man in London fall at her feet.

But he's the only one I want, a mournful little voice answered. At the thought, something suspiciously like a tear dripped down her cheek.

Angrily she smeared it away, putting her other hand to her stomach to quell the sick churning there. As for this absurd sense that her world had just tilted and nothing would ever be the same again, doubtless she was merely a trifle faint from rushing off without breakfast.

She was guiding Diablo around a turn, ostensibly searching for her missing hat, when the conclusion she'd been trying to suppress ever since the colonel's departure finally elbowed its way into consciousness.

No, she couldn't be *in love* with the colonel!

Chapter Fifteen

Her head immediately set about denying the uncertain welter of emotions confusing her heart. Surely she couldn't have the colossal, totty-headed, wisp-witted idiocy to fall for Sinjin Sandiford. The one man in London who despised her.

Pulling right against the command that would have urged him left into a tree, Diablo snorted and shook his head at her. Even her horse was disgusted. Hands trembling, Clarissa let the reins fall slack.

Oh, she was in lust with the man, that she readily admitted. But love?

Just because he seemed to have winkled his way into her thoughts in nearly every waking moment didn't mean she loved him. She was merely…entangled by the novel predicament of wanting a man who desired but did not like her. And what matter that in spite of his faults—surely if she were in love with him she'd think him flawless—she still found him the most accomplished and compelling man she'd yet encountered?

And as for the absolute bleakness that invaded her heart at the idea of him happily married to the Virgin, that was doubtless pique that he found another—especially that insipid chit who'd probably bore him senseless in a month—superior to herself. She'd recover.

Wouldn't she? Desolation settled on her like morning fog, its chill penetrating to the bone.

She tried to feed a fortifying anger. Clarissa Beaumont, reigning belle of the ton, did not go about sighing over a man like some weepy-eyed heroine in a Maria Edgeworth novel.

Drawing the reins taut, she urged Diablo onward, forcing her mind to focus on the memory of Maddie's bloodstained hands wrapped in the harness. Clarissa Beaumont had matters more important than heartache to attend.

Sarah received her in her upstairs sitting room, to which she'd returned after seeing Aubrey settled for a nap. Squelching her disappointment over not being able to cheer herself with a romp with her favorite, Clarissa consoled herself with the offer of tea.

"Why so solemn a face?" her friend asked.

The impulse to confess her dreadful suspicion in Sarah's discerning and sympathetic ear tempted, but she refrained. First, she'd come here on Maddie's behalf, and second, she was a bit uncertain how her friend would react to the idea that Clarissa might be in love with Sarah's old sweetheart. Would it distress her? Particularly now, Clarissa couldn't face the thought of alienating her one true friend.

So she related to Sarah the unexpected events of the last evening. Her friend listened without comment—until Clarissa told her what she'd done with Maddie.

Sarah's eyes widened. "You brought her home with you?" she repeated blankly, and then burst out laughing. "Really, Clare, you are the most complete hand! Whatever will you do with the girl now?"

"I've decided to have her trained as a maid. 'Tis what

she came to London for, she told me, to go into service with the family that employs her cousin.''

''A noble intent, but a devilish tricky business. How did Timms and Mrs. Woburn react?''

Clarissa smiled ruefully. ''Initially as you might expect, especially as the poor girl came clad only in the scandalous gown the procuress had forced on her. But after I related the circumstances, she reluctantly came around. She'll train Maddie and ensure she's treated by the staff as well as can be expected.''

Admiration warmed Sarah's clear gray eyes. ''How kind you are—and clever. Bravo, Clare!''

The aching sadness she'd bottled up deep within warmed slightly at her friend's rare praise. ''More must be done, though,'' she replied. ''Maddie told me at least two other girls at the brothel had been tricked and abducted as she was. 'Tis an outrage, and someone must put a stop to it!''

''I've heard tales of such deplorable acts, but never known if they were true. You're right, it is outrageous and illegal besides.'' Sarah's face turned pensive, and she tapped one finger against her chin. ''The charge would be kidnapping at the least, but to prove it you'd have to have credible witnesses. Given the girls' unfortunate situation, I doubt their stories alone would be enough, even if they could be induced to testify.''

''So Maddie believed.'' For an instant, Clarissa remembered the sly rumors and innuendo about her own behavior. Yes, men would ever think the worst of a woman. ''Furious as it makes me, I'm afraid I must agree. To stop the bauds, I think I shall have to catch them in the attempt.''

''Catch them?'' Sarah stared at her in dismay. ''Clare, what mad scheme have you hatched this time? Don't misunderstand, I think your aim admirable, but the people who would commit so despicable an act must be totally without scruples! I can't believe one procuress alone could run such an operation. Doubtless she has a whole network of accomplices, all of them as unprincipled as she. Trying to stop them would be both difficult and dangerous.''

Clarissa waved an impatient hand. ''Really, Sarah, I'm not a complete looby. I know all that, and I don't propose to try to catch the woman out myself. I've hired a Bow Street runner to loiter about the coaching inn when the Mail arrives and watch out for the baud. If she approaches any unaccompanied young females, he can warn them off.''

''That sounds feasible,'' Sarah admitted. ''Still, I cannot help feeling uneasy. You have no experience dealing with people as ruthless and immoral as these.''

''I have a little, you will remember.''

Understanding flashed in Sarah's eyes. ''Ah. So that is why you cannot let this rest. But please, for me, will you be very, very careful? And I should feel much better if you would consult Nicholas about this.''

''Englemere? He'd either laugh, or frown me down in the particularly irritating way he has and tell me to mind my own business.''

''I don't think so. Really, Clare, you must admit I know him better than you! He will find this of grave concern, and he can advise you much better than I.''

''Oh, Sarah, Englemere and I have never rubbed well together. He only tolerates me for your sake.''

''Nonsense, Clare, he's very fond of you.'' At Clarissa's look of patent disbelief, Sarah added, ''It's been some years since your broken engagement. You've both grown beyond that.''

The mention of engagements brought her sorrow, never pushed very far out of mind, rushing back. Yes, she and Englemere had both quickly recovered from their ill-advised betrothal. Why should they not, since neither's heart had been engaged? She was painfully certain she would never get over the colonel.

Her inner distress must have been mirrored in her face, for her too-perceptive friend widened her eyes in concern and seized Clarissa's hand. "What is it, Clare? What's wrong?"

The desire to be stoic and strong warred with a cresting tide of misery. Weary of trying to stem it, Clarissa let the wave wash through her, filling her once again with desolation and bringing weak, despicable tears to her eyes.

She managed to produce a wobbly smile. "N-nothing of importance, really. It's just I'm terribly afraid I've gone and done something s-stupid."

"Nothing you and I together cannot mend. Haven't we always managed to fix everything?"

Tears came in earnest now. "I d-don't think anyone can f-fix this. It's…it's your f-friend Sinjin."

Sarah paled. "What about Sinjin? He's not injured!"

"N-no. The sh-shoe is rather on the other foot." Clarissa fisted away the tears and took a huge gulp of air. "You see…Sarah, are you all right?"

Perhaps Sarah suspected what Clarissa was about to confess, for her friend had gone linen-white. She brought one trembling hand to her lips. "I'm fine. Please, continue."

Clarissa still wasn't sure it was wise to tell Sarah everything, but having confessed this much, she could hardly turn evasive now. "'Tis sheer idiocy, I know, given his opinion of me, but I rather think I've, well, fallen in love with Sinjin.'' She said the last words in a rush.

Sarah lurched past her, seized the china pitcher on the dressing table, and cast up her accounts.

''S-sorry!'' Sarah gasped a moment later, wiping a handkerchief against her brow. ''The sickness comes and goes at odd times. A child is a joy indeed, but the business of making one is sometimes less than pleasant.''

Wretched as she felt, Clarissa had to laugh. She poured her friend a glass of water and waited for her to sip it. ''Better now?''

''Better. And I'm so sorry. You were—''

''Confessing my heart has been broken for all time, which moved you to vomit. That's Englemere's brat you're carrying for sure.''

''Rubbish. Clare, you're much too severe with poor Nicholas. He is all sympathy and concern,'' Sarah protested. Ignoring Clarissa's unladylike snort, she continued, ''So you think you love Sinjin. And I take it by your distress you do not feel he returns your regard?''

Clarissa laughed again, this time without humor. ''Returns it? Recall he is the one who found me that night at Covent Garden! He thinks me vain, rash and spoiled. We cannot seem to have a single conversation that does not end with us snarling at each other.''

''And yet you believe you love him?''

Clarissa sighed. ''I surely hope I'm wrong. But as much as he aggravates me, I cannot help admiring him. To the point that he so invades my thoughts I can scarce concentrate on anything else. And when I see him, even though I know he doesn't approve of me, even though I know we'll likely quarrel, still there's this—leap of joy. I crave being near him. No other man has ever affected me like this.'' At that admission, tears stung her eyes yet again. "Pathetic, isn't it? The heartless Clarissa Beaumont, who's left a trail of rejected suitors in her wake, at last succumbs. To a man who doesn't want her."

"Are you so sure he doesn't?"

"Oh, he desires me. There's fire enough of that sort between us whenever we meet. But as he's pointed out in no uncertain terms on several occasions, I'm too pretty, impulsive, extravagant, spoiled and aristocratic to meet his requirements for a wife."

Sarah patted her hand. "Perhaps. But you are also brave, loyal, devoted to your friends and family, and utterly unflagging in pursuit of what you feel is right."

Clarissa gave her friend a hug. "Dear Sarah. Even if what you say were true, Colonel Sandiford wants a wife who is quiet, calm, frugal and biddable. I'm certainly none of that. And why shouldn't he have an excellent woman possessed of every virtue. He deserves someone like you."

"Tush, we both know I'm no paragon either. Still—"

A niggle of panic touched Clarissa's heart. "Sarah, I absolutely forbid you to mention anything of this to him! 'Tis bad enough to pine away in foolish infatuation. I would not have his pity."

"Calm yourself, my dear. I trust I'm old and wise enough not to meddle in affairs of the heart. But surely all is not lost yet. And you're a very persuasive lady when you wish to be."

A wild hope flared and was as quickly dashed. "Even were that true, which in his case I sincerely doubt, there isn't time. He's already found a suitable candidate. I saw them in the park today, and by the way she clung to his arm as they walked together, I'd guess an announcement will soon be forthcoming."

"You're that sure?"

Clarissa nodded, finding it suddenly impossible to speak. Voicing the idea of the colonel marrying another was simply too difficult to manage.

Well, she'd have to manage it...but later. Surely with time she could learn to mask and control her unruly emotions. With a sigh, she gave Sarah another hug. "I must be going. I promised Mama a book from Hatchard's, and if I don't hurry, I shall be late for luncheon."

"We'll talk more of this later. But Clare, about the first matter, will you humor me and speak with Nicholas? I know you feel you must deal with it, and I applaud your good intentions, but I would feel easier if I knew you weren't proceeding all alone."

Clarissa shrugged. "If it will ease your mind. After all," she added with an attempt at humor, "since I already feel lower than the Thames at ebb tide, his ridicule or criticism can't make it any worse."

"He shall do neither, I promise. He's in the library, I believe. Won't you take a moment and speak with him now—for me? After all, I'm a lady in a delicate condition and I shouldn't be made to worry."

"Lest you cast up your accounts yet again." Clarissa smiled gamely. "Very well. I'll bait the bear in his den immediately if 'twill make my Sarah happier."

And so a few minutes later, she knocked at the door to Englemere's library. Though his brows shot up in surprise at seeing her, he quickly recovered, cordially inviting her to join him. After the usual exchange of civilities and her refusal of tea, he invited her to a wing chair before his desk. "To what do I owe this unusual honor, Clare?"

"Only Sarah's insistence that I consult you about a matter of some...delicacy." Bracing herself for Englemere's disdain, with a touch of defensiveness Clarissa recounted the story of Maddie's abduction.

To her surprise, he listened to her entire tale without once interrupting, his face grave. After she concluded, he remained silent for several minutes.

"I'm glad Sarah induced you to consult me," he said at last. "The situation may well be more dangerous than you're aware. We've had some reports of abductions such as this. Even the smuggling of young women to dens of vice abroad. The interior ministry is looking into it, but quite frankly their efforts are concentrated more at sniffing out insurrection at home—drat the Levellers for fomenting the fears of all the conservatives."

He sighed. "Men who can scarcely be moved to consider the plight of jobless, homeless returning soldiers are unlikely to work up much sympathy about the activities of a baud. Not when her victims are country serving maids. But that does not mean persons of conscience can allow such a situation to go unchecked."

"So you approve my plan?"

"Let me consider it further. Hiring runners to watch the posting inn when the Mail arrives seems prudent. I'm not sure how far the runner could intervene in the baud's affairs without endangering himself, however. The woman undoubtedly has enforcers to discourage interference, and probably financial backing as well. I've long suspected some man of prominence must be behind the overseas scheme. It may be necessary to take more precautions. And I must warn you the efforts may be futile in the long run. The procuress will probably simply shift her 'recruiting' efforts to another inn."

"Perhaps, but if I can save even one innocent, the effort far outweighs the risk."

"Of course. The runners are a good starting point. I'll

check my sources and let you know what else might be prudent.'' He paused, then said, ''You have a good heart, Clare.''

Clarissa looked up sharply, but found no mockery in the faintly smiling glance Englemere rested on her. Tentatively she smiled back.

Perhaps Sarah was right. Perhaps she had allowed their past history to color her opinion of Englemere for too long. Now that she considered it, in the years since he'd married Sarah she couldn't remember one instance of his being the dictatorial, overbearing, stuffy autocrat to whom she'd been so briefly betrothed.

How vain and self-absorbed she'd been then, no doubt all too transparently pleased with herself for garnering a proposal from so rich and prominent a suitor. The realization made her wince. Had she ever even considered his feelings? Thank heavens she'd matured with the years!

Then a flash of insight, sudden and startling as unexpected thunder, rattled her mind.

In consternation, she stared at Englemere and blurted, ''You *wanted* me to cry off! That's why you turned so disagreeable after we were engaged.''

The look of guilt she surprised on Englemere's face confirmed that lowering suspicion.

Obviously realizing it was too late to prevaricate, he held up both hands. ''Unfair of you to catch me unawares. And if it is possible to atone for so unhandsome an admission, I must say that on numerous occasions, the woman you've since become has made me regret doing so.''

That could only be a polite fiction, but nonetheless her eyes burned. ''Considering you have Sarah, that's ridiculous, but I thank you for it anyway.''

He took her hands and kissed them. ''Someday you

will find a man you truly care for. And he will love you, as Sarah and I both do, for the wonderful lady you are.''

I already have, and he doesn't want me. But of course, she wasn't about to whine to Englemere about that. She pasted a smile on her face and bid him goodbye.

But once she'd collected Diablo and guided him toward Hatchard's, the unhappiness that by force of will she'd suppressed just below the level of consciousness surged up to swamp her in a tide of uncertainty and despair.

Try as she might to deny, ignore, or explain it away, in the hidden depths of her heart, the awful conclusion resonated true. She had indeed been foolish enough to fall in love with Sinjin Sandiford.

What was she going to do about it? A rapid review of her options revealed she had none. She simply wasn't the kind of woman he sought, and no amount of wishful thinking, no depth of pain could alter that grim fact.

Sarah was. No wonder the colonel had loved her. Sarah possessed all the virtues he sought, with gentleness, empathy and a loving heart thrown in besides.

For the first time in her life, Clarissa found herself envying the poorer, plainer, less dashing friend to whom, she realized with mortifying insight, she'd always felt superior. Now she'd gladly give away any of her supposed advantages—looks, fortune, the adulation of the gentlemen she met—to be the kind of woman, like Sarah, that Sinjin Sandiford could love.

Although a future without the colonel seemed desert-bleak, she had too much pride to confess her love and throw her money and her heart at the feet of a man who'd doubtless throw them both back. Didn't she?

The truly awful truth was, if she thought there was even a prayer that such a degrading gambit might work, she probably would try it. But it wouldn't. With the colonel about to offer for the Virgin, time was desperately short, and she had nothing with which to deter him from proposing save the passion he had already scorned.

The absolute dearth of any hope that she might find a way to win the man she loved slammed her against a wall of desolation so absolute that for a moment she simply sat motionless in the saddle, paralyzed by the pain of it.

A dizzy faintness seized her and she realized she'd stopped breathing. She gasped in a lungful of air. *You will get through this. He will go on with his life, marry the Virtuous Virgin he deserves, and you will go on with yours. You are tough, stubborn, and determined, and you will survive.*

Just don't ask how.

Having slept badly, Clarissa pulled herself out of bed before dawn. Walking to the windows, she threw open the casement and breathed in a lungful of chill morning mist, its swirling vapor barely illumined in the darkness.

The ball she'd attended last night had been every bit as tedious as she'd feared, leaving her with a colossal headache that sent her to bed uncommonly early. Better get used to it, she told herself as she rested her chin on her hand and stared out into the dimness. *The rest of your life is like to hold nothing better.*

Irritated, she slammed the window closed. Enough whining. Striding back to her bed, she rang the bell pull to summon her maid.

She always took a morning ride in the park, and so she'd ride. At the idea of the park, though, her pulses commenced thrumming and her stomach took a shuddery flip. The colonel often rode in the park early, Sarah had told her.

She tried to squelch an absurd burst of excitement. Probably he didn't ride every day. Certainly he didn't ride so early. She absolutely, positively would not ride in the park hoping she might encounter him.

Being too honest to lie to herself and too desperate to scorn any chance of meeting him, Clarissa wrenched her habit from the wardrobe and began to pull it on.

Chapter Sixteen

Mist made opaque by the struggling early sun hung damp about the treetops as, brow knit in thought, Sinjin guided Valiant into the deserted lanes of Hyde Park. He hoped to call upon his mother this morning with some interesting news about their financial status, but with his mind churning, he was too impatient to sit in his rooms until the hour when his mama, never an early riser, would likely be ready to receive him.

With the intention of encouraging Lady Sandiford to refurbish her wardrobe and begin attending some of the parties he knew she so loved, after his walk with the Motrum ladies yesterday he'd paid a call on his solicitor to ascertain the current status of his funds.

To his surprise, that question elicited a broad grin from Mr. Manners and a hearty invitation to join him in some port. Over that fortifying beverage, Mr. Manners confided that, in the mysterious way of the world, news had already circulated the city that the impecunious Lord Sandiford was courting the daughter of the very rich Mr. Motrum—with that gentleman's approval. Even better, Mr. Motrum had apparently assured some of his banking and trading partners that whether the former soldier became his son-in-law or not, Colonel Sandiford was a steady man who'd make good on any sums he was advanced. With backing from such a source, Mr. Manners informed him, Sinjin could now draw on his bank for whatever he required.

Grateful as he was for the unexpected financial reprieve, Sinjin left Mr. Manner's office embarrassed and with a deepened sense of unease—an unease born of his talk with Miss Motrum.

To be brutally honest, it appeared that young lady did not possess those housewifely virtues he'd been so supremely confident he'd find in a well-brought-up middle class maid. And during their second meeting, he'd felt as uncomfortable with the Motrum party as he had at the first, struck ever more forcibly by both Mrs. Cartwright and the erstwhile suitor Mr. Wickham that he was out of place.

Lastly, though, it was the least of considerations, and probably not gentlemanly to judge, he had to admit he found Miss Motrum, well—*dull.*

The memory of a young lady who was decidedly not dull flashed through his senses like a Congreve rocket.

Apt, he thought, trying to squelch the thought. The lady in question was just as likely to erupt unpredictably and go streaking off in the wrong direction.

Not that Miss Beaumont didn't possess some virtues worthy of admiration. After further thought, he'd had to concede she had likely assisted Alex in full awareness of the positive attention it would generate for him. She might be reckless and extravagant, but she had also shown herself courageous, witty and kind. To his considerable surprise, she had treated the Motrum party throughout their encounter with the same courtesy she would have extended another member of the haut ton. Still, she was hardly the sort of wife he'd envisioned.

He had to chuckle wryly at that conclusion. What widgeon-headed notion possessed him to think a Beauty courted by the wealthiest and most eligible bachelors of the ton—and one he'd treated on several occasions with less than courtesy—would entertain for an instant the idea of marrying a scarred old soldier with barely a pound to his name?

Somehow, that indisputable observation left him feeling more hollow than amused.

Dismissing with difficulty the image of Miss Beaumont, he considered once again what he must do. He needed a wife who was serene, hardworking and dependable. He'd been so sure that a moderately accomplished middle-class girl with sufficient dowry would be his best choice.

Two meetings with the Motrums had shaken that notion to its foundations. Where had his reasoning been in error?

Was it that outside the extraordinary circumstances of an army on the march, men and ladies from different classes did not normally associate closely enough to become comfortable? And could it be those same circumstances, rather than their middle-class origins, that had perfected in Mistresses Trapper and Fitzwilliams the virtues he so admired?

Or was it that the daughter of a rich middle-class magnate was raised, not to master the skills her less advantaged sisters possessed, but to be in every way but birth identical to a lady of the aristocracy?

Sinjin prided himself on analyzing the evidence and prudently choosing a course of action. As a soldier who'd built a reputation for getting the maximum number of his men through a battle safely, he'd learned that if one discovered flaws in one's original tactics, one must alter them on the spot to meet the changing threat.

Though he hung on grimly to the hope he'd not made such a tactical error when determining his choice of a bride, a prudent officer always maintained a reserve. Which meant he'd best begin considering alternatives to Miss Motrum before the courtship reached the point where he could not, in honor, withdraw.

Valiant had begun his second circuit of the park when Sinjin spied a distinctive black stallion, its rider just kicking her mount from a canter to a gallop. His pulses leapt, and without further thought he urged Valiant in pursuit.

At first he thought she was not aware of him riding behind her, but as Valiant narrowed the gap between them, she glanced back, then gave the black the whip. He grinned, set his spurs to Valiant, and the race was on.

Boney's hatband, but she could ride! With a recklessness he had to admire as much as he deplored it, she leaned low over the black's neck, counterbalancing her weight in the sidesaddle until she seemed almost to become one with the stallion.

Trees and benches flashed by as galloping hooves ate up the greensward. Caught up in the sheer exhilaration of the ride, he felt a sharp pang of disappointment when all too soon the park gates hove into view, and then a rush of satisfaction as Valiant reached and overtook the black.

He pulled his stallion up just before the gate posts, patting his mount's neck as he rounded back to Miss Beaumont.

He couldn't accuse her of enticement today, garbed as she was in a severely-cut habit of charcoal gray, her flame-red hair hidden beneath a simple black shako and matching veil. The plainness of the gown, however, seemed to set off the excellence of the figure it outlined and drew attention to the classic purity of her face, just as its somber hue set off the brilliant green of her eyes.

Which were now regarding him warily.

He felt again that automatic, unbidden sense of connection. Given his previous discourtesy, she'd probably be anxious to escape at the earliest polite moment. Suddenly, he wanted more than anything to have her linger. Could he but provoke that fiery temper, he might delay her departure.

"Caught you," he announced. "A capital race, however. For a lady on a sidesaddle."

To his delight, she immediately stiffened. "You think so? As it happens, I was pulling up when you passed me."

"Doubtless," he agreed with a blandness he hoped would further ruffle that temper. "Would you walk with me a moment while the horses cool?"

At first he feared she'd decline, but with her groom now following at a respectful distance, she apparently couldn't find a polite reason to refuse. "I'm returning to breakfast, but I suppose I could spare a few moments."

Sinjin dismounted quickly, and before she could call to her servant, reached her side. "Allow me."

With a groom nearby to perform the office and given that the willing widow he so desperately needed to assuage his lust was no closer in view, he must be a masochist to have sought out this opportunity to hand her down.

Even knowing that, nothing save trampling by a runaway stallion could have kept him from the ill-advised delight of clasping her slender waist and savoring the feel of her as he lifted her down from the saddle.

She was no lightweight, but even after her booted feet gained their balance he couldn't seem to pull his hands away. She glanced up, startled. Some words, a protest probably, parted but did not exit her lips.

As it had once before in her phaeton, a powerful desire swept through him to pull her closer, to feel the warmth of her down the whole length of his body as he tasted the berry brightness of that mouth. His muscles clenching with the urgency of his need, for some timeless moments they both stood motionless, staring blue eyes to green as his nostrils drew in the soft rose scent of her.

Then she stumbled back from him and grabbed her trailing rein with one shaky hand. "Y-you wanted to talk?"

That's the least of all I want. Trying to beat back his baser instincts, he struggled to remember just what it was he'd meant to tell her.

Alex, the thought finally issued from his muzzy brain. He stilled his trembling lips and cleared his throat. "I wanted to thank you for taking Alex up with you at the park—and apologize for my unhandsome accusations."

He was both pleased and shamed at the astonishment that lit her fine eyes. "Apologize? To me? Indeed, Colonel, you confound me!"

"Nonetheless, keeping Alex at your side brought him a great deal of favorable notice. He's since gotten some flattering invitations he'd not otherwise have received."

She shook her head. "You underrate Lieutenant Standish's charm. He's a handsome, intelligent, witty man and a hero besides. I'm sure any advantage he's obtained was based on his own considerable appeal alone."

Sinjin felt a brief surge of—gad, it couldn't be jealousy! Damping down the uncomfortable feeling, he continued, "With no disparagement to Alex, I must disagree.

More important, however, since the afternoon of your drive he's been less...haunted than I've seen him at any time since Waterloo. For that, I cannot thank you enough. He's had a rough go of it, as I imagine you can guess.''

Her face softened. "I can well imagine. He went down during Uxbridge's charge?''

"Yes, he was riding with Ridgeby's guard and—'' Sinjin caught himself. "You are acquainted with the battle?'' he asked, astonished that so beautiful and socially prominent a lady would have any interest in military affairs.

"Me and the half of England that read the daily accounts in the *Tribune*. I can read, you know.''

He flushed. "I seem to be continually underrating your talents, Miss Beaumont.''

"You have no idea how much." She smiled then, and he felt the warmth of it seep into him, as when, after a night of bitter cold spent huddled under a threadbare blanket on rocky ground, the fierce Peninsular sun had at last risen to warm his weary bones.

A man could lose himself in that smile, as Alex had observed... "If I could beg a favor, Miss Beaumont,'' Sinjin said, regathering the threads of his argument, "Please try not to...dazzle Alex too much. Flesh and blood can resist just so much of your charm. He's already suffered a great deal. I wouldn't want to see him hurt.''

"Would you believe me if I swore I intend him no harm?''

He studied her solemn face. "I believe you,'' he said, and to his surprise, meant it. Once again her eyes captured his and he felt the flash of attraction crackle between them. Miss Beaumont capricious was enticing, but Miss Beaumont noble was nearly irresistible.

Get hold, man, he admonished himself. Captivating

though she be, Miss Beaumont, the flower of London society, was not the kind of woman to live happily in a half-ruined manor house far from the diversions of the city, trading her expensive gowns for a dusty housedress as she helped restore a dilapidated estate.

"If I can be of any help to Lieutenant Standish, I should be very pleased. Those of us who benefit from our gallant soldiers' efforts can never do enough to repay you." She sighed. "I only wish I had been a man, that I might have served. As long as there is an England, men will tell tales of Waterloo."

He stared at her, incredulous. Aside from the ludicrous vision of such a ravishing female turned into a man, something in her tone pricked at all the ugliest of his memories of that carnage.

"Thank a merciful God you were not there."

"How can you say so, you who were one of the valiant ones who prevailed, besting Boney for good and all?"

"Is that how you imagine the battle—a glorious charge of cavalry, the flash of guns, the thrill of bringing home victory? Merciful Heavens, woman, did you not read the death rolls? Can you imagine what the stump of a man's shoulder looks like when his arm's been blown off, or how a horse shrieks as it's dying? What it's like to ride an endless field of bodies frozen in death's contortions, uniforms too covered with mud to be able to identify the army, much less the unit for which the man fought? Thousands upon thousands of bodies…"

His voice died away as he suddenly perceived her emerald eyes fixed on him, wide with shock, her lips parted in dismay as she listened to an account no gently-bred female should ever hear. "F-forgive me, ma'am, that was unconscionable! I should never have spoken thus."

She took a trembling breath. "I suppose you must

speak of it to someone, or go mad. No, I'm not foolish or naive enough to believe it was all glory. Battle must be terrifying, so awful I wonder that any man can bring himself to it. And yet—to pledge oneself to so desperate an enterprise and pass the test, to stand fast with one's fellows in a cause one believes worth more than his life—that is glorious.''

Her soft comments left him speechless. *Though she'd never experienced it, she did understand.* Taken unawares, he felt a deeper bond weaving itself between his spirit and hers.

And then she placed her hand on his arm. ''I admire you so much, Colonel.''

The tightness in his chest seemed to crack, releasing a melting sensation that turned his blood to fire. It took every iota of his willpower to resist seizing that gloved hand and pulling her into his arms.

Get away, the voice of self-preservation rose from somewhere deep within him. *This unusual woman cannot be yours. Leave before your fraying control disintegrates entirely.* ''Again, my apologies, Miss Beaumont. For my careless words, and for doubting you. Now, I should allow you to return to your breakfast.''

So strongly felt was that urge for self-protection that his next actions made no sense. For when Miss Beaumont, with a hesitation that seemed almost shy, stuttered out an invitation for him to break his fast with her in Grosvenor Square, instead of returning a sane and rational refusal—he said ''yes.''

Chapter Seventeen

They spoke little on the transit back to Grosvenor Square, occupied with guiding their tired but still spirited horses through the swirl of carts, tradesmen and carriages congesting the streets.

Thank heaven for the respite. Clarissa rode with every nerve on edge, intensely aware of the horseman beside her. She'd pushed Diablo to the limit in an attempt to outrun her despair, then looked back to find the colonel, pursuing *her*.

Like the proverbial moth, she simply couldn't make herself withdraw from the flame, even though she, unlike the moth, was fully aware of the fire's destructive power.

And so, stuttering like a half-wit, she proved her idiocy by inviting him for breakfast.

She still felt at her shoulders, her sides, the imprint of his fingers where he'd helped her from her horse. The kiss he'd almost taken—nay, that she'd almost stolen—hung between them, both threat and prize. Knowing she could never be more to him than a temporary diversion, to be discarded when he went on with his life, it was madness to toy with an attraction that, on her part at least, was powerful enough to consume her.

But a demon rode her now, and it wanted that kiss.

Botheration, she was half-charred already. He'd likely either avoid or despise her for it after, but she'd have one searing memory from the wreckage to warm her the rest of her empty life.

Seeing to the horses, ushering him in, calling for fresh coffee occupied some moments, and then they were in the small parlor where breakfast had been set out. She scarcely knew what commonplace trivia she prattled, so strongly was desire thrumming in her blood. Today she would feel those lips, those hands on her. *Today. Soon.*

Though her wits were too scattered to discern whether his conversation was as stilted and unnatural as hers, surely he felt it too, that irresistible pull smoldering between them. She wondered the footmen bringing and removing dishes were not singed.

She must have eaten something, for James removed her plate as well. She knew to a crumb what the colonel had consumed, having watched each move of his tanned hands as he placed toast, eggs, sausage on his plate, each twist of lip as he spoke to her while disposing of his meal, each movement of his throat as he swallowed his coffee.

It struck her to wonder if her intense scrutiny made him uncomfortable, and she grinned wolfishly at the thought. Good. Hunter or hunted, they would end this thing that had hung between them for days. *Today. Now.*

"Would you like to see the garden? It's particularly lovely now with the bulbs just out." Beckoning, she walked to the French doors leading to the terrace.

Mercifully he followed, sparing her the necessity of deciding whether, had he refused, she would have actually attempted to haul him out bodily.

At the door he took her arm with a touch that simmered on her skin and any lingering doubts evaporated. Ah yes, he felt it too. And this time, today, he would not resist.

She blessed some ancestor who must have designed the small townhouse garden with dalliance in mind. After traversing the small back terrace, they passed a curtain wall of wisteria fronted by a multicolored array of tulips which blocked the view of the garden beyond. And down a short path flanked by awakening roses, sheltered by another hedge of yew, sat a conveniently placed garden bench.

Silently he walked her down the garden path. Every sense acutely alert, she heard each chatter of birdsong, each sharp clip of riding boot against stone. The sweet violet scent of woodland iris filled her head.

After rounding the yew hedge, the colonel stopped abruptly. "Miss Beaumont," he said, his voice thick.

"'Tis r-rather warm here in the s-sun," she stuttered, though more likely it was the heat within that prompted her to shed her wool spencer and toss it on the bench.

She looked back up into blue eyes smoky with desire, and the demon exulted. *He would kiss her. Now.*

"Miss Beaumont—" he began again.

"Clare," she whispered. For a fierce moment she held his gaze with eyes that begged him to resist no more, then tilted her head up, letting her eyelashes drift shut, offering.

Still he hesitated. If he didn't kiss her soon, she would scream. She opened her eyes again, desperate with wanting, furious at the delay.

His entire body stood tensed, hands now clenched at his sides, even the muscles at his throat corded with effort, as if he were about to fight—or flee.

Trying to deny temptation still, she realized. Damn him

and his dedication to his dull, virtuous virgin. Before she could think what she did, Clarissa reached up and jerked that golden head toward her.

His lips made rough, uncertain contact. But after an instant's touch, growling deep in his throat, the colonel wrapped her in his arms and hauled her where she craved to be, hard up against the lean muscled length of him.

The kiss she'd wanted, shamelessly begged for, was an assault, a take-no-prisoners charge meant to overwhelm resistance and breach any defenses. She reveled in it, matching him thrust for tongue-thrust, on fire to ravish every scorching surface of his mouth.

Like iron against iron, the friction of their clothed bodies struck sparks that flamed and sizzled against her skin at every point of contact, heating her blood and sending it coursing, molten, to every vein. When he brought one hand up to caress the aching tip of her breast, she cried out as sensation spread in dizzying circles from the peaked nipple to the burning, melting center of her.

She wanted the thin, teasing barrier of fabric removed, craved the feel of his hand against her bare skin. Before she could utter an impassioned plea, he brought his teeth, hot and wet from the efforts of her tongue, to nibble at her ear.

Then he began a slow, agonizing march from the soft skin at the curve of her jaw to the pulse at her throat, lower still across her bared collarbone, sizzling the skin at the edge of her bodice, using tongue, lips and teeth in a rapturous torture.

One hand inched down the fabric of her gown and his lips followed, his teeth nipping the material to pull it against her skin, then his tongue sliding under to push the fabric back, allowing air to shiver on the skin's wet surface.

She clawed at fistfuls of golden hair to hold him there against her. With an inarticulate mutter that might have been approval, he pushed his tongue deeper, playing in the moisture that bedewed the hollow between her breasts, then gliding over her skin, closer, closer by infinite degrees to the pulsing nipples.

"Please," she gasped, "oh, please."

At last he plied one hardened nipple with soft, liquid pressure. Pleasure exploded like a rifle shot and rippled outward, deadening her muscles, paralyzing breath. She would surely have fallen if he had not supported her, his tongue still tracing around and over the tip in unimaginably torturous caress.

She wanted…oh, she wanted! To be freed, her skin bared and open to his hands, his mouth. Her fingers flailed, then caught the top of her bodice and jerked it down.

The gown, still fastened in back, strained at the pull, but she managed to free the breast he'd kissed, the taut material under it lifting the rounded globe up to him like an offering.

He'd halted in his pleasuring, but before she could whimper a plea, he murmured something that sounded like "yes," slid his hands up to support her back, and took the whole of the nipple into his mouth.

She was galloping on Diablo, faster, faster, approaching some distant obstacle. She could feel a tension mounting in her body like that of her horse as he gathered himself for the jump, her muscles locking, pressure spiraling tighter and tighter to an almost unendurable peak, and then…

Air. Cold, vacant air when abruptly the colonel staggered away from her, nearly unbalancing them both as he set her back on her feet.

No! she wanted to scream. He couldn't stop—not now, not with her heart thundering in her chest, her breath coming in gasps, not when she was so close to reaching that elusive something toward which every nerve and muscle strained. She'd...she'd kill him if he stopped now!

It appeared murder would be required, for to her anguish and fury, the colonel continued to retreat. Shaking, gasping, hands trembling and apparently as unsteady on his feet as she, but definitely backing away.

Could she have gathered breath enough she would certainly have screamed then, except she heard it. Faintly at first, and then with increasing volume as her roaring pulse slowly quieted, unstopping her ears.

"Clarissa? Are you in the garden, dear? Clarissa?"

Mama. Had the colonel heard her too? Was that why he'd left her so suddenly, bereft and demented with need?

His face unreadable, he was staring at her, shaky fingers fumbling with his flattened cravat. Staring at the naked breast still outlined by her straining bodice.

With a muttered oath she jerked the material back up to cover herself, a suffusion of hot embarrassment replacing the cooling embers of desire.

Thank heavens Mama never proceeded beyond the terrace. Readjusting her neckline, which was now stretched sadly out of shape, she snatched the jacket off the bench and pulled it on. As she re-looped the buttons, she took a ragged breath and called to her mother.

Her second attempt produced sound. "H-here, Mama. I'm coming."

Refusing to glance at the colonel—or worry what havoc he'd wreaked on her hair or face, she stalked down the path back to the terrace.

She'd at least got her breathing under control by the

time she reached her mother. Before she could turn to introduce the colonel, who'd followed silently in her wake, Lady Sandiford's brow creased in concern.

"Are you all right, dear? Your color is alarmingly high."

If she could have done so undetected, she would have kicked the colonel with the hard heel of her riding boot. "The, ah, sun is rather hot in the back garden, Mama. Let me introduce Colonel Lord Sandiford, lately of the Tenth Hussars and recently returned to London."

"The handsome young soldier you were describing to me in such glowing terms the other night? Then I'm—"

"No, Mama, that was someone else."

Her expression puzzled, Lady Beaumont nonetheless extended a hand to be kissed. "Charmed, Colonel."

"Madam," he replied shortly, and bowed.

Leaving her remark unexplained, Clarissa fell silent. She absolutely would not look at the colonel.

Lady Beaumont's eyes, slightly myopic without the spectacles she was still too vain to wear except in the privacy of her room, attempted to focus on him. "Yes, it must be warm, Clarissa. The colonel is looking alarmingly flushed as well. Come, let us get out of the sun. Won't you join us for some refreshment, Colonel? I'm sure Cook could have some lemonade made up in a trice."

"Very kind, ma'am, but I…I have business elsewhere. Another time, perhaps. I must bid you ladies goodbye."

Another time? After that—Clarissa couldn't think what to call the interlude in the garden—he thought he could just walk out without a word?

Not in this life. Pasting on a smile for Mama's benefit, she grabbed the colonel's arm. "I'll see him out, Mama. Would you have Timms, ah, check with Stebbins in the stables to see if Diablo is all right? I believe he may have strained a hock on his gallop this morning.''

''Yes, dear. I'll order lemonade, too. So cooling. It's quite dangerous to get overheated, you know.''

Oh, she knew. Was the colonel already regretting the rash passion he'd encouraged her to display, had succumbed to himself? The thought was almost unendurable. However, having cleverly cleared the front hallway of attendants, she intended to find out before she'd allow the colonel to make his escape.

But when they reached the entry he forestalled her, holding up a hand. ''Please, let me speak, Miss Beaumont. Our behavior—'' his eyes dropped to her bodice and she could almost feel her breast once more bare beneath his gaze, ''—ah, that is, my behavior in the garden was reprehensible. I...I simply can't find words to excuse it.''

He held himself as stiffly upright as an outraged spinster kissed under the mistletoe by the neighborhood lecher. The regret she'd dreaded to see was painted plainly on his face, shaded by...disgust? Though he'd disdained and disapproved of her before, somehow this time the distaste cut right to the quick.

Pain spiraled deep, and without even thinking, she reached out to him. He recoiled. He desired her, his accusing eyes said, but only as he would any other wanton. In the ashes of passion, he abhorred her touch, this supposed lady who'd shown herself every bit the whore the clubmen claimed.

Something small, frail and helpless deep within her bled. And as always, she found refuge in anger. Had she a small-sword, she could have run him through on the spot.

''No need to apologize,'' she said through clenched

teeth. "After all, I practically begged for what I got, didn't I? But there is a silver lining to this rather tawdry episode. Just think how amused all your fine friends at White's will be as you describe how Miss Beaumont moaned and writhed under your hands. You should be able to dine out on the story for weeks."

His face went white, and for a moment she thought he would strike her. Instead, he turned on his heel, stalked out the door and closed it with a slam.

Well, she'd told him. Lips trembling, hands beginning to shake, she knew she'd never make it through a pleasant morning chat with her mama, not when her world had just shattered into irreparable fragments in front of her eyes.

His white-faced fury spoke more eloquently than any words. He despised her for breaking his control and himself for succumbing. If he never saw her again, it would be too soon.

For her as well. How could she see him and not remember the feel of his lips, his hands. In spite of his disapproval and disgust, she knew to her shame she would only want to feel them again, longer, harder. Writhing with frustration and fury, she gathered her skirts and ran up the stairs to her room.

Then stopped with horror inside the door as she caught sight of her reflection in the pier glass. Her lips were reddened and swollen, her cheek chafed where the scrape of his beard must have rubbed it. Rosy blotches decorated her neck, and the loops on her jacket were done up wrong.

For a silent moment she blessed her mama's deteriorating eyesight and the servants' discretion. Then she fell on her bed and wept.

* * *

Considering he'd left the Beaumont townhouse in a daze of fury so impenetrable as to be almost a stupor, it was something of a miracle that he ended up a short time later at the mews behind his Audley Street rooms. Thank Heaven Valiant knew where his oats were kept.

Too bad Sinjin hadn't been as wise in knowing where to keep himself. He wouldn't then have had to endure a wounding reminder of the frequent hospitality poverty compelled him to accept, or worse—the jibe that he had so little honor he would first compromise a lady and then boast of it at Whites. That comment had so incensed him that he'd nearly been induced, for the first time in his life, to strike a woman.

Not that he hadn't deserved a stinging rebuke. Even now, he had difficulty imagining how he could have been so lost to all sense of decorum, propriety and sense as to have almost ravished a woman in full daylight in her back garden, with servants, tradesmen and her own mother but a few steps away.

Knowing the effect she had on his senses, he should never have come back with her from the park. Certainly he ought to have avoided that secluded back garden. He'd been lost the moment his boot trod the first stone.

How was it that she managed time and again to bewitch him, he the most dispassionate and rational of men?

Ah, but how marvelous the fall had been. Close his eyes and he could savor again the taste of her passion-dewed skin, thrill to a response so heady he'd been driven nearly to frenzy. Just the thought of how she'd ignited in his arms set his pulses hammering while the tightness of his breeches reminded him of the sudden, unwelcome termination of that delicious journey of exploration.

Thank Heaven the acute senses he'd sharpened over

six years of campaigning hadn't failed him, even if sense and reason had. If he'd not been distracted by the soft pad of Lady Beaumont's leather slippers on the brick terrace, heaven knows what unpardonable sin he'd have committed.

Having been moments from disaster should prove a signal lesson. In future, he would steer well clear of the dangerously alluring Miss Beaumont.

He was halfway up the stairs, congratulating himself on that impossibly narrow escape, when the unpalatable truth slammed into him like an incoming French twenty-pounder.

Whether or not Lady Beaumont had discovered them in the garden didn't matter. Miss Beaumont wasn't a discreet, willing widow, though she'd certainly been willing enough, nor a camp follower, nor a Society wife of compliant virtue. She was an unmarried young woman of quality. And what he had done with her in the garden had, for a man of honor, irretrievably compromised her.

For which offense there was only one remedy. He would have to marry her. Whether she wanted him or not.

He staggered into his rooms, fumbled some brandy in a glass and downed it in one gulp. Making his way to the wing chair by the fireplace, he sank into it and put his aching head into his hands.

How had he stumbled into such folly?

Yes, there was enough fire between them to set off a regiment of musketry, but to make a marriage work required so much more. After the tumult of war, he wanted serenity in a life's companion, not constant alarms, comfort rather than confrontation. He required a partner with the skill and desire to help him rebuild the wreckage of his estate, not an unpredictable, irresponsible, town-bred flirt who'd sulk in the country and drive him mad flirting with everything in pants back in town. He didn't want a wife with a pack of courtiers attached.

He'd better get used to it, though. There was no way to avoid marrying her without ignoring his duty and forfeiting his honor. Which, of course, was unthinkable.

As he proceeded to empty the brandy decanter, he considered the implications. Miss Beaumont was rich, thank heavens. He'd really be in a pickle if he'd blundered into compromising a penniless young lady. And marriage would free him to indulge all the passion he'd been riding on so tight a check-rein practically from the moment he saw her.

Once again a vision of the perfect, beautiful breast she'd bared to him in the sunlight recurred, fogging his brain and swamping him in heat. Having her ravishing, responsive body beside him, under him for the rest of his life would be sweet recompense indeed.

There were others. She was gallant, courageous and honest—all rather rare qualities in a woman. She'd neither whined nor complained on several occasions when many would have done both.

And she certainly didn't bore him. He recalled that mad gallop through the park and his lips curled into a smile. No, life with Clarissa Beaumont would be anything but dull.

Her quick, demanding wit would keep his mind sharp. She might kick at being dragged to the country, but if he could persuade her to it, she would probably be a hard and tireless worker. She certainly threw herself passionately into whatever she began.

Remembering her reaction to his initiatives in the garden, his smile broadened. He had a few ideas on how to go about persuading her.

And hadn't he felt, almost from the beginning, this

deep sense of comradeship, almost the sort of bond fellow soldiers share? He'd probably have to be ever on the lookout to restrain her madder impulses, and keep a loaded pistol to discourage the scores of men foolish enough to consider making a cuckold of him, but all things considered, perhaps this marriage wouldn't be such a disaster after all.

Disaster or not, neither of them could escape it now. Though he expected Miss Beaumont would try.

Indeed, tendering her a proposal of marriage at this tardy moment was probably going to be rather hazardous. Miss Beaumont had been furious with him when he left, which was no less than he deserved. After his unforgivable treatment of her, the longer he waited to make a declaration he should have offered her on the spot, the angrier she would have reason to become.

Glancing at the mantel clock, he ran a hand over his cheek, noting the rough feel of the stubble there. He'd best shave again, then dig out his regimentals, and for the first time in his life, go deliver a proposal.

Two hours later, gold polished, boots shined to such a gloss he could see himself in them, Sinjin presented himself at Miss Beaumont's door. When Timms indicated that neither of the Beaumont ladies were in to callers, he informed the butler he had no intention of leaving until he saw Miss Beaumont. Ordering the man to show him to a room and bring wine, with a grin Sinjin followed the disgruntled servant into the parlor.

He didn't think he'd have to wait long. His Miss Beaumont wasn't the coy sort to sulk and delay. No, she'd probably be only too willing to seize another opportunity to flay his hide with the whip of her tongue.

Imagining other things he'd teach that tongue to do

provided pleasant occupation. As expected, he was very soon interrupted.

His whole body tensed with anticipation as he heard her quick, light step approach. His eyes on her as she entered, he barely heard the butler announce her. The breath he'd been holding eased out in relief, however, when he noted she did not bring a trail of chaperones in her wake. He relaxed even further after she ordered Timms to withdraw and leave them alone.

So she was expecting his proposal and did not intend to fight him. Everything, Sinjin thought with a grin, was going to be fine.

Slowly he raised satisfied eyes from her delectably heaving bosom (ah, soon to be fully explored!) to her kiss-bruised lips (his lips now, to kiss and kiss again) to her stormy eyes—and his jocular mood faltered. Miss Beaumont's lovely green eyes were sheened with tears.

Remorse struck him. Of course, after he stomped out without so much as a word, she must have thought the worst, that he had used her abominably and did not intend to make it right. Without even thinking he reached out to touch her cheek. "I'm sorry, sweetheart."

She batted his hand away. "Say what you came to say and be gone." Crossing her arms, she averted her face.

She'd not taken a chair, nor had she invited him to do so. Did one go down on one knee in front of a standing maiden?

Arms crossed over her chest, trying hard to draw in even breaths, no easy task when one's lungs felt as if squeezed in a vice, Clarissa stood and waited. She'd been sorely tempted to let the arrogant colonel idle downstairs till he rotted, but by now she knew the wretch was as stubborn as she. The blasted man would probably sit in her parlor until doomsday.

Only the certain knowledge that should she allow him to do so, sooner or later Mama would learn of his presence and become upset, prompted her to reluctantly receive him.

If he'd come to do what she feared—to deliver a pro forma proposal—she would flay him alive. But first, she'd not make uttering those sham words of devotion easy.

She kept her head averted.

She heard him shuffle about and clear his throat twice. Blast, but she wished she dared take a good look at him in his regimentals. But then, given his effect on her it was probably best to refrain. She waited.

He cleared his throat once again. "Miss Beaumont, it may have come to your attention that though we have been acquainted but a short while, my, um, regard for you has steadily increased."

Like a brain fever, she thought.

"In view of the, um, experiences we have recently shared, I feel it imperative to demand you do me the honor of becoming my wife."

Through your wanton behavior I've been led to action that compromised you, so knowing my duty, I am forced to ask for your hand, she translated mentally.

Not even the vestige of pretty words about affection, no false promises to honor and cherish. In some detached part of her brain she had to admire his brutal honesty. Still, the reality of that forced proposal was ever so much more degrading than her imagining.

Too desolate to utter words, she remained silent. The colonel shifted once more, then said impatiently, "Did you not hear me, woman? I've just asked you to marry me!''

She whirled to face him. '''Asked?' I believe 'demand' was the word you used, Colonel. But let me hasten to assure you such a great sacrifice as you seem willing to make—to bind yourself to a wanton just to secure her fortune—is entirely unnecessary.''

He knit his brow, as if trying to make sense of Greek. ''Bind myself to a... When did I say anything about wantonness or fortunes?''

''I read between the lines,'' she said sweetly. ''Now, you have made your offer, I have refused it, and you are free to go. Goodbye.''

She turned to step away, but he grabbed her arm. ''You cannot mean to refuse! What about your reputation?''

''Is it mine you worry about or your own? Considering the offence occurred in my own garden with nobody to observe but my own family and servants, I think I can assure you your precious reputation is safe. No hint of your dallying with an unmarried miss will pass their lips.''

He frowned, still holding her arm. ''But I know of it. You know of it. There can be only one honorable recourse.''

Oh, for a moment she nearly gave in. The colonel, every glorious tempting inch of him, every aggravating atom of him, could be hers merely for voicing of a simple ''yes.''

The old Clarissa, supremely confident in the power of her body to charm, mold and change a man, would have taken that offer and worried later about the consequences.

But the new Clarissa realized she could not force his love. And the new Clarissa knew she could not bear to have his body, his name, perhaps even his children, without an affection that at least in part matched the all-consuming passion she felt for him.

Besides, she knew what sort of wife the colonel desired, and even at the cost of her own happiness, the new Clarissa wanted the colonel to be happy.

Swallowing a sea of misery, she struggled to keep her tone tart and accusatory. "A fine honor that allows you, for the price of a few kisses, to conveniently claim a rich girl's fortune." Pleased to note the stunned reaction to that salvo, she finished him off with a final one. "I can protect my own reputation, thank you, Colonel, and you may recoup your fortunes elsewhere. I recommend you fill your coffers with the virtuous virgin's money. Before anyone else leads you astray."

He was tight-lipped in anger now. "You are adamant in refusing an offer honorably given?"

She made an elaborate courtesy, a portrait of mockery. "I am. Honor has been satisfied," she deliberately employed the terminology of the duel. "You may withdraw."

He glared at her a long moment, as if he would once more bare her not just to the skin but to the soul. Almost she quailed before it, but nowhere this side of hell would she let him see how much she longed for that which he so casually, callously offered, how cut to the very marrow she was that he would offer her his name but not the love she craved more than she'd ever wanted anything in life.

Damn him. If he didn't leave this instant, she'd take the fireplace poker to him.

When at last he broke the tension of their gaze, she almost slumped backward. "As you wish then, madam," he spat out, and strode from the room.

Her legs suddenly rubbery, her vision blurring, Clarissa held herself upright by force of will.

Let him believe she thought he'd tried to compromise her to gain her fortune. He'd hate her for it, but that was better than his tempting her to accept from him a marriage without the love he could not give. Touched on the quick in the pride and honor he so valued, Clarissa doubted he'd propose again.

Thank a merciful God. When at last she heard the slam of the front door heralding his departure, Clarissa slid to the floor where she stood and bent her bowed head to her hands.

If this misery was what being in love entailed, the state was vastly overrated.

Chapter Eighteen

He was, Sinjin told himself once his anger cooled enough that he could think, enormously relieved. He had made the offer honor required, and been refused. And in such an insulting manner! As if he, he! an officer of the Tenth, would ever stoop so low as to trick a woman into marriage for her money. Thank heavens he need never speak to that red-haired virago again.

At the thought of that valiant spirit and passionate body claimed by another man, his fingers clenched on the reins, causing Valiant to prick up his ears and whinny. Well, perhaps he was a little disappointed.

Was he not in fact trying to lure another young lady into marriage for her money? But both parties in that transaction understood his circumstances from the start. If they did make a match, it would be an honorable bargain. Even if the idea still left a sour taste in his mouth.

Realistically, did he have any other choice? An idle ornament from the ton would be of no use to him. Surely under the surface veneer that ladies' academy had painted on, surely beneath the airs and graces Mrs. Cartwright tried to convey to her, he would find in Miss Motrum a kind, industrious soul who would be a helpmate. And if the lady was a trifle—placid, after the fits and starts of the tempestuous Miss Beaumont, that must only be welcome.

Besides, Mr. Motrum's kindness in intervening with the bankers only reinforced the imperative that his benefactor's daughter become Sinjin's wife.

He laughed shortly without humor. Such a signal honor he'd convey, to offer her a loveless match with a penniless aristocrat.

But then, there was always the possibility Miss Motrum might also refuse him. His bruised spirits lit with a glow of…surely not hope.

He sighed. A good commander moved swiftly, using the resources he had available. And, as Miss Beaumont so nastily reminded him, he did need to settle his future—not just his, but that of his mama and any future generation of Sandifords. He'd reexamine the matter, but if no better plan presented itself, he would offer for Miss Motrum this very week.

Clarissa raised her head from her lap. She could, of course, sit here in a soggy heap until one of the maids found her, thence to spread the word throughout the house that not only had Miss Beaumont come in from the garden all red-cheeked and rumpled, she later received a call from the gentleman in question and been prostrate with grief after.

Not Clarissa Beaumont. Bad enough her fair skin betrayed her with a telling redness about the eyes. She'd not have the rumor spread to the ton through the subtle network of servants' gossip that Miss Beaumont had been disappointed in love. Especially since it was true.

Too agitated now to tolerate the idea of returning to mope about her rooms, she rose, her legs cramping a little. What she needed was some occupation, some task to take her mind off her own misery.

A mail coach would arrive soon. Perhaps this evening she could check with the runner on their progress there. And though at the moment she was thoroughly disenchanted with the business of love, she still had Lieutenant Standish's affairs to settle.

The groundwork for that had been well laid. Perhaps it was time to pay a visit to Lady Barbara herself. And given the swirl of grief, anguish and anger tightening her chest, seizing the opportunity to rout the girl's top-lofty mother would be most satisfying.

She felt the blood lust of battle rise within her. She might not be able to entice one unmentionable colonel, but the Countess of Wetherford was about to discover that Miss Clarissa Beaumont usually got what she wanted.

Eyes bathed with lavender water and arrayed for social combat in her most modish new gown, an hour later Clarissa presented herself at the Countess of Wetherford's townhouse. The drawing room was so full of guests, young ladies and gentlemen clustered around Lady Barbara and society matrons about the Countess, that Clarissa was forced to make polite chat for some minutes before being able to insinuate her way close to Lady Barbara.

The Countess followed her progress with a narrowed eye. No doubt the fastidious old beldam thought Clarissa Beaumont, with her scandalous gowns and flamboyant behavior, much too ''fast'' to be a fit companion to her delicate daughter.

Oh my, she was correct, Clarissa thought, tossing a savage smile in that lady's direction.

With her usual precision she quickly flattered, redirected or intimidated away the knot of young people about Lady Barbara, then honed in on her target.

"Would you not take a turn in the garden with me, Lady Barbara? The plantings are so lovely just now."

Ruthlessly suppressing the pain of what had occurred when she'd used that ploy just this morning, she made herself beckon to the door.

Countess Hawk Eye swiveled her head around. "Another time, perhaps, Miss Beaumont. It would be rude of Barbara to abandon her other guests."

Who are far better companions for her than you, Clarissa finished the unspoken phrase. "Countess, the tulips bloom but a few days merely. I've heard such high praise of the superior arrangement of your garden, I should be vastly disappointed to miss the display."

The Countess twitched her lips, unable to extend the blooming time of tulips and unwilling to protest her garden was not out of the ordinary. "Perhaps one of the gentlemen could escort you."

Clarissa had no intention of carrying along excess baggage, even as several gentlemen eagerly indicated their willingness to oblige.

"And have them abandon the other young ladies? That *would* be rude. No, the walk shall take but a minute. Lady Barbara, do you require your shawl?"

Given Clarissa's recent highly publicized excursions with Lieutenant Standish, it was no wonder the look Lady Barbara cast her was distinctly hostile. "I suppose so, if Mama permits."

"Of course she does. Come, we can fetch it in the hallway. I'll bring her back to you, ladies, gentlemen, in a trice." With that, she stood and tugged with unladylike force on Lady Barbara's arm.

With honeyed words and ruthless precision she got

Lady Barbara out of the room, had her shawl fetched and propelled her into the garden. As soon as they walked beyond hearing of the gardeners, Clarissa began.

"I suppose you may wonder why I sought you out. I wished to speak with you about Lieutenant Standish. He used to be a particular friend of yours, did he not?"

Lady Barbara stiffened. "Since you've spent so much time with him, I should think you know him better than I."

So the little cat had claws. "Such a charming young man. As you've just noted, I have spent time with him of late. Indeed, I begin to consider him a serious suitor."

Lady Barbara's eyes widened. "A s-suitor?"

"Yes. So of course I'm anxious to know if my impressions are correct. He appears to be a kind, honest, intelligent, charming gentleman. Amusing, and yet ever mindful of a lady's sensibilities. Did you find him so?"

Lady Barbara was beginning to look stricken. "Y-yes."

"And so handsome." Clarissa gave a delicious chuckle. "He kisses divinely, do you not think?"

"Yes! No!" Lady Barbara went pink, then white. "How should I know anything about his kisses?" she declared hotly, tears glistening at the corners of her eyes.

"No? I thought you might have some experience." Clarissa sighed. "His having been wounded has made him so much more compelling than other young men. He understands endurance, perseverance, and loyalty. Qualities that will make him an excellent husband, don't you think?"

Lady Barbara, her glance full of loathing, did not answer.

"Though it's a shame the lady he really loves won't have him, eventually he shall have to marry someone. I'd best entice him before that black-haired granddaughter of Lady Arundell does. Thank you, Lady Barbara, you've been most helpful. Shall we return to the house?''

Lady Barbara seized her arm. ''He…he is still is love with someone else?''

Clarissa felt it time to drop the pretense. ''Don't you know the answer to that better than I?''

For a long moment the girl was silent. ''I…I had hoped he was.''

''Then what do you intend to do about it?''

''I—I don't know! If only Mama weren't so set against him! I keep hoping if I follow her wishes now, and wait long enough, she'll eventually see what a fine man Alex is, and…and give him her blessing again.''

Clarissa sniffed. ''If some other young lady hasn't snapped him up first. Do you really believe his injured arm makes him less a man?''

''Of course not! Why, he's a hero!''

Clarissa smiled, her last doubt removed. ''Then if you love him, you must let him know that, disapproving mama or no. If you don't think him worth defying your mama to love, perhaps another woman deserves him.''

''I don't want another woman to have him!'' Lady Barbara burst out.

''Then you must act. Now.''

''But how can I approach him? Mama forbids it!''

Clarissa sighed. The girl was such an infant. ''Send him a note, asking him to meet you at the park, or Hatchard's, or some other place your mama permits you to go without her.''

Lud, was she going to have to write the note as well?

''I—I don't know. I shall have to think of a way.''

''My dear Lady Barbara,'' Clarissa replied impatiently,

"In whose affection would you prefer to bask for the rest of your days? Your mama's? Or Lieutenant Standish's?"

The dark, troubled eyes cleared. "I'll send the note. If you would be so kind as to get a message to him?"

Spineless still, Clarissa thought with disgust, and then caught herself. She had not grown up overshadowed by a domineering mother, so who was she to judge? At least the girl was making the right choice now, while still at considerable risk of her mother's ire.

Botheration, was that tolerance and compassion speaking? She was in danger of turning into Colonel Sandiford's saint. The memories of that conversation, before she could extinguish them, cut deep.

She surfaced from that anguished thought to find Lady Barbara's eyes on her. "Why are you doing this for me?" the girl asked softly.

Clarissa managed a slight smile. "Lieutenant Standish is a fine soldier, an admired friend. He loves you. And I want the people I care about to be happy."

Once you've inspected the battlefield and written your orders, implement them—another good commander's axiom. Having arrived at no feasible alternative to offering for Miss Motrum, Sinjin set his plans in motion.

He sent her flowers the first day, a small book of poetry the next. This morning he'd sent around yet another floral tribute which included a message informing Miss Motrum he would call upon her this afternoon at two.

It being nearly the appointed hour, he had dressed with care—in his best blue coat, not his regimentals—and ordered a bouquet of roses to bring with him.

Did Miss Motrum like roses? The scent of them on another woman's passion-dewed skin wafted up from memory.

Shaken, he banished it. Thinking of one woman while preparing to offer for another simply wouldn't do. He owed Miss Motrum better than that.

Yet, with still certainty, do what he might to squelch the memory after, he knew the scent of roses would forever conjure up one certain face.

Ridiculous, to be turning sentimental now, when he needed his wits about him to phrase a proper proposal. After all, he'd not done so well with his first. He'd best insure this one was better.

To keep the dust of the road off his pristine coat, he took a hackney. And occupied the journey rehearsing perhaps the most important short speech he'd ever give.

Miss Motrum and Mrs. Cartwright were expecting him, the butler told him. Feeling as nervous as he had on the eve of a battle, he paused at the threshold.

Somewhat to his surprise, another visitor occupied the sofa in the parlor. At his entrance, an older lady dressed in rich brocade ornamented with braid and buried beneath the weight of so much expensive jewelry he wondered she could walk, turned to eye him avidly.

"So you're Mr. Motrum's lordling," the woman said after the introductions had been made. She gave Miss Motrum an arch look. "I'd say your papa's bought himself a prime one." She turned to give Sinjin an exaggerated wink.

Affronted and uncertain what he should reply, Sinjin stood speechless. With a hasty glance at him, Mrs. Cartwright interposed, "Mrs. Wintergreen was just leaving. Do let me escort out, dear ma'am."

"I'll be sure to see you again Friday at Mr. Motrum's turtle-dinner. And maybe you, too, eh, my lord? Close as my Henry is to Mr. Motrum, I dare swear we shall meet again often.'' Mrs. Wintergreen gave Sinjin a broad wink.

With proper expressions of delight, Mrs. Cartwright ushered out the visitor, whose inquisitive glance rested on Sinjin all the way to the door. As if judging whether a shipment of goods had been worth its price.

Wonderful. Unless after their marriage he forbade Miss Motrum to attend her father's entertainments, or sent her to them alone—a rude and insulting gesture—he'd be enduring the woman's stares in future. Would she wonder whether his services in the bedchamber gave full value?

Dismissing that distasteful thought, he glanced at Miss Motrum's serene face.

Surely she understood his reason for coming here today.

Mrs. Cartwright apparently did, for she remained standing by the door. After Mrs. Wintergreen's heavy tread and strident tones faded away, she turned to them. ''I believe I left my needlepoint in the library, Anne, dear. You two will excuse me while I fetch it, won't you?''

The soft tap of the closing door echoed unnaturally loud in his ears. Miss Motrum sat beside him, her face demurely lowered.

This was the moment. Should he go down on one knee? Or did one not do so until the actual proposal?

Sweating now in his fine wool coat, Sinjin combed his memory for the well-rehearsed opening line. ''Miss Motrum, as we've become acquainted, you may have noticed my regard for you has steadily increased.''

No, drat—that was how he'd begun his other, disastrous speech. A little rattled, he remembered he must add something about growing affection. Women expected that.

"I'm honored, my lord," Miss Motrum replied, startling him.

He cleared his throat. "That is to say, I admire your character and think my regard could grow into a warm affection. That we might share. Ah, both of us."

There, 'twas badly done, but he'd said it. The only thing remaining was to deliver the proposal. Just go down on one knee and get it over with.

He shot a quick glance at Miss Motrum. Hands clasped in her lap, she waited expectantly.

But his legs seemed cast in iron, and the words stuck to the roof of his mouth.

He simply couldn't do it.

He felt heat rise up the back of his neck, suffuse his face as he tried to get control of his tongue. He dared not even look at Miss Motrum.

At that moment, the door burst open and Mr. Wickham fairly flew into the room. Here, Sinjin realized immediately, lay Salvation.

"Jeremy!" Miss Motrum exclaimed, her cheeks pinking as she looked uncertainly from Sinjin to her father's assistant and back. "What an…unexpected pleasure."

"Miss Motrum, Lord Sandiford," Mr. Wickham gasped. He caught his breath and bowed, the smile he offered Miss Motrum fading to a frown as he faced Sinjin. "When I asked your papa if you would be walking in the park this morning and he informed me you were…entertaining instead, I hastened to, um, pay my respects."

Miss Motrum giggled. "Jeremy, I saw you just last night."

"That was last night, and besides, 'tis only correct that I call and thank you for the invitation."

"Excuse me, please," Sinjin interrupted. "I have a

question for Mrs. Cartwright. I believe I shall go in search of her.''

Miss Motrum looked puzzled, then torn as she realized his odd intention would leave her alone with Mr. Wickham. Obviously unable to decide if she dared countermand his desire, or should merely seek to delay him, she stuttered, ''Sh-shall I fetch her for you?''

''Oh, no, I couldn't permit you to abandon your hostess duties.'' Sinjin moved his gaze to Mr. Wickham, who was staring at him with wary uncertainty. *This is your chance—now use it,* he silently signaled the surprised young man. Then, with a bow, he strode out.

He met Mrs. Cartwright on the threshold of the library. ''Lord Sandiford! Is anything amiss?''

''Not at all, ma'am. Indeed, I believe that everything shall soon be put perfectly to rights. I wished to inquire which brand of cigar Mr. Motrum prefers, and from which shop he procures them.''

''Cigars?'' she echoed, a touch of aggravation in her tone. ''He obtains his from Wendover on King Street, of course.'' Then a pleasanter thought must have occurred, for her face lit. ''You wish to speak privately with Mr. Motrum? Excellent! Am I to wish you happy? Oh, I shall be in raptures—''

''Naturally, I'm delighted by the cordiality the Motrum family—and your gracious self—have always shown me.''

Mrs. Cartwright's rapture faded. ''Then you and Anne have not…? Well, let us return to the drawing room! Anne can tell you just how Mr. Motrum likes his tobacco blended. Such a clever girl!'' Mrs. Cartwright motioned him along.

Sinjin followed, keeping his steps deliberately slow.

"Where on King Street? I must send a servant and don't wish him to mistake the shop."

"If I may be so bold, simply send him to me, dear Lord Sandiford. I should be happy to direct him."

As they neared the drawing room, a murmur of voices emanated from behind the half-closed door. Mrs. Cartwright halted, her brow creasing. "My, we must have other guests," she exclaimed, looking none too pleased. "Anne, dear," she called as she pushed the door fully open, "who are you—Anne!"

With a gasp, Mrs. Cartwright went motionless, her hand frozen on the doorknob. Over her shoulder Sinjin could see Miss Motrum locked in Mr. Wicham's embrace, his fingers twined in her golden hair as he kissed her thoroughly.

So absorbed were the two it wasn't until Mrs. Cartwright shrieked her charge's name a second time that the couple sprang apart. Putting hands to cheeks flushing scarlet, Miss Motrum stepped hastily back, while a grinning Mr. Wickham caught her with an arm about her waist and drew her back beside him.

"You wicked, wicked girl!" Mrs. Cartwright wailed. "And you, Mr. Wickham, are a…a viper!" Only then did she seem to remember Sinjin standing behind her. "My dear Lord Sandiford," she cried, whirling to face him, "you mustn't think…only allow me to explain!"

"No explanations necessary." Sinjin smiled at Mr. Wickham, who flashed him a look of bemused gratitude over Miss Motrum's downcast head. "It's time I took my leave."

With a bow, he turned and walked into the hall.

Mrs. Cartwright scurried after him and seized his elbow. "Please, my lord, do not hasten off! Let me ring for tea! I'll deal with you later, missy,'' she threw over her shoulder.

Deftly Sinjin extracted his coat sleeve. ''Thank you, ma'am, but I mustn't tarry.'' He accepted the hat and gloves offered by the waiting butler. ''A very good day to you, Mrs. Cartwright, and my compliments to Miss Motrum.''

Silencing the lady's protests with his sternest colonel's look, Sinjin bowed once more and strode out the door, his spirits lightened by a wholly irrational sense of deliverance.

He should be downcast and ashamed, he chastised himself as he took a hackney back to North Audley Street. For the first time in memory, he'd failed to perform his duty.

Like the greenest cavalry officer caught up in the excitement of the charge, he'd overrun his lines and was now alone, without visible reinforcements, deep in dun territory. Given his failure and the perilous financial state it now left him in, there was no reason whatsoever for the sense of euphoria filling him.

Still, he had to chuckle at the neatness of his maneuver, irrational as it may have been. He'd managed to outflank Mrs. Cartwright's aspirations and bring Mr. Wickham's big gun to bear in a way that made the outcome of an engagement unavoidable.

Though Miss Motrum might initially be dismayed at losing her aristocratic suitor, he felt certain the lady herself would end up satisfied by the turn of events. He hoped so, since unlike a certain tempestuous woman he could mention, she had neither the spirit nor the resourcefulness to extract herself from the situation.

He amused himself another few moments considering how Miss Beaumont might have gotten round the incriminating circumstances. Clever and determined as she was, he had no doubt she'd have managed it somehow.

Ah, what a woman!

And then it hit him, like a lance blow from his flank he should have foreseen. He'd not been able to propose to Miss Motrum because he'd already made the only proposal his heart wanted. To Miss Beaumont.

The realization settled in, deep and satisfying as a well-executed attack, even as his head protested. Miss Beaumont possessed not a single trait he'd professed to seek in a wife. As he knew only too well, she was extravagant, impulsive, short-tempered, sharp-tongued, both ton and town-bred. They couldn't be in the same room for more than a few minutes without clashing.

Ah, but some of the battles…

For a moment the taste, touch and smell of her suffused him. Hunger for her, a need that encompassed soul as well as body, filled him.

He didn't want a willing widow. He craved the greedy, heart-stealing innocence of Miss Beaumont's passionate body. And the fierce, courageous spirit that inhabited it.

Had Sarah sensed how well they might deal together when she asked Clarissa help him find a bride? He braced himself for the grief that always cut at him when he thought of his lost love, but this time the pain was muted.

Find another love, and be happy, she'd advised him. Aye, sweet Sarah, so I shall, he promised.

Giddy, he laughed out loud. "I love you, Clarissa Beaumont," he whispered, and then said it again, louder. Lud, he wanted to shout it to the treetops.

His hunting instincts screamed at him to seek her out, now, this instant, to end what they'd begun in the garden and change her answer to his proposal.

However, he thought, grinning into the darkness of the

hackney, one small impediment remained. At the moment, the lady in question despised him.

Of course, he'd given her every reason, criticizing and insulting her practically from his first breath. But the fire that consumed him burned in her too, he was sure. For a delicious moment he relived the scene in the garden as she held his greedy lips against her bared breast.

A deeper connectedness linked them as well, one he'd sensed and fled from so many times over these past weeks. She felt that, too. He'd read it in her eyes.

She'd accused him of using seduction to gain her fortune. He wasn't above using it to win her heart.

Like it or not, Clarissa Beaumont, he swore to himself, you're going to end up marrying me.

But this time, unless he wished to foolishly mount a suicidal charge against defenses well fortified by anger, hurt, and outrage, he'd better plan his campaign carefully.

First, he must deliver the final salvo in the drawing room encounter by dispatching a box of Mr. Motrum's favorite cigars along with a note of gratitude—and a formal notice that he was withdrawing his suit. Mrs. Cartwright's ambitions notwithstanding, there'd be no further impediments to Mr. Wickam achieving his aims.

And then, he'd take on the battle for Miss Beaumont.

Chapter Nineteen

Leaning back in a wing chair in her sitting room, Clarissa contemplated the enormous bouquet Timms had just brought up, and smiled. The card from Lieutenant Standish that had accompanied it bore a single phrase, "thank you," written over and over across the entire surface.

Apparently the note from Lady Barbara she'd had Maddie deliver to him had done its work. Truly, she was happy for them. When she considered how affronted the Countess of Wetherford would be when she found herself outmaneuvered, her smile widened.

And then wobbled. She took a deep, painful breath. She wouldn't think of all the reasons she had not to smile.

Maddie, her soft brown hair shining under a crisp white cap and her gray uniform buttoned up to the chin, entered after a brief knock. "Yer horses be ready, Mistress."

"Thank you, Maddie. Tell Stebbins I'll be down directly," she told the girl, who was gazing at her with awe in her eyes. At least someone thought well of her.

Indeed, Maddie seemed to be always in the hallway when Clarissa passed, alert for any small service she might do, though running her mistress's errands was not part of a parlor maid's duties.

Not that the girl neglected her other chores—quite the contrary. To Clarissa's delight, Maddie worked so hard at whatever task the housekeeper set her to that within the week she'd turned Mrs. Woburn from unwilling sponsor to warm advocate. The housekeeper had praised her to Clarissa on several occasions, even adding a gruff apology for her initial reluctance to take the girl on.

Maddie's pretty face and slender figure hadn't gone unnoticed by the male staff either. Though now she shrank from any contact with men, Clarissa had reason to hope that perhaps in time, the happy future of courtship and marriage her brutal abduction had initially stolen from Maddie might become a reality after all.

Another success. Would that her part of the adventure could have had so happy an ending. Her momentarily buoyed spirits sank once more.

"Be there anything else, Mistress?"

She must rally herself out of the dismals into which she'd sunken when Colonel Sandiford stalked out of her parlor.

Oh, she'd mouthed brave words to herself at the time, but the truth was that same evening, faced with the prospect of dancing, smiling, and chatting her way through Lady Carleton's ball, she'd pleaded a headache—no invention, that—and stayed home. The next night, though she forced herself to attend Mrs. Wendfrow's musicale, she left directly after the music, waving off her hostess's plea that she stay for refreshments and card play. She'd skipped her normal at-home this afternoon, and now, although Alastair and Mountclare both expected her to drive her phaeton to the Park for the promenade hour, she couldn't bring herself to go.

She was still too distracted, she told herself. Driving a high-perch phaeton with a pair as spirited as hers required absolute concentration.

Missing so many social events was bound to cause talk, but just now she simply didn't care. Let them gossip. Only one person knew the reason for her sudden reticence, and despite her hateful words to the contrary, she knew the colonel would say nothing.

At the mere thought of him, her heart contracted painfully and tears stung her eyes.

Botheration! No, she would not hide herself away in her chamber and weep like some weak, spineless watering-pot. Clarissa Beaumont would wrap up the splintered pieces of her heart, hide them away, and present to the world a bold face.

"Mistress? Be ye all right?"

Maddie's concerned voice cut through her abstraction. She swiped the moisture from the corners of her eyes and straightened. "F-fine, Maddie, thank you."

She would go out, but not to parade among that simpering, posturing, gossiping gaggle of fashionables gathering at the park. As she recalled, the Mail Coach arrived about five.

"Maddie, tell Stebbins I'll not need the phaeton after all. Have Timms summon a hackney. And would you tell me how to get to the coaching inn where you were, um, taken?"

Maddie's face paled. "Oh, no, Mistress! I cannot go with ye there!"

"Calm yourself, Maddie. I've no intention of forcing you to return to a place that must bring back painful memories. I need the direction only—I'll take a footman."

Maddie ran over to throw herself at Clarissa's feet and

seize the hem of her gown. "Nay, Mistress, ye must not go! 'Tis much too dangerous."

"Nonsense. In a heavy cloak and bonnet, I'll look like any other traveler, and the footman will be standing by. I spoke with Mr. Beemis, the runner, two days ago, and you'll be happy to know he was able to forestall what he suspected was an attempt to entice a young girl from the Mail coach that arrived that afternoon. Mr. Beemis should be at the inn as well, so I shall be perfectly safe."

Maddie, her fingers still tugging Clarissa's hem, looked up, tear-filled eyes imploring. "Please, please, Mistress, ye must not go!"

In spite of herself, Clarissa was touched. She had a house full of servants, a wide circle of friends, but who other than Sarah—and this damaged girl—had ever seemed to care for her welfare?

She bent down and gently pulled Maddie to her feet. "You mustn't worry. I won't be all alone, as you were, and I know what's about. I will be fine."

"Ye cannot know..." Maddie shuddered, clutching Clarissa's fingers.

A sharp memory returned—rough hands holding her close, foul breath panting into her face.

"I know more than you may think," she said softly. And pulled her fingers free. "Now, go have Timms summon that hackney. If I arrive too late, the runner will have already gone and I won't be able to consult with him."

Maddie looked as if she'd like to protest further, but after a moment, she curtsied. "As you wish, Mistress."

After the girl left, Clarissa rummaged in her wardrobe for her thickest, plainest cloak and a bonnet that fully covered her flaming hair. Not that she expected to meet anyone she knew in so unfashionable a locale, but best to appear as unobtrusive as possible. Some might call her reckless, she thought, lifting her chin, but she wasn't such a looby that she thought to take a hand in the business herself, nor did she wish to upset any plans Mr. Beemis might have. She just wanted to see for herself the machinery she had set in motion.

Whistling, Sinjin sprinted up the stairs into White's, a spring in his step. He'd order some celebratory wine, contemplate his plans for the subjugation of Miss Beaumont, and hope to find Hal Waterman and Englemere. After all they had done on his behalf, he wanted them to learn straightaway of the wreckage of their initial plans and from him, rather than from a possibly displeased Mr. Motrum or some other source.

He was therefore happy to discover Hal sitting alone in the card room, flipping cards over in a desultory manner, an expression of infinite boredom on his face.

Hal brightened immediately when he saw Sinjin approach. "Join me!" the big man invited. "Cards dashed dull," he added as Sinjin brought up a chair. "Nothing for it. Reception." He rolled his eyes and shuddered.

Sinjin stared at Hal thoughtfully for a moment, trying to knit together the pieces. "Your mama is entertaining?" he hazarded as last.

Hal nodded. "Cronies…daughters…marriages. Had to escape."

Sinjin considered this new information. "Your mama and her friends are discussing the possible nuptials of their daughters?"

"Dreadful business," he pronounced, then took a long swallow from his wineglass. "Poor men."

Intrigued despite himself, Sinjin asked, "Who?"

"Dunno yet. Still planning."

The waiter arrived with Sinjin's champagne and a pair of glasses. Hal said nothing as the man uncorked the vintage and poured out two frothing glasses. Once the waiter had departed, he raised his glass to Sinjin.

"Wish you happy?"

"Not exactly, though I'm certainly exalted at the moment. You and Englemere may be less than happy after I confess that I...well, I just couldn't bring myself to propose. In any event, unless I miss my guess Mr. Motrum's assistant Mr. Wickham is about to do so."

Hal nodded sagely. "Good choice."

Not sure whether his friend meant Mr. Wickham's boldness or his own reticence, Sinjin felt moved to add, "You must not think I do not value all the efforts you and Englemere expended on my behalf. I'm fully cognizant—"

Hal waved him to silence. "Happy to help. Think naught of it."

Sinjin chose to believe Hal meant not to worry over his inability to claim the heiress. For a moment, the two drank in companionable silence.

Then something seemed to strike Hal, for he straightened and looked directly at Sinjin. "Not Miss Motrum." He lifted his glass to toast. "Why champagne?"

Sinjin chuckled. "Deliverance from an unwanted fate. And," he swirled the bubbly wine in his own glass, "hope for the future."

Hal studied his face for a long moment, then grinned. "Another lady. Congratulations! Declared yet?"

"Is it declarations we're celebrating?" Englemere asked as he walked over to join them. "By all means, pour me a glass!"

"Not Miss Motrum," Hal inserted helpfully.

Englemere raised his eyebrows. "Not Miss Motrum? Now that's a surprise. Who, then?"

Sinjin flushed. "As I told Hal—"

Mr. Waterman waved him to silence. "Nicky's fair. Had your choice. Didn't choose her. No harm done."

"It's a bit more complex than that," Sinjin said. "I fully intended—"

Englemere, too, made a deprecating gesture. "No need to explain, Colonel. We made the introductions only. Whether the matter progressed further was always entirely between you and Miss Motrum." He paused to take a sip. "Which brings me back to my first question. What declaration are we toasting?"

Sinjin felt his flush deepen. "In view of my earlier preferences, I imagine you will find this rather surprising, but actually I've determined to wed a lady of the ton after all."

Englemere raised his class in tribute. "I always felt that would be a more comfortable choice. Who is the lady?"

Such a radical turnabout might make him appear the idiot, but he could never be embarrassed about his choice. "Clarissa Beaumont," he said proudly.

Englemere froze, his glass halfway to his lips, and Hal choked on his wine. For a moment neither man uttered a word. Then Englemere burst out laughing.

"Clare? By heaven, Colonel, she'll lead you a merry dance!"

Sinjin grinned at him. "I fear you're entirely correct. Nonetheless, I'll have her and no other."

"You've already offered for her, then?"

Sinjin thought of the stilted two-sentence proposal he'd uttered and the quite predictable response. "N-not exactly. I've made some...tentative moves, which I have to confess did not meet with entire success." An understatement, that. "But I have hopes of a happy outcome in the near future."

Hal poured himself another glass, raised it at Sinjin and downed it in one gulp. "Brave man," he said.

"Nonsense," Englemere said. "Hal finds Clare a bit...spirited for his taste, but I heartily approve your choice. I've known the young lady for some years and have watched her grow from a striking but somewhat shallow girl to an intelligent, resourceful, dynamic woman. I wish you both very happy."

Delighted to have reached an understanding with the two men who'd been so instrumental in helping find a way out of his financial difficulties, Sinjin poured another glass all around. As they were about to drink, Alex Standish walked in, a beaming smile on his face.

"Ah, Colonel, you've broken out the champagne! You must have heard the news!"

Sinjin poured him a glass and handed it to him with a quizzical look. "What news is that?"

"Lady Barbara has accepted my hand. I spoke with her father this morning, so it's official. Gentleman, you see before you the happiest man on earth!"

Of course, this announcement required the ordering of additional champagne. While the friends were pouring another celebratory round, a waiter approached Alex.

"Lieutenant Standish, there's a young...person outside with a message for you which be accounted most urgent."

The lieutenant looked up, startled. "Urgent? Send him up at once, man."

"Beggin' your pardon, Lieutenant, but I cannot do that. Club rules. The young person is a female."

Alex's face paled. "A lady?"

"No sir, a servant girl, I'd say."

Frowning, Alex set down his glass. "If you gentlemen will excuse me, I think I'd best go outside."

Hal rose too. "Go with you," he offered. "Help."

Had it been anyone else, Sinjin thought, his lieutenant might have stiffened with affront at the insinuation he might not be capable of handling whatever situation had arisen. But with Hal, it was impossible to take offense.

"Sounds havey-cavey," Englemere agreed. "Shall we all go?"

A few moments later, all four men exited the rear stairs to find a young girl in a gray housemaid's uniform waiting by the gate, a stout footman standing guard nearby. As soon as Alex, limping on his weak leg, made it to the bottom of the steps, she rushed over to seize his arm.

"Please, Lieutenant, ye must come at once." Her eyes were red from weeping and fresh tears sheened their surface. "It's the M-Mistress!"

"What is it, Maddie? What's happened?"

"Oh, sir, I begged her not to go, but she wouldn't listen! Now she's been gone since afore five, and the footman too, and ain't nobody seen 'em since, with it goin' on seven. Please, ye must go to the inn!"

Clarissa struggled to open her heavy eyelids. A glimmer of light pierced the gloom, threatening to make her queasy stomach revolt, and she hastily closed them again. Her pulse unsteady, she took long careful breaths in the darkness, waiting for her stomach to calm, trying to determine where she was and remember what happened.

She'd taken a hackney. To the coaching inn. Maddie had watched her depart. Though the inn bustled with travelers, customers at their dinner, and locals raising a pint of home-brewed, she spied the runner straightaway.

He'd frowned when she nodded to him, obviously not happy to have her there, though she slipped at once to a side table where, in the midst of so busy a crowd, she didn't see how her presence could interrupt his work. Then in the corner she spied the dark-haired woman who'd claimed Maddie as her runaway apprentice.

She'd hunched in her chair, pulled her collar higher, and sipped tea brought her by a scowling barmaid, grateful for its warmth and her footman on watch nearby. The woman circled to a girl with wide, frightened eyes who'd just entered the inn, a large basket bound up with rope in her hands. Spoke with the girl, patted her shoulder.

Clarissa had tensed, waiting. Surely the runner would make his move. But then the scene started to go hazy, dizziness stole over her. The last thing she remembered was her head hitting the hard wooden table…

She opened her eyes wide, wincing at the light. Someone must have drugged her tea!

As quickly as she could given the queasiness in her gut, she looked around her. She lay on a narrow wooden bed with a lumpy straw mattress covered by an ancient, dusty coverlet. Mercifully she still wore her own garments, though her cloak and bonnet were nowhere to be seen in the small, bare room whose only other furnishings were a table topped by a washbowl and a chipped pitcher.

Somehow she'd always imagined a brothel would be gaudier.

Before that useless and hysterical thought popped out of mind, the door opened and a short, slim man dressed in the first style of elegance walked in.

"My, what a prize the bauds have brought me tonight," Lord John Weston drawled. "Miss Clarissa Beaumont."

She sat up straight, the hair on the back of her neck bristling. "L-Lord John?"

He made her a bow. "Kind—if unexpected—of you to drop by my humble establishment. When Maisie told me some fancy woman had stolen away one of her girls, I thought she was simply telling me a Banbury tale to excuse her own incompetence. So it was true."

Somehow, seeing Lord John here instead of some unknown villain calmed her. Lord John she could deal with.

"Where is my footman and the runner?" she demanded in as imperious a tone as she could command.

He laughed. "Still playing the high-and-mighty Miss Beaumont, Diamond of the Ton?" He swept her with a glance from head to toe. "You'll soon find out, my aristocratic beauty, that I rule here."

"You cannot think to hold me. My household knows where I went. If I do not return promptly, they will mount a hue and cry, which will eventually lead them here. Surely you cannot want that."

He shrugged. "An inconvenience to Maisie, perhaps. I shall merely accelerate the plans already in motion. Adding your loveliness to the fortune I'll carry with me, ah, that makes the game even better."

He walked over to the bed and reached out his hand.

"Don't you dare touch me."

He held his hand motionless, a bare inch from her face. "Oh, I shall touch you. In every conceivable way I shall touch you, whether you desire it or no. You've taunted, teased, rejected me for years. You're in my power now, and the reckoning will be all the sweeter."

"You would be much wiser to let me go." If she could keep him talking, she might be able to get past him to the door.

"A fine one to prate of wisdom you are, my sweet.

But who am I to complain of the foolish, passionate nature that brought you to me? Not when I will soon savor the taste of it myself.''

She stood up, hoping despite her disheveled gown to act the picture of dignified hauteur. ''Nonetheless, if you hold me against my will, you'll pay an even higher price. Abducting a powerless country lass is one thing. Attempting to abduct a member of the aristocracy is sheer lunacy.'' She edged toward the door.

''Transportation at the least, if not the hangman,'' he agreed, and then grabbed her shoulder. ''Which is why you're going nowhere—just now. Tomorrow morning, very early, we'll leave together. I've a hankering to see the exotic lands of the far east, where I've done... business.''

Remembering Englemere's words, she could well imagine what sort of business it had been. But he was a coward, and all bluster. Surely he wouldn't dare kidnap her! ''I wouldn't cross the street with you.''

She struggled to break his grip, but he held on, surprisingly strong. Sick fear coiling in her stomach, she whirled suddenly to throw a punch at him.

The blow struck off-center, and while he reeled from it, he did not go down. She scrambled to the door, wrenched the knob.

He reached her before she could open it, grabbed her and jerked her to face him. With the back of one hand he dealt her a stunning blow, then dragged her to the bed.

''So you like it rough?'' he panted as he forced her back. ''Happy to oblige, when I come back to take you.''

Despite her fear, disgust rolled through her. She'd die before she submitted to this miserable muckworm.

''You'd better bring pistol and knife, for I'll never submit to you any other way.''

"That can be arranged," he snarled, his hot breath scorching her face. "Or perhaps I'll bring back several of the hearty gentlemen we employ to guard our noble portals. Large, unwashed, rather rough types they are, and generally not fussy in their requirements. Two of them holding you down should do it. Such a show you'll provide them while I take you. Think of it, Clarissa, their crude hard members stiffening as they watch me strip you, plunge into your maidenhead. I might even let them have a go, once I'm finished."

"You are despicable."

He laughed. "You've not even begun to discover." Before she could flinch away, he touched her jaw where a throbbing bruise had already begun to form. "Remember my little love tap. I'll be back, very soon, my sweet angel, to finish what I started. And don't bother wondering if you can escape my hospitality. The door will be locked, the windows are barred, and even were they not, this room is three floors up."

He walked to the door, then turned to stare at her, his insolent gaze raking her from slippers to forehead. "You belong to me now, Clarissa, without hope of escape. Think about it. I certainly shall." He slipped out the door, and she heard the bolt slide in place.

Fear and fury held her motionless for a moment, but then she leapt from the chair and ran to the door. Unlike the other flimsily-made objects in the room, it was constructed of solid oaken planks, its hardware of iron that didn't budge when she rattled the handle. Pressing her ear to the rough surface, she could hear only the shuffle of feet, a groan about whose origin she preferred not to speculate, and distant, raucous laughter.

If this house were indeed owned by Sir John, no one within its walls would dare help her anyway.

Heart pounding, she scurried to the window, which was barred as he'd described. Peering out between the wooden slats, in the darkness she could just barely make out the street far below.

She sank to her knees, hands on the window frame, fear accelerating to terror in her heart. How could she have been so stupidly naive? Hadn't Englemere warned an operation as complex as the one that had captured Maddie would be well-funded and well-run?

At least some of the posting inn's employees, if not the owner himself, must be part of the ring, must have seen her nod to the runner when she first came in. Or the black-haired woman remembered her from the night in Covent Garden. How one disaster had led to another.

The bawd must have sent over the drugged tea. But what had happened to the runner and her footman?

For her to have been taken, the perpetrators must have incapacitated those two men first. She felt the sting of remorse through her fear. Bad enough that her impulsive, ill-thought-out escapade had landed her in peril. What havoc had she brought into the lives of James and Mr. Beevis with her well-meant but disastrously naive intervention?

And was she now to suffer the same fate as Maddie— or worse? Drugged or beaten into submission for Sir John's pleasure, taken abroad to use until he tired of her and then sold to some potentate's brothel?

Tears blurred her eyes and her heart raced so fast she thought she would faint. She gripped the windowsill until her nails bit into the wood.

Enough. Her reckless, thoughtless, stupid behavior had landed her here, but Clarissa Beaumont would not succumb without a fight. There had to be some way out.

Sir John wouldn't return for a while—clearly he

wanted to give her time to worry over her fate—but she couldn't count on his absenting himself for too long. And though there was a slim chance she might be able to break free from a man of his slight build, he'd promised to bring back reinforcements.

Panic rippled up from deep within her and shuddered through her entire body. What would happen then didn't bear thinking of.

Act now. Hurry. She took a gasping breath, grabbed the edge of a window barrier and willed her mind to focus as she pulled herself up off the floor. The slats barring the glass weren't nearly as solid as the oaken planks of the door. Could she find something to pry the boards loose, or something hard with which to smash through them, the window would break. The opening was rather narrow, but she was reasonably sure she could fit through it.

She peered once more out of the narrow gaps toward the street far below. She couldn't jump from this height without killing herself, or breaking a leg at least. Once she got the window cleared she'd need a rope.

She whirled around, searching for any object in the meagerly furnished room that might be of use.

Sprinting to the bed, she ran her fingers under the mattress. As she expected, a rope lattice supported the thin straw pallet. She yanked the mattress aside.

The rope appeared sturdy. She need only unknot it from the frame and tie the individual cords together.

But what to free the window?

She jumped to the table, but though rickety, its legs and top were too thick to be of use prying loose the slats. The only remaining objects in the room were the sad-looking coverlet and the washbasin.

She grabbed the bowl, wrapped it in the coverlet and

tossed it to the floor, where it shattered with a muffled crash. Scratching aside the material, she seized the flat bottom piece and smashed the remaining side sections away, then scrambled to her feet and went to attack the window slats.

Sweat making her fingers slippery, she cut her palm against the ragged edge of the bowl as she tried to force the broken pottery piece between the slat and the window. At first it seemed the shard was too thick, that she'd never be able to fit it into the space, and she cursed, wishing she'd thought to conceal something—a small knife, a nail file—somewhere on her person. Finally, blood from her palm mingling with pottery dust and the tears of frustration dripping off her cheeks, she succeeded in prying up one corner of the board.

After that, the work went more quickly. Once she'd freed the first slat she used that as a lever to free the rest. Then to the bed, to unknot rope with fingers made clumsy by desperation, and then swiftly knot the free pieces together.

How much time had elapsed? Twenty minutes? An hour? She had no idea, knew only a driving imperative to get out of the room as soon as possible. Once Sir John came back, she was lost.

She ran to the window, set down her coiled rope. She'd need something to anchor it on. Looking around wildly, she chose the bedstead and ran back to drag it close to the window. Even should her weight pull it downward, it was too large to fit through the window frame.

As a clock in her head ticked away the precious minutes, she stationed her rope, grabbed the pitcher off the table and peered through the dirty glass into the street below. As soon as there was enough activity there to mask the sound of breaking glass, she would strike.

Nerves stretched to the breaking point, she was almost ready to jump regardless when the dim sounds of a scuffle on the street below caught her ear. Peering out, she could see people gathering near the main road on which the house stood. Taking a deep breath, she smashed the pitcher through the window.

Chapter Twenty

In the flickering torchlight of White's back entrance, Englemere stepped closer and gave the servant girl a swift inspection. "Are you the young lady Miss Beaumont rescued?"

Sinjin, who had been standing by listening with polite interest, felt a shock jolt through him. "What has Clarissa to do with this?"

He advanced on the girl, who shrank away from him toward the footman.

"Colonel, please," Alex cautioned, moving between him and the cowering Maddie. "Are you saying that Miss Beaumont went to the coaching inn where you were abducted?"

A second shock hummed through Sinjin's nerves. "Abducted?" he almost shouted.

Englemere moved closer to the girl. "Don't be frightened, Maddie. My wife is your mistress's closest friend, and these other gentlemen are her friends too. It may be essential for Miss Beaumont's safety that you tell us everything you know, as quickly as possible."

Maddie looked over at Lieutenant Standish, who gave her an encouraging nod. "Like I told the lieutenant, Mistress said as how she'd go to the inn and talk with that Bow Street feller what was watching out fer Maisie. Done stopped her once from takin' a girl already, Mistress said. She said she weren't goin' ta do nobbit but watch, but ah, sir, she don't know these people! And now she be gone near on two hours, and I was so afeared, I had to come look fer ye. Ye must go help her, please sir!''

"Where is the inn?" Sinjin demanded. "Take us there."

Maddie's eyes widened and a single tear streaked down her cheek. "Don't worry none, Maddie," said the footman waiting beside her. "I'll be with ye, and I won't let nobody touch ye."

"I know this is difficult, but we need your help, Maddie. Will you do this, for your Mistress's sake?"

The girl took a deep, shuddering breath. "Aye."

To travel more discreetly they summoned a hackney, and during the drive Alex and Englemere related the circumstances of Maddie's rescue. Cursing Clarissa for her foolhardiness, under his breath for Maddie's sake, Sinjin nevertheless had to admit her stubborn courage.

Surely they would find her, either already safely back home or at the inn, conferring with the runner. After all, people of quality did not simply disappear, like street corner vagrants. But even as he assured himself that all would soon be well, a nameless terror ate at his gut.

When they found her, he was going to shake her until her teeth rattled.

After halting in Grosvenor Square to determine Clarissa was still missing and at Curzon Street to pick up several sets of pistols, they sprung the horses and headed south. Arriving soon thereafter at the inn, they found in the dining room only a handful of passengers awaiting the next day's mail coach and a gathering of local boys raising a convivial pint. Neither the barkeep nor any of the serving maids professed to know anything of a woman fitting Clarissa's description, the servant attending her, or a small mustachioed man from Bow Street.

Hal and Lieutenant Standish were all for hauling the innkeeper into the back alley and offering a bit more persuasion, but urging restraint, Englemere herded them back into the hackney where Maddie and her footman waited.

"Not unexpected that they'd deny all knowledge," Englemere reasoned. "The bauds couldn't be working from here without complicity on the part of someone at the inn. Quite probably whoever is backing the whole enterprise has the inn's employee on the payroll as well."

"Very true," Sinjin agreed. "Which means we can't afford to waste time, when at this moment they are probably already sending word through their network that someone is searching for Clare. We must find her and the others as soon as possible." He turned to Maddie. "Please, do us one more favor. Lead us to the brothel where they took you."

Maddie choked on a sob. "Oh, sir, I cannot! I...I dunno how to get there. I was drugged when they took me."

"Can you find it from Covent Garden Square?" Lieutenant Standish interposed. "The place where we met you that night?"

Tears dripped down the girl's face. "I dunno, sir! When I got away, I ran and ran. I dunno if I could find my way back or not."

"Lieutenant Standish will help you, Maddie," Sinjin said, keeping his voice gentle. "You can do it. I know you can."

Maddie glanced at Alex, who nodded encouragement. She took a shuddering breath. ''I'll surely try.''

Once more they set the carriage at a reckless pace. Trying to stave off the nightmarish visions the notion of Clarissa's capture propelled to his brain, Sinjin forced himself to occupy the transit by discussing how best to infiltrate the brothel once they found it. Bowing to his superior military knowledge—and perhaps understanding he must do something or go mad, Englemere and the others fell in with Sinjin's plans for the assault.

It took two false starts, by which time Sinjin was ready to roar in frenzied frustration, but finally they were able to locate the baud's establishment.

During six long years of war, Sinjin had lost count of the number of battles in which he'd fought. He'd spent countless nights huddled on rocky ground, trying to snatch a fitful sleep despite the uncertainty of the carnage to come. Never before a battle had fear shredded his nerves like it did this night, contemplating the awful reality that the woman he'd finally come to realize he loved was held captive somewhere, perhaps beaten, raped or…he couldn't allow himself to think of worse.

Halting the carriage several streets away, they left the footman to guard Maddie and approached quietly on foot. Now at last, Sinjin could turn his anguish into action.

''When we reach the door, Alex distract the guard, and Hal take him out. Englemere, follow me inside. Watch out for any other guards, and shoot anyone who resists. I'll continue straight through the building and then rejoin you in the front. Everyone ready?''

Pistols cocked, they approached on silent feet. A heavyset man stepped aside from the doorway to allow one obviously inebriated man to leave. At a nod from Sinjin, Alex raised a shout. When the guard turned toward him, Hal barreled into him, the full weight of his massive body slamming the man into the wall. Sinjin, trailed by Englemere, ran past and into the house.

Racing back from the kitchens, where he'd discovered nothing more threatening than a cowering cook and several scantily-clad women, Sinjin skidded to a halt in the main parlor. To his astonishment, along with more weeping, half-naked women, Hal stood guard over Lord John Weston.

Sinjin turned to Englemere and jerked a thumb at Weston. "Customer?"

Englemere shook his head. "Found him in the back office with the charming proprietor, Miss Maisie. If my suppositions are correct, Lord John is the owner of this establishment and the director of the whole operation. In fact, with the lovely Maisie's cooperation, I'm confident he'll soon be leaving his native shores for a long residence at Botany Bay."

Hal grunted and backed Sir John, his nose bleeding and his face cut, against the fireplace wall and held him there with a contemptuous glare, as if daring the man to reach for the poker so Hal would have an excuse to finish him.

"He'll need a send-off before we deport 'em." Hal reached out and rubbed one huge fist under Lord John's already damaged chin. "Call it…a thank you from all those poor girls."

"Later, Hal." Sinjin sprinted to the cornered man. Fear and defiance still mingled in his eyes.

"I should have smashed you the first night we met, you miserable worm," Sinjin said through clenched teeth. "Where is she?"

"Sweeter than I ever expected, she was," Lord John gasped, struggling in Hal's grip but still defiant. "You should have seen her open her legs to—'' Whatever else he meant to say was lost in the crash of Sinjin's fist.

''Manage here,'' Sinjin snapped to his compatriots. ''I'll find Clarissa.''

He spun on his heel and ran. As his boots pounded up the steps, a harrowing memory recurred of mounting the stairs in a much richer mansion, racing down a hallway three years ago to find the woman he loved unconscious, brutalized by another such villain.

Blood lust hotter than any that had ever seized him in battle blurred his vision. If that swine Lord John had harmed her in any way, there'd be no deportation, no hanging. Sinjin would kill him where he stood.

And if, please merciful God, Sinjin found her unharmed, he would strangle Clarissa for putting him through this.

Methodically, floor by floor, he ran down hallways, jerked open doors. Though he surprised several couples in delicate embrace, he did not find his lady.

Finally, fear swelling his throat so that it was hard to breathe, he reached the narrow, short-ceilinged top floor. Only four doors opened on the hallway, one of which was bolted. He went immediately to that one.

''Clarissa!'' he yelled. ''Clare, it's Colonel Sandiford—Sinjin. Are you in there?''

He waited a second, hearing nothing but the echo of his shout. Then bracing himself, he shot out the lock. Although the explosion brought a round of shrieks from the floors below, from behind the door he heard only silence.

Kicking it open, he ran into the room, and his heart nearly stopped. It looked as if a desperate struggle had taken place. The single bed in the room had been nearly dismantled, its straw mattress flung to the floor, the rope supports themselves destroyed, and the bed frame pushed up against the narrow window nearly bare of glass. Wooden planks lay scattered about amid the shreds of a tattered coverlet and shards of glass and broken crockery.

And then he saw, tied in a crude knot to one bedpost, a ragged rope that led from the bed out the window.

His heart commenced to beat again and hope soared aloft, lifting his lips in a fierce smile.

Damn and blast, but she was magnificent.

The window was almost too narrow to accommodate his shoulders, and he had to use strip rags from the coverlet to protect himself from the jagged edges of the broken glass, but he managed to push himself out. The rope ended a full eight feet above the ground. Sinjin's fear rebounded. Had she managed the drop without injury? If so, where had she fled?

"Clare!" he yelled as he descended the rope, leapt lightly to the ground. "Clare, where are you? It's Sinjin! Come out, love, you are safe now!"

This side alley had no streetlights. Peering into the gloom, he could see several smaller alleyways leading off it. There was no sign of Clarissa.

Hearing his shouts, several members of the small crowd gathered at the entrance of Maisie's shuffled closer, but he ignored them. He was about to set off exploring the first alleyway when a shaky voice called out.

"S-Sinjin? Is it you?"

From behind a pile of reeking rubbish bins a figure straightened and walked out with clumsy steps. Shoving his pistol back into his belt, he ran toward her.

Gown bedraggled and sooty, half her hair pulled from its pins, and smelling faintly of garbage, Clarissa Beaumont threw her arms around his neck.

Lifting her up, he carried her to the carriage where

Maddie and the footman waited. After racing inside to tell Englemere and the others he'd found her and would convey the ladies home immediately, he leapt back in the jarvey and ordered the driver to take them to Grosvenor Square.

He found Maddie weeping over her mistress's bloody, rope-burned, lacerated palms and face while Clarissa tried to reassure the girl her injuries were minor and would quickly heal. In spite of all the horrors she must have suffered this night, she was still the one giving comfort.

His heart swelled with love and pride. Still, she had much to answer for.

"Let me see your hands," Sinjin ordered.

For a moment she resisted, but at last she held them out for his inspection. "Worse than last time," she said gruffly, a wobble in her voice.

He wanted to rage at her for scaring him to death, then seize her in his arms and kiss her senseless, but the presence of an audience deterred him. Best to get rid of it as speedily as possible. And implement his newest plan.

"Definitely worse than last time," he agree. "These cuts will need tending. We'll drop your staff at Grosvenor Square, that they may assure everyone you are well, then proceed for some nursing."

"Like before?"

Not exactly, but she didn't need to know that yet. He'd done enough fighting for one night. "Like before."

Except for patting Maddie and whispering soothing words, she remained silent the rest of their journey. At Grosvenor Square he hopped out to escort Maddie and the footman inside, then spoke quietly to the driver before climbing back into the jarvey. Once freed of the necessity of making a show of cheerfulness, Clarissa had slumped back in her seat, looking exhausted.

He let her rest in silence, hoping she might fall asleep, which would make this next phase easier, but evidently—and with good cause—too shaken for that, she remained silent but awake until the carriage slowed once more.

He leaned to lift her in his arms, but she pushed him away. "I can walk."

"I'm sure. But your appearance is…somewhat alarming. The state of your garments would be less noticeable if I carry you in, claiming you felt faint."

She must truly be exhausted, for she gave him no further argument, allowing him to exit the carriage and then reach back to lift her in his arms.

Since she'd leaned against his chest, sighing, and closed her eyes, he was able to make it halfway up the steps to his rooms before her eyes opened with a snap. "This isn't Sarah's house. Where are we?" she demanded.

"Englemere was with me looking for you. There's no one to fetch Becky without alarming Sarah, so I thought it better to bring you back to my rooms." When she stiffened as if in alarm, he quickly added, "I'm quite a competent doctor, I assure you. Once Englemere reaches home and sends me word, I'll convey you to Sarah's."

And so he would—much later. And hopefully after he had the answer he wanted.

But she'd been through a harrowing evening, and seduction would have to wait until her wounds, both physical and mental, had been tended.

He deposited her on the sofa in his sitting room and had his batman, who raised his eyebrows but said nothing further, bring clean water, unguent, bandages and brandy.

While he tended her cuts, he encouraged her to sip the warming spirits and tell him what had transpired.

With obvious reluctance she related the story, attributing full blame to herself for her recklessness and lack of foresight. Several times he had to grit his teeth to keep from crying out his rage, and when she related Lord John Weston's plans for her, he could not restrain an oath. He would see the bastard hung for this.

Not until he assured her Englemere had discovered the runner and her footman, bound but otherwise unharmed, did she relax.

"Should you like to bathe?" he asked, once her hands had been cleaned and her glass drained.

Her eyes, which had been drooping, snapped open. "Here? Now?"

He nodded. "There's no telling what time Englemere will return. He and Hal must settle the prisoners with the magistrates, tend to the runner and your footman, and settle the, ah, ladies somewhere. I'm sure you cannot be comfortable in that gown."

She shuddered. "I shall burn it. But to bathe here? It's quite improper, as you well know. Indeed, I shouldn't even be here."

"Given the activities of this evening, it's a bit late to worry about propriety, don't you think?"

She sighed. "I should love a bath. But what shall I put on after?"

"I'll lend you a robe," he replied, trying to keep his tone nonchalant and brotherly, while entirely unsibling-like excitement shimmered up his nerves and pooled in the pit of his stomach.

Amazingly, she didn't balk at that.

"I'll bring you a blanket. Rest a bit while I have Jeffers prepare the bath."

He hastened to have a now thoroughly disapproving Jeffers drag the hip bath before the fire and fill it with hot water. When all was in readiness, he woke her.

"I'll leave you to it. If you require anything, call."

It was all he could do to walk from the room, his senses swimming with the image of her naked body submerged in hot, soft scented water. But soon—soon, he promised himself.

After what seemed an hour of impatient pacing, he finally heard the call he'd been awaiting. "Colonel. I...I can't seem to reach the towel. Would you be so good as to place it closer?"

He wiped his sweating palms on his trousers. Having her remain here for the night would be enough. She'd just been through a wrenching, traumatic experience that would have reduced most women to screaming hysterics. Without question, this was not the night for seduction. He would wrap her in the towel and leave.

Stand an arm's length away and wrap her soft, warm, naked body in a towel...and then leave without touching her?

He took a ragged breath. He could do it. When at last they lay joined, it would be at a moment they both fully desired. He would not seduce her into marriage when she was weakened and distraught.

Another night, he vowed. Soon.

Disappointment coursed through his body even as he acknowledged the rightness of the decision. Steeling himself to the torture of it, he walked into the room, picked up the towel in shaking hands and brought it to her. Beneath the suds he caught tantalizing glimpses of a flat belly and rounded hips, while two soft, full globes floated just below the surface of the water.

With a groan he averted his eyes. "The towel," he

gasped, words nearly sticking to the dust-dry roof of his mouth.

"I'm a little unsteady," she said, her words wobbling in truth. "I fear I must hold on to something in order to stand up. Would you lend me a shoulder, and then wrap the towel around me, please?"

Why hadn't he sent for her maid before beginning this torture? "Y-yes, of course." He gulped in a breath, clutched the towel in nerveless fingers and stepped closer. "I'll close my eyes."

She smiled. "Certainly." And placed one passion-damp hand on his shoulder.

As she stood up, he slammed his eyes shut...except for one teeny, tiny peek, which under the circumstances must surely be justified.

Botticelli's Venus, arising from the bath. So perfect, so flawlessly perfect was she that he forgot about closing his eyes altogether, staring down in openmouthed wonder at the smooth curve from neck to back to buttocks, the long, long, slender legs. Reverently he wrapped the towel about her shoulders.

He stepped back and saw a rosy glow on her cheeks before belatedly snapping his eyes shut.

"You weren't supposed to look." Her tone was reproachful.

"I didn't."

"Liar."

"Well, only a glimpse."

Bare naked hand still on his shoulder, she shivered.

"Colonel, I fear I'm beginning to suffer a...delayed reaction from my unspeakable experience today."

"Quite understandable."

"You were so comforting before. Do you think you could...hold me as you did then?"

"Now?" With only the thin barrier of a towel between her luscious body and his ravenous manhood?

"Now. Please."

He swallowed hard. Of course he could do it. Small wonder she wanted comfort, and as a gentleman, he would give it to her. Even if it killed him.

Slowly he pulled her against him. But instead of keeping the towel wrapped about her, at the last moment she pulled it back so that he clasped against him only warm, damp skin.

The feel of her burned into his body—heavy round globe of breasts, slight swell of stomach, smooth length of thighs. He forgot how to breathe, and his brain was surely melting.

"Colonel." Her voice, whisper-soft as a breath over bare skin.

"Y-yes?" he responded, amazed he was still capable of speech.

Dropping the towel altogether, Clarissa pulled his head down to meet her lips.

The only thought remaining in the steamy puddle of his brain was that, brilliantly passionate though she be, this gallant woman who would be his wife was still a virgin, and must be taken gently.

Butterfly kisses, light, soft, he placed on her lips as he carried and laid her gently on the bed. But an urgency shimmering in her heated skin, she pulled him down beside her, tongue delving into his mouth, hands pulling at his waistcoat, his shirt, until she'd freed it from his trousers. Dispensing with buttons, she merely slid one hand under the material, tugging it loose, and then brought her fingers up in a slow spiral across his chest until they found the tight nub of a nipple.

He groaned into her mouth, his tongue now seeking to

master hers, advancing and retreating in cadence to mimic the motion he would teach her body. She wrapped one leg around him, pulling his torso closer, until the hardness of his erection throbbed against her thigh.

She moved her hand down to touch him, and his muscles clenched as he fought to retain control.

She broke the kiss and looked at him, her damp dishevelled hair a flaming cloud across the pillows. "I want all of you. Now. Please."

He moved her hand to his trouser buttons, helped her to one by one free the straining cloth. He savored for a moment the erotic feel of her fingers on his bare flesh, but she was right. This partial, hidden groping wasn't enough.

He rolled away from her to the side of the bed, shucked off his boots and stripped down his breeches. She moved to sit behind him, one hand caressing his chest as he struggled with the buttons of his shirt and waistcoat, the other continuing to explore the long, hard length of him from shaft to smooth, pulsing tip.

He flung the garments aside and pushed her back against the pillows. "Now you," he growled.

Her kiss-reddened mouth faintly smiling, she watched as, beginning with her toes, he ran the slightly calloused smoothness of his fingers over her skin. When he reached her knees, parting them with methodical hands, her lips parted too, her eyes gone glassy and her breath coming in shortened gasps.

"Better," he murmured, and bent his head to apply his lips and tongue to the smooth skin of her inner thighs.

Her hands, damp now, clutched at his shoulders while he used one hand of his own to cup and caress her breasts. Nipping, sucking, laving, he slowly advanced up her thighs, toward the heat and scent of her that cried out her readiness.

With an inarticulate sob she protested his hand abandoning her breast, but she was a virgin, and he must prepare her. When he moved his fingers into her warm, damp passage she cried out and arched into him.

"Better, better still, sweetheart," he encouraged. Easing into her tightness, he accustomed her to the feel and touch of possession. Then, still working his fingers in ancient rhythm, he moved his lips to possess the tight bud hidden above.

She convulsed then, every muscle going rigid as she sobbed out his name, her cries resonating deep into his soul.

His beautiful, passionate vixen. He'd give her a lifetime of such moments.

When she lay limp, he moved back beside her, rolling her slack figure into his arms. While her breathing steadied and slowed he kissed her neck, her shoulders, murmuring inarticulate love words.

At last her brilliant eyes opened and looked at him, slightly dazed, astonished. Strong emotion he dare not put a name to swam in her eyes. "Ah, Colonel."

He kissed her. "A moment ago you called me Sinjin."

"I didn't know...I never suspected." She sighed rapturously. "No wonder a maiden is always surrounded by chaperones. If she were ever to learn...that...existed, the world would contain naught but wantons."

He chuckled. "Perhaps it's not like this for every woman."

"No? Ah, what a tragedy!" She shifted, leaned up on one elbow. "Speaking of which, though I have no actual knowledge of the subject, shouldn't there have been more—for you?"

Her fingers trailed down his thigh to find his still-pulsing hardness, and he gasped. "More...for both of us."

"Show me." She pulled his head back to hers, reached out her tongue to trace his lips as her fingers slowly stroked his length. "Show me now."

He hastened to oblige.

Much later, dawn sun crept over the pillow, its rose glow turning Clarissa's tangled hair to flame. So like the eternal flame that now consumed his heart.

There'd been little sleep, but he'd never felt so refreshed and revitalized. His vixen had begged for repeated lessons, and he'd not been about to deny her.

And as for the other lady who had held his heart so long—this must indeed be what she'd hoped for. "How can my happiness ever be complete until you too are happy?" she'd told him.

Be happy now, sweet Sarah.

He still felt a bittersweet ache to think of her, that inextinguishable human longing for things lost that could never be. A part of his youth, his past, and his first love, she would always be dear to him. Just as, he suspected, he was dear to her.

He touched a finger to the soft cheek of the woman who would be his bride, and lost himself in imagining a lifetime of nights like the one they'd just spent, a lifetime of days in which to work and plan and argue and love together. And children—saucy red-haired daughters, strong, green-eyed sons—

His thoughts halted, caught up in contemplating the deceptively mild appearance of Clarissa sleeping. Given the tempestuous nature of the woman he loved, perhaps he'd best hope only for daughters.

She began to stir, and he grinned in anticipation.

There'd be a battle here this morning, but he'd arrayed his forces in so impregnable a position, he had no doubt of the outcome.

Those entrancing green eyes opened, at first befuddled in sleep, then snapping wide as she realized who stared down at her—and where she was. She sat up so quickly, he caught a glimpse of her magnificent breasts before she belatedly snatched the sheet up to cover herself.

To his utter delight, a deep blush rose from her neck to her cheekbones, which deepened when she glanced over and realized he sat clothed only in the full magnificence in which God had created him. She jerked her gaze away.

Ah, yes, he grinned, a shameless wanton, his Clare.

He could have spoken, eased the awkwardness of this moment for her—a gently-bred, unmarried maiden awakening in full daylight after a night of passion to find herself naked in the bed of her lover. To his shame, he remained silent, consumed with curiosity about how she'd react next.

She moistened her lips nervously, which nearly broke his resolve, and then cleared her throat. "It's…it's nearly daylight."

"I believe dawn is usually considered such, yes."

That brought a flash of indignation to her eyes, and she straightened, sheet well in hand this time, unfortunately.

"If you would be so good as to hand me my clothing, I should return home now. As soon as possible, before too many people are stirring on the streets."

He couldn't help it then—he grinned. "The items are rather widely scattered, but I shall do my best." Taking pity at last on her flaming face, he pulled on a robe and went to the sitting room to retrieve her gown.

* * *

Wrapping the sheet under her arm, Clarissa put a hand to her scorching cheeks.

When first the colonel had brought her to his rooms, she'd been too shaken and demoralized to realize that a merciful God had given her one last opportunity to taste passion with the man she loved. Last, for certainly after this episode, so much more tawdry than the first, he would avoid her tainted presence.

Not until he'd charitably offered her a bath, and she thought of the possibilities, had the notion swept through her mind like a whirlwind. Even then, badly as she wanted to feel his touch in every possible way, she'd almost lost her nerve. What if he simply threw her the towel and walked away, disgust and condemnation in his eyes?

But after the first touch, her worry dissolved. They might be unsuited in every other way, but in passion they were perfect partners. His lips took hers as if by right, his body fit with hers as if completing the missing half of a single whole. She'd had a night of love fiery enough to warm all the lonely tomorrows of her life, unforgettable enough to leave her the strength to do what she now must.

Which was to leave quickly and before going, to withstand the renewed offer of marriage on which the good, dutiful soldier would now feel honor-bound to insist.

A tear trickled out and she slapped it away. No weakness now. The colonel was going to marshal every argument he could summon to try to persuade her, and she needed all her wits to resist. She could not endure having the price of her passion be his entrapment in marriage to a woman he did not want, nor the torture of living each day with a man she adored who desired but could not love her.

Sinjin—ah, Sinjin, she whispered the name one more time. She wanted all of him, body, soul, heart, mind. All or nothing.

So it must be nothing. If she left immediately, before fashionable London was stirring, no one but the good friends who had come to her rescue need ever learn of her visit. The colonel himself was too much a gentleman to ever boast of compromising her. All she need do was remain strong and say "no."

She wrapped her arms about herself, basking in the bittersweet memory of the touch, taste, feel of him. Despite the years empty of husband or lover stretching before her, the possibility that rumors might emerge to blacken her reputation, never would she regret last night, when in his arms she fully experienced the intensity of love that through the centuries men and women had fought for, died for, and celebrated.

Sinjin entered, a small bundle of clothing in his arms. "I think I've located your slippers and undergarments. The gown itself is torn and soiled. Why don't you wear one of my robes, and send to Sarah's for other clothes to be brought?"

He wore his dressing gown casually wrapped, revealing a large vee of tanned, muscular chest. She shouldn't stare at him like a starving vagrant at a banquet, but she couldn't seem to help it.

"I'll make do with that. The sooner I depart, the better my chances of salvaging some shred of reputation."

He tossed the bundle on a side chair and came to sit beside her on the bed. Immediately heat flared in that hidden place he'd explored so well throughout the night.

He picked up one bandaged hand and kissed it, rattling

her so much she almost forgot to clutch the sheet. "You know it's too late for that," he said quietly. "Clare, you will have to marry me."

She edged away. "We've played this scene before. Since my nerves are too shattered to argue, let me say 'no' again and leave it at that. Now, my gown, if you please."

He hopped up, gathered her dress, and threw it in the fireplace. "I don't please."

"Sinjin, be reasonable. You know you do not want to marry me. I'm...I'm headstrong, reckless, used to doing exactly as I please."

"You do need a keeper."

"I cannot abide restraint!"

"You will when I impose it."

Choosing not to argue that point, she continued, "I buy what I like, never thinking of cost."

"I'll teach you economy."

"I have a wretched temper."

"I've noticed."

"Men call me wanton."

He grinned. "I especially noticed that."

She sucked in a breath and resisted, just barely, the urge to punch him in the jaw. Why was he making this difficult when she was trying so very hard to do the right thing? "So you agree it's impossible. You need a calm, frugal, proper wife to help you rebuild your estate, not someone embroiled in scandal. Despite what happened last night, I intend to continue rescuing girls like Maddie."

"It's a good cause. If the ton disapproves, to hell with 'em."

Hands shaking, she summoned her last, best argument, determined to voice the words despite the pain. Even so, her voice wobbled. "You shouldn't have to forfeit the rest of your life to preserve your honor. You deserve a wife of your own choosing. You deserve someone like S-Sarah."

All the teasing light left his eyes. "Clare, I admit when first I returned there was a...shadow haunting my dreams. I was angry with the world, feeling it had stripped me of everything I care about save duty. But over the weeks I've known you, frustration and outrage and fury and joy have burned all that away. What's left is a bright flame that draws me, scorches me and lights my life with a brilliance I cannot imagine living without. You, Clare. You brought me back enjoyment and excitement." His serious tone lightened and he waggled his eyebrows at her. "You make me want to get up in the morning."

Oh, that. "Passion's not enough—"

"Hear me out," he commanded, stilling her lips with his finger, " and believe what I say. No, you're not the proper, obedient, thrifty wife I thought I wanted. But I've come to realize you are exactly everything I need."

He took her nerveless hand and looked into her eyes, pinning her motionless. "I love you, Clare, only you. Marry me. Please."

Sincerity vibrated in the timbre of his words, in the stark unsmiling gaze. He really wanted her—not his middle-class virgin, not a lady like Sarah.

Shock and euphoria beating dizzy wings at her chest, she stared dumbstruck at the man for whose happiness she'd gladly lay down her life, her fortune, and very soul. Who by some miracle of bad judgment had just admitted to loving her, unsuitable as she was.

An upsurge of emotion made her giddy, as if she'd been suddenly carried aloft by angels.

The old Clarissa would have drawn out her answer,

teased and tormented her suitor to ever more extravagant vows. The new Clare had no intention of risking that.

Still, she thought, her needy soul feasting on the devotion shining in Sinjin's eyes, a little reassurance wouldn't come amiss. And what better way to solidify a bond meant to last for all time than by returning where they had truly became one flesh?

"If I promise to say 'yes' later, will you continue trying to convince me?" She drew her finger down his neck to part the cloth of his robe, then traced down the matted hair of his bare chest to the smoothness of his abdomen and lower still, until with a groan he stiffened.

A thrill spiraled through her at the sound. "Wanton that I am," she murmured, "I find passion so very persuasive." She touched her tongue to the pulse at the base of his throat.

He shuddered, then pulled her roughly back into his arms. "Let it never be said that I failed to persuade."

Epilogue

Several weeks later Clarissa sat at her dressing table while Sarah finished pinning a wreath of coral roses in her hair. "There, you're perfection. Sinjin will be so dazzled by his bride he'll scarce be able to speak."

"Leave him enough breath to say his vows," Clarissa grumbled. "I've waited long enough."

Sarah laughed. In fact, the betrothed couple's first argument had been over Clarissa's desire to seek a special license and marry immediately, while Sinjin urged a calling of the banns and the staging of at least a small wedding to gratify the lifelong dreams of Lady Beaumont.

"At least he hasn't changed his mind," Clarissa said as she rose to give her friend a hug.

"As if he would! One needs only to look at his face to know he's totally besotted with you."

Clarissa turned anxious eyes to her friend. "You... you're not upset, are you?"

Sarah shook her head. "You widgeon, have I not said from the beginning my fondest desire was for him to find another lady to love? And I couldn't be more delighted that he eventually had the good sense to choose my dearest friend."

Clarissa studied Sarah's face. "You're sure?" Knowing Sarah had once held unchallenged sway over Sinjin's heart, she could not imagine anyone relinquishing that cherished position without some pangs of regret.

Sarah smiled. "Clare, could you envision having in your heart, your bed, your life, any other man but Sinjin?"

"Absolutely not!"

"Then you know how I feel about Nicholas. But we'd best be going. After all," she winked, "the sooner the wedding ends, the sooner the honeymoon begins."

Clarissa grinned and took Sarah's arm. "Amen to that."

Waiting in the Beaumont parlor with Nicholas, Hal, and Sarah's brother Colton, Sinjin paused in his pacing to greet Sarah's arriving sisters. The chattering twins, Cecily and Emma, both about to make their debuts, were followed by older sister Meredyth, who ushered them to their seats while their youngest sister, Faith, bounded over to hug first him, then Hal.

"Mr. Waterman's going to marry me when I grow up," she announced, beaming up at her towering escort. "He promised I could keep frogs in my room, ride whenever I wished, and never embroider again."

Hal gently detached the girl and grinned. "Might as well wait. Like frogs and horses."

As Faith skipped off, her sister Elizabeth, the acknowledged beauty of the family, approached on the arm of her elderly husband. The look in Hal's eyes as they rested on Mrs. Lowery made Sinjin wonder with a touch of sadness if his massive friend would ever marry.

But then the vicar arrived, wiping every other thought from his head.

Clare in her peach gown eclipsed even Elizabeth, and except for Aubrey taking a fancy to the Sandiford bridal ring and needing persuasion to relinquish it, the ceremony went well. Much as he enjoyed the company of his family and friends, having—over the strenuous objections of his bride—insisted on chastity for the month preceding their wedding, he was more than anxious for the reception to end so he might bear his wife away.

He had to chuckle. Announcing she'd be too... preoccupied by his company to much notice her surroundings, with a sparkle in her eye that promised infinite delights, Clare had insisted they skip an elaborate wedding trip and proceed straight to Sandiford Court.

Trust his Clare to be impatient with fripperies and anxious to throw herself immediately into the tasks of their life together.

Finally, after toasts and well wishes and a teary farewell from Lady Beaumont, they stood beside the coach that would carry them to Sandiford. Leading her son Aubrey, Sarah walked over.

Sinjin held her at arm's length, the touch bittersweet. "How does it feel to be proved right—again?" he asked gruffly.

"Wonderful," she said, and kissed his cheek.

Aubrey squirmed from his mother's grasp and threw himself on Clare. "An' Clare stay!" he sobbed.

Clarissa bent to pat his back. "Don't cry, poppet. Mama will bring you to visit us soon."

Sinjin knelt beside the boy. "Come now, my man, bear up. Besides, what you need is not Aunt Clare, but a little cousin to play soldiers with whenever you wish." Ignoring the kick Clarissa gave his knee, he continued, "Does that not sound like a good battle plan?"

Aubrey raised brilliant green eyes to him, apparently

considering the notion, and then bobbed his head. "Aubrey want now."

Sinjin laughed. "I shall do my best. Come, Clare, let's be off. I fear this young fellow is impatient."

"So am I." The smoldering look his bride gave him sent a burst of heat through his veins that owed nothing to the liberal quantities of champagne he'd imbibed.

"How fortunate," he rasped as he handed her into the coach, "that we're traveling in a closed carriage."

She glanced at him over her shoulder. "Why do you think I ordered one?"

After a final wave to the wedding guests, he settled beside her and let down the shade. "Ah," he murmured as he leaned over to help her unlace the fastenings of her satin gown, "the benefits of choosing a most improper wife."

* * * * *

*Be sure to look for Julia's next
sensational Regency Historical,*

MY LADY'S TRUST,

*available in book stores
in early 2002.*

**Please turn the page for
a sneak preview...**

Prologue

Soundlessly Laura crept through the dark hall. Having rehearsed—and used—the route before, she knew every carpet, chair and cupboard in the passageway, each twist of the twenty-nine steps down the servants' stairs to the back door. Even had their old butler, Hobbins, and his wife not been snoring in their room just off the corridor, the winter storm howling through the chimneys and rattling the shutters would cover the slight rustle of her movements.

Just once she halted in her stealthy passage, outside the silent nursery. Lean towards the door and she could almost catch a whiff of baby skin, feel the softness of flannel bunting, see the bright eyes and small waving hands. A bitter bleakness pierced her heart, beside whose chill the icy needles being hurled against the windows were mild as summer rain, and her step staggered.

She bent over, gripping for support the handle of the room where a baby's gurgle no longer sounded. Nor ever would again—not flesh of her flesh.

I promise you that, Jenny, she vowed. Making good on that vow could not ease the burden of guilt she carried, but it was the last thing she would do in this house. The only thing, now, she could do.

Marshalling her strength, she straightened and made her way down the stairs, halting once more to catch her breath before attempting to work the heavy lock of the kitchen door. She was stronger now. For the last month she'd practiced walking, at first quietly in her room, more openly this past week since most of the household had departed with its master for London. She could do this.

Cautiously she unlatched the lock, then fastened her heavy cloak and drew on her warmest gloves. At her firm push the door opened noiselessly on well-oiled hinges. Ignoring the sleet that pelted her face and the shrieking wind that tore the hood from her hair, she walked into the night....

Enchanted by England?

Take a journey through the British Isles with Harlequin Historicals

ON SALE JULY 2001

THE PROPER WIFE
by **Julia Justiss**
Sequel to **THE WEDDING GAMBLE**
(England, 1814)

MAGIC AND MIST
by **Theresa Michaels**
Book three in the Clan Gunn series
(Scotland & Wales, 1384)

MY LORD SAVAGE
by **Elizabeth Lane**
(England, 1580s)

ON SALE AUGUST 2001

CELTIC BRIDE
by **Margo Maguire**
(England, 1428)

LADY POLLY
by **Nicola Cornick**
Sequel to **THE VIRTUOUS CYPRIAN**
(England, 1817)

HARLEQUIN®
Makes any time special®

If you enjoyed what you just read,
then we've got an offer you can't resist!

Take 2 bestselling
love stories FREE!
Plus get a FREE surprise gift!

Clip this page and mail it to Harlequin Reader Service®

IN U.S.A.
3010 Walden Ave.
P.O. Box 1867
Buffalo, N.Y. 14240-1867

IN CANADA
P.O. Box 609
Fort Erie, Ontario
L2A 5X3

YES! Please send me 2 free Harlequin Historical® novels and my free surprise gift. After receiving them, if I don't wish to receive anymore, I can return the shipping statement marked cancel. If I don't cancel, I will receive 6 brand-new novels every month, before they're available in stores! In the U.S.A., bill me at the bargain price of $4.05 plus 25¢ shipping and handling per book and applicable sales tax, if any*. In Canada, bill me at the bargain price of $4.46 plus 25¢ shipping and handling per book and applicable taxes**. That's the complete price and a savings of over 10% off the cover prices—what a great deal! I understand that accepting the 2 free books and gift places me under no obligation ever to buy any books. I can always return a shipment and cancel at any time. Even if I never buy another book from Harlequin, the 2 free books and gift are mine to keep forever.

246 HEN DC7M
349 HEN DC7N

Name	(PLEASE PRINT)	
Address	Apt.#	
City	State/Prov.	Zip/Postal Code

* Terms and prices subject to change without notice. Sales tax applicable in N.Y.
** Canadian residents will be charged applicable provincial taxes and GST.
   All orders subject to approval. Offer limited to one per household and not valid to
   current Harlequin Historical® subscribers.
   ® are registered trademarks of Harlequin Enterprises Limited.

HIST01   ©1998 Harlequin Enterprises Limited

Harlequin invites you to walk down the aisle...

To honor our year long celebration of weddings, we are offering an exciting opportunity for you to own the Harlequin Bride Doll. Handcrafted in fine bisque porcelain, the wedding doll is dressed for her wedding day in a cream satin gown accented by lace trim. She carries an exquisite traditional bridal bouquet and wears a cathedral-length dotted Swiss veil. Embroidered flowers cascade down her lace overskirt to the scalloped hemline; underneath all is a multi-layered crinoline.

Join us in our celebration of weddings by sending away for your own Harlequin Bride Doll. This doll regularly retails for $74.95 U.S./approx. $108.68 CDN. One doll per household. Requests must be received no later than December 31, 2001. Offer good while quantities of gifts last. Please allow 6-8 weeks for delivery. Offer good in the U.S. and Canada only. Become part of this exciting offer!

Simply complete the order form and mail to:
"A Walk Down the Aisle"

IN U.S.A
P.O. Box 9057
3010 Walden Ave.
Buffalo, NY 14269-9057

IN CANADA
P.O. Box 622
Fort Erie, Ontario
L2A 5X3

Enclosed are eight (8) proofs of purchase found in the last pages of every specially marked Harlequin series book and $3.75 check or money order (for postage and handling). Please send my Harlequin Bride Doll to:

_____

Name (PLEASE PRINT)

_____

Address   Apt. #

_____

City   State/Prov.   Zip/Postal Code

_____

Account # (if applicable)   **097 KIK DAEW**

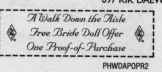

HARLEQUIN®
Makes any time special ®

Visit us at www.eHarlequin.com

A Walk Down the Aisle
Free Bride Doll Offer
One Proof-of-Purchase

PHWDAPOPR2

New York Times bestselling author

Kasey Michaels

& RITA Award-winning author

Gayle Wilson

spin wonderful stories that range from historical times to the best of contemporary feelings. In this special collection, we are proud to highlight both authors—and styles of stories.

TIMELY MATRIMONY
by **KASEY MICHAELS**

He was the perfect Regency hero— who stepped out of his time into a bewildered, charmed and *very* independent woman's life!

&

RAVEN'S VOW
by **GAYLE WILSON**

They'd wed for duty and for freedom—then desire awakened within them. Now danger was about to follow....

A Timeless Love

Silhouette®
Where love comes alive™

Available in July 2001 wherever Silhouette books are sold!

Visit Silhouette at www.eHarlequin.com

BR2TL